W9-BYH-117

She stared at the broken idol and frowned.

"Unfortunately, we do not carry items like this, so I cannot offer a replacement. You must have purchased it elsewhere."

He was surprised at how pleasant her light voice sounded and how well-spoken she was. Not the sort of tones one usually encountered in this quarter of London. Though if her father had been an antiquarian, she was likely better brought up than most of the locals. An antiquarian? What was he thinking? The man had been a charlatan and a thief, and a pair of pretty dark eyes was not going to divert him from getting his money back.

She raised her gaze to his and smiled.

His mind went blank.

For what felt like a very long space of time but could only have been a second or two, he could do nothing but stare at the way her smile lit her whole face and added sparkle to dark velvet-blue eyes— not brown as he had first thought.

Pulling himself together, he gave her his best haughty stare. "I am certainly not mistaken as to where this item was purchased, and if you do not refund my money, I will see you arrested for fraud."

Author Note

By the time you are reading this, our days of all-out social distancing should hopefully be over, and I send my sincere hope for your health and safety and that of your families.

It was at the request of several readers that I wrote Red's story. He thought his future was set in The Widows of Westram series but it seems my dear readers had other plans for him. They were right; he did deserve his own happily-ever-after.

I do hope you enjoy his journey as much as I did.

I do love hearing from readers and it is easy to reach me though my website, annlethbridge.com.

If you purchased this book without a cover you should be aware
that this book is stolen property. It was reported as "unsold and
destroyed" to the publisher, and neither the author nor the
publisher has received any payment for this "stripped book."

HARLEQUIN®
HISTORICAL™

Recycling programs
for this product may
not exist in your area.

ISBN-13: 978-1-335-50583-5

A Shopkeeper for the Earl of Westram

Copyright © 2020 by Michéle Ann Young

All rights reserved. No part of this book may be used or reproduced in
any manner whatsoever without written permission except in the case of
brief quotations embodied in critical articles and reviews.

This is a work of fiction. Names, characters, places and incidents
are either the product of the author's imagination or are used fictitiously.
Any resemblance to actual persons, living or dead, businesses,
companies, events or locales is entirely coincidental.

This edition published by arrangement with Harlequin Books S.A.

For questions and comments about the quality of this book,
please contact us at CustomerService@Harlequin.com.

Harlequin Enterprises ULC
22 Adelaide St. West, 40th Floor
Toronto, Ontario M5H 4E3, Canada
www.Harlequin.com

Printed in U.S.A.

ANN LETHBRIDGE

A Shopkeeper for the Earl of Westram

In her youth, award-winning author **Ann Lethbridge** reimagined the Regency romances she read—and now she loves writing her own. Now living in Canada, Ann visits Britain every year, where family members understand—or so they say—her need to poke around every antiquity within a hundred miles. Learn more about Ann or contact her at annlethbridge.com. She loves hearing from readers.

Books by Ann Lethbridge

Harlequin Historical

It Happened One Christmas
"Wallflower, Widow...Wife!"
Secrets of the Marriage Bed
Rescued by the Earl's Vows
The Matchmaker and the Duke

The Widows of Westram

A Lord for the Wallflower Widow
An Earl for the Shy Widow
A Family for the Widowed Governess
A Shopkeeper for the Earl of Westram

The Society of Wicked Gentlemen

An Innocent Maid for the Duke

Visit the Author Profile page
at Harlequin.com for more titles.

This book is dedicated to all those people who helped us through these terrible times, the frontline workers who risked their lives so that others could remain safe.

Chapter One

'**W**ell? What do you have to say about it?' Portly and red-faced, Mr Josiah Featherstone looked grim. While he held no title, he was descended from dukes and earls on both sides of his family. A landowner of enormous influence among the *ton*, he demanded the respect of all he met.

Surrounded by the imposing linenfold panelling in Featherstone's study, Red gazed in shock at the broken Egyptian goddess on the mahogany desk. The head, now separated from the body, revealed the artefact was not solid gold, but actually gilded lead. He felt ill. 'I do not know what to say. I sold it to you in good faith. I assure you, my father believed it to be genuine Egyptian grave goods or he would not have set such store by it.'

'Save it for a rainy day, my boy. It will stand you in good stead.'

It was one of the few things he had not sold off to pay the creditors.

Red had sold it to Featherstone, his future father-in-law, when he'd been left with a mountain of debt run up by his deceased younger brother, Jonathan, since the Westram estates, while improving, had not been yielding enough to cover such an enormous sum. Not to mention that along with Jonathan's widow, he'd also been left with financial responsibility for his older sister, Marguerite, and his younger sister, Petra, whose husbands had been killed alongside Jonathan by a company of French infantry. At the time, everyone had thought it was all over a ridiculous wager. The *ton* had dined out on the gossip for weeks. Only later had Red learned that Jonathan and Petra's husband, Harry, had gone after Neville Saxby, after witnessing his physical abuse of their sister Marguerite.

When Red had learned the truth, he had felt like an utter failure as head of his household. How could he not have known what was going on in his own family? Why had Marguerite not come to him for help? He had vowed then that he would not be fooled by anyone again, the way he had been fooled by Neville Saxby.

He had also decided it was time to take the bull by the horns and marry Eugenie Featherstone, as had been arranged by their parents before they were out of the schoolroom. His marriage to their neighbour's only child and the heiress of the Featherstone fortune would finally put the Westram title and the Greystoke family on a sound financial footing. Something he and his father had being trying to do since the ramshackle Fifth Earl, Red's grandfather, had let the estate spiral into debt.

And now this.

'I really do not know what to say, sir. I thought it was the genuine article and so did my father.' And so had Featherstone when he saw it.

Featherstone waved an impatient hand. 'Reimburse me and we will say no more about it.'

Pride stiffened Red's backbone. 'Naturally, I will refund your money.'

His gut dipped. How the hell was he to put his hands on a thousand pounds, in short order? A hundred pounds, he could manage easily, or even two hundred, but a thousand pounds would wring the estate dry and leave it in very bad shape, if he could manage it at all.

Every heirloom of value, not covered by the entail, had been sold to pay off his wastrel of a grandfather's debts years ago. His father had put his all into making their seat in Gloucester self-sufficient and had left Red to finish the task, but there was still much to do and repairs to the old house were a constant drain on any income they received. Marriage to Eugenie, the portion she would bring to the family coffers, was intended to solve all his financial problems.

His father had made him promise not to let himself be lured into a disastrous match by the sort of romantic nonsense his grandfather had engaged in. The old Earl had spent every penny to keep his wife happy. And after seeing the wreck his grandfather had become after his wife died, Red had no intention of allowing the same thing happen to him. He would follow in his father's footsteps and make a good marriage, for the benefit of the estate.

Devil take it. 'Naturally, I do not have that sort of

sum ready to hand,' he said stiffly. 'Perhaps after the wedding—'

Featherstone's jaw hardened. 'You plan to pay me with my own money? What sort of fool do you take me for? I will be a laughing stock, if word of that got out.'

Red's mouth dried. Featherstone set great store by his reputation for shrewdness. Indeed, he was known for his business acumen and for getting the best of any bargain. Many would delight in seeing him get his comeuppance. 'I certainly do not intend to discuss it beyond these walls, sir. It does not reflect well to my credit or that of my family.'

Featherstone frowned. 'I believe we should postpone any thoughts of a wedding until this matter is settled, don't you?'

Red gaped at him. He had never seen this side of Featherstone. The old gentleman had always been ready with advice and guidance with regard to the estate and matters of business, perhaps a little too ready, but Red had quelled his impatience at the attempts at interference. On the other hand, he had more than once seen Featherstone bluster and rage about being overcharged. He'd tended to ignore it, since it did not affect him personally.

'You surely do not think I deliberately sold you a fraud?'

Featherstone made a face of distaste. 'Whether you intended it or not, I am defrauded. Am I to think you are no better than your grandfather?'

The accusation caught Red on the raw. Yes, he'd sown a few wild oats while at university and had kept a mistress or two before he had formally offered for Eugenie, but compared to his grandfather, and his younger brother Jonathan, Red had led an exemplary existence.

His heart sank. Was it possible his father had known of the fraud? God, he hoped not.

'You will have your money. I swear it, upon my honour. But I will need some time—'

'Next week, then, after which we can announce the date of your marriage to Eugenie.'

The engagement had never been formally announced, though it had been understood for years. It should have been celebrated two years ago, but two deaths in the Featherstone family had forced them to put it off.

Still, Red had considered himself betrothed. He gritted his teeth. If he had to negotiate a loan, it would likely take more than a week. 'I need two weeks at least.'

Featherstone shook his head slowly. 'Very well, but not a day longer.'

He really did not like Featherstone's begrudging tone. 'Does Eugenie know?' His fiancée was exceedingly strict in her notions of propriety. Like her father, she set great store by the Featherstone name and abhorred any sort of scandal. He had been fortunate she had not changed her mind about marrying him when there had been so much gossip caused by his siblings. First his brother's death, along with his sisters' husbands, then his sisters' mad idea about going into trade.

'Eugenie was the one who discovered the forgery,' Featherstone said. 'She dropped the blasted thing. She is as shocked at the deception as I am.'

Not nearly as shocked as Red. 'May I speak with her? Explain?'

Featherstone made a gesture of assent. 'Two weeks, remember.'

How could he forget? Fuming, Red bowed and left. Outside the door he discovered Eugenie, hovering anxiously. Tall and slender to the point of thinness, she looked as if a stiff breeze might blow her away. She looked harried, when she usually looked calm and cool.

He reached out and took her hand. 'My dear Eugenie,' he said. 'I—'

Her hand was as cold as ice and limp in his grasp. She slipped out of his hold and twisted her hands together. 'I am shocked, Westram. Truly I am.'

'You cannot believe I knowingly sold your father a forgery.' He softened his tone. 'You must trust that I would never do such a thing.'

Her gaze slid away. 'I do not know what to think. Papa is quite put out.'

His spine stiffened. He had expected her to be supportive. Sympathetic to his situation given their impending marriage. But they were not married yet and Eugenie would never go against her father while she still lived under his roof.

He smiled encouragingly. 'I intend to see your father repaid.'

She gestured to the door. 'I heard. It is all so very unfortunate.'

Unfortunate. She had said the same thing when his sisters had been widowed and again when they had gone into trade, trying to establish their independence. She'd used those very words. She spoke them now, as if she thought this was his fault. Unease filled him.

She turned her face away. 'I also heard him say he was putting an end to our wedding plans.'

So that was the reason for her upset. Poor Eugenie. Their marriage plans had been put off several times. First to give him time to put his finances in order, then because she had been in mourning. He, too, had thought they had resolved every impediment and had been looking forward to bringing home his bride. Not only because all his financial problems would be solved, but because it would fulfil his most important duty to the earldom, providing the next generation of Earls of Westram.

'It is a temporary setback, I promise you.'

'I do hope so.' She turned back, lifting her chin and looking down her nose in a manner that always reminded him of a queen observing the lower orders. It was a mannerism, nothing more. 'There have been so many scandals attached to the Greystoke name. Your brother. Your sisters' husbands. Should I now fear for my reputation, I wonder?'

He had always admired her high standards. But right now her attitude was like salt in a wound. Anger, which was as hot as his hair was red, rose in his gorge. With difficulty he squashed it. He'd learned to control his temper over the years, but right now it seemed to be slipping its leash. And he had never discussed with Eugenie the real reason his brother had left for France with his brothers-in-law. After all, she was not yet a true member of his family. 'Come now, you must admit that my sisters have made the most advantageous of matches and their new husbands are beyond reproach. All of that other nonsense is in the past.'

Her eyes narrowed a fraction. 'Yes, of course. But you know how the *ton* likes to dredge up past transgressions if there is even the hint of a scandal.'

His jaw tightened. 'There will be no scandal, Eugenie.'

'I am glad to hear it,' she said. 'I look forward to your return.' She gestured to a footman who ushered him out of the room.

Dammit all! He was going to find out who had defrauded his father and bring him to justice. Then there would be no possibility of scandal and Eugenie's worries would be put to rest.

Harriet hummed as she dusted the china shelf, making sure the prices were clearly visible. Today had been an excellent day. Two giggling housemaids out on their day off had decided that miniature erotic statuettes would make excellent gifts for their beaux and a gentleman dandy had discovered the naughtiest snuffbox to show his friends.

Trade was looking up. Hopefully those satisfied customers would send other customers her way. If her shop caught on with the well-to-do, she would never need to worry about money again.

It had taken a lot of scrimping and scraping to make a go of this little shop. She had to throw out all her father's lofty ideas about antiques and stock items that cost a whole lot less and that people could afford. One thing she would never do was let herself get into debt the way her father had. She never bought anything unless she could pay for it right then and there.

The string of bells attached to the door tinkled. She pinned a welcoming smile on her face and turned to attend to her customer. She relaxed. 'Mother. I did not expect you back for an hour or more.'

Small and frail with faded brown hair and hazel eyes, her mother always reminded Harriet of a wren, whereas her own black hair, dark eyes, and sturdy frame must likely remind others of a crow. Black hair ran in her father's family. Papa had often remarked that she was the spitting image of his own sister, Harriet's Aunt Maud.

Not that the Godfreys recognised Harriet as a relation. A third son of Admiral Lord Godfrey and slated to join the navy, her father had abandoned his family's plan for his future when he discovered a fascination for the ancient world and took a ship heading east. When he returned, his marriage to her mother, the daughter of the owner of an antique shop in Bond Street, had been the final straw for his parents. They had disowned him.

Unfortunately, Father's enthusiasm for antiques had far outweighed his head for business and, after inheriting the shop and running it for many years, he'd sunk into debt. After the family had spent months in one of the worst debtors' prisons in London, he was forced to sell everything at a loss and move to these smaller and less well-appointed premises. She could still feel the anger rising in her breast at the memory, the anger tainted by the fear she had felt when locked up in that dreadful place. Up until then, she had thought her father could do no wrong. When she learned that her mother had begged him not to invest every penny in items that were touted as coming from Versailles, but were, when they arrived, very poor imitations of French master-pieces, she could not forgive him. If he had listened to his wife, they would never have ended up in the King's Bench prison.

While Mother had forgiven him, Harriet had never been able to see him the same way.

When he became ill, not long afterwards, Harriet had taken over the shop, determined they would never get into debt again. Papa's sudden death a year ago had been a huge shock. She wished she had told him she had forgiven him, even if she could not quite let go of her resentment. And, unlike her mother had, never would she give a man the power to decide her fate.

But she had pulled things together and now it seemed that they were emerging from the mire because she had a flair for finding 'unusual objets d'art'.

Mother drifted along the shelves and peered at the pewter mug with a phallus for a handle. 'What is this?' she asked, tilting her head this way and that. Over the past few years her vision had deteriorated badly.

'It is a mug for ale, Mother,' Harriet said.

Mother nodded. 'You will never guess what Mrs Beasley told me?'

Mrs Beasley was the cobbler's wife, and his prem-ises were a few doors away. The two women took tea together once a week followed by the reading of the leaves. Mrs Beasley was famous for her predictions.

Harriet repressed a smile. 'Well, if she told you our fortunes are secure, I shall be very happy.'

'I am not talking about what she saw in the leaves, though I want to discuss that with you also. No, lovey! It is about the robberies.'

Harriet's stomach dipped. 'Robberies?'

'Yes. Three shops were robbed this week, one of them only half a mile from here. There is talk of a gang. All the shopkeepers are taking precautions.'

Harriet's stomach churned. 'A gang?'

Mother nodded vigorously. 'According to Mrs Beasley, the constables are involved.'

Harriet would not be in the least bit surprised. 'What sort of precautions are the other shopkeepers taking?'

'The jewellers have hired men to stand watch at night. Mr Beasley is having a locksmith add new locks to his doors, front and back. Mrs Beasley says that is what most of their acquaintances are doing.'

The lock and bolts on their doors were sturdy enough. 'I doubt they will trouble with us. We have very little worth stealing.' A fence would give little more than a penny or two for most of their stock and anything valuable was locked away in their safe upstairs at night. One of Papa's more practical purchases.

'How do *they* know that?' Mother asked. 'We could be murdered in our beds. We have no man to protect *us*.'

One of Mother's frequent complaints. 'You are not suggesting we hire a watchman? We can barely manage the rent as it is.'

'No, of course not. But if you found a husband... Mrs Beasley saw I would become a grandmother if you followed a difficult path. It made me think now was the right time for you to approach your granddad.'

Harriet's stomach plummeted. 'Mother, dearest—'

'Your father always said you ought to have a proper come out. If we do not do it soon, it will be too late.'

Harriet sighed. This old desire of her father's was completely impractical, like so much of what Papa had wanted for his family during his lifetime. Unfortunately, it was plain to Harriet that while her father's parents might, just might, take Harriet under their wing, they absolutely would not accept her mother. The snobs.

Her mother was a kind, sweet, loving woman, and was far more important to Harriet than trying to join a social circle that would never accept her as one of their own.

'It is already too late,' she said, more calmly than she felt. 'I am four and twenty and long past the age for come-outs. Even if I wanted one. I am happy here, Mama. If things continue as they have, we will be able to buy the shop and then we will be set for the rest of our lives.' Never again would they have to fear the land-lord increasing their rent.

'Nonsense. Four and twenty is no age at all. You must marry. Someone your father would have approved of. Perhaps if we moved to Bond Street…'

Her mother had this odd idea that a nobleman would only have to catch a glimpse of her daughter and be smitten. Well, they were beginning to attract some of the lesser nobility to this shop and, so far, not one of the gentlemen who had browsed her wares had given her so much as a glance.

Nor she them.

The only man who had shown a romantic interest in her, and on whom she had begun to rely, had announced that when they married he had grand plans for her shop and was not interested in the least in her opinion on the matter, despite the fact that his ideas were unrealistic. It was then that she realised it was the shop he wanted, not her. And, of all things, he fully intended to turn it into a butcher's shop when it became *his*. The disappointment had cut deeply. She'd felt like a complete idiot.

Why did she need to marry? She was providing for herself and her mother very well and no man making protestations of affection was going to lay his hands on her hard-won earnings.

Marriage would not suit her one bit.

Although, she had sometimes thought about the idea of taking a lover. Given some of the artefacts her father had brought back from the East and some of the curiosities she carried in her shop, she was no stranger to erotic images. Visions of them had returned to her in the dark reaches of the night and left her restless and intrigued. But so far, she had not met a man who intrigued her nearly as much as her own imaginings.

'Write to your grandfather, lovey,' Mother said. 'Admiral Lord Godfrey would surely want to see you suitably wed.'

She shook her head. 'I am perfectly happy as we are. Please do not mention the Admiral again.'

Mother sighed. 'One day you will come to your senses and regret not taking my advice.'

'When that day comes, I will let you know. How is dinner coming along?'

She would not eat until after the shop closed. Trade was always brisk in the evenings and they did not close the shutters until nine.

'We are having the rest of the stew I made yesterday. There is enough left, if I add a couple more potatoes. I will have it ready for when you close up.'

They always had leftovers on the days Mother went to Mrs Beasley's. Not that it was a hardship, Mother was a wonderful cook though her bad sight slowed her down.

'I shall look forward to it.'

Mother gave her a hug and disappeared through the curtain that separated the shop from the stairs to their living apartment above.

This business of robberies was worrying. But what could Harriet do? Hope and pray the burglars did not choose this shop for their nefarious activities was about all.

The string of bells attached to the door tinkled and a broad-shouldered, tall gentleman strolled in, glancing about him with emerald-green eyes that seemed to miss nothing. He removed his hat and revealed a head of neatly styled dark auburn hair.

Her heart missed a beat. He had to be the handsomest man she had ever seen. Her pulse speeded up. Her throat dried as if she had swallowed a feather from her duster. Heat flowed up from her belly all the way to the top of her head.

Shocked by the intensity of her reaction, she turned away, flicking her duster wildly over the articles on the shelf. So aware of his presence was she that she had no clue whether she had cleaned this shelf before or not. Every fibre of her being strained to sense his movements as he strolled around her little shop.

Her hand was trembling so hard, she dropped the duster. She bent forward.

Her forehead knocked against a forearm that had appeared from nowhere. Prickles darted across her shoulders, painful little stabs of pain. Red-faced, she stumbled back and collided with an umbrella stand. Knobby sticks and parasols clattered to the floor.

'Allow me, miss.' His voice was deep and smooth and, of course, terribly refined. The sort of manly voice one could listen to all day.

With a grace she could only gawp at, he picked up the duster and held it out to her with an incline of his head.

When she did not move, he lifted her hand by the wrist and pressed the duster's stick against her palm. Somehow, she managed to close her fingers around it. She watched dumbfounded as he righted the stand and scooped up its contents.

The charm of his smile when he had completed this task was like a vision of heaven.

'I beg your pardon,' he said. 'I did not mean to startle you.'

Her whole body sighed with pleasure at the sight of that smile.

Oh, good Lord, what was the matter with her? She gave herself a mental shake. He must think her a complete nodcock standing here staring at him as if he had arrived from another planet.

He might just as well have done so. From the quality of his coat and the elegance of his manners, he was clearly a gentleman from the highest of society. The sort who only shopped on Bond Street and likely belonged to all the best gentlemen's clubs. He must have lost his way to have ended up here.

'I—' she stuttered. She inhaled a deep breath and started again. 'May I be of assistance?'

His mouth hardened. He looked a little less friendly than he had a moment before.

'I seek the owner of this establishment.' He nodded at the sign behind the counter. 'H. J. Godfrey.'

A chill went down her spine at his icy tone. Why on earth would a man like him be seeking her father. 'H. J. Godfrey passed away last year, sir. I am H. A. Godfrey.'

'I see,' he said, pointing at the sign with the tip of his cane. 'Then the son will do.'

Papa had had the sign made before Harriet's birth in a burst of hope. Unfortunately, no son had ever been born to her parents.

'I am his daughter,' she said. 'His only offspring. How may I help you?'

The gentleman looked shocked. 'You are the owner of this business?'

'I am, sir.' She could not understand his strange reaction. Was he embarrassed to purchase one of her novelties from a woman? Could he have such delicate sensibilities?

He dropped a black velvet bag on the counter with a

solid-sounding *thunk*. 'I am returning an item purchased here and I would like my money back.'

She frowned. She did not recall selling him anything. She would certainly have recalled him had he ever set foot in her shop. 'What is it?'

When Red had entered the establishment, the woman, whom he had assumed was a shop girl, had turned and gazed at him. Despite the anger burning low in his gut, he could not help noticing she was remarkably pretty with large luminous eyes and black glossy hair pinned neatly beneath a lacy cap. Roses had bloomed on her cheeks.

The fact that she was the proprietor was an unpleasant surprise. He would much rather deal with a man than this young woman. Still, needs must.

He emptied the velvet bag on to the battered wood of the counter.

She stared at the broken idol and frowned. 'A copy of Egyptian grave goods.' She picked up the body and turned it around, regarding it closely. Her hands, as he had already noticed, were elegant, but work roughened.

'Did you drop it?' she asked. 'Unfortunately, we do not carry items like this, so I cannot offer a replacement. You must have purchased it elsewhere.'

He was surprised at how pleasant her light voice was and how well spoken she sounded. Not the sort of tones one usually encountered in this quarter of London. Though if her father had been an antiquarian she was likely better brought up than most of the locals. An antiquarian? What was he thinking? The man had been a charlatan and a thief and a pair of pretty dark eyes were not going to divert him from getting his money back.

She raised her gaze to his and smiled.

His mind went blank.

For what felt like a very long space of time, but could only have been a second or two, he could do nothing but stare at the way her smile lit her whole face and added sparkle to velvet-dark blue eyes, not brown as he had first thought.

Pulling himself together, he gave her his best haughty stare. 'I am certainly not mistaken as to where this item was purchased and, if you do not refund my money, I will see you arrested for fraud.'

She recoiled from him, clutching at the counter as if needing support.

Every instinct made him want to offer that support, but he knew better than to give in to it. He was the victim here and was not about to be gulled by a fraudster's play-acting.

Her gaze shifted from the broken statue on the counter to his face. Her full lower lip trembled. She straightened her shoulders and took a deep breath. 'What proof do you have that you bought it here?' She folded her arms across her chest in a most challenging manner.

Good God, did she actually have the temerity to accuse him of lying? He'd had quite enough of people impugning his honour. What with Featherstone and then Eugenie—his chest tightened for a moment at the thought of the disappointment in Eugenie's eyes. All the fault of this woman's father.

Heat rose up from his chest. He clenched his fists at his side to hold his temper in check and forced himself to calm. He'd been so utterly furious after going over his conversation with Featherstone in his mind, he'd been almost blinded by rage. He'd given vent to his feelings by a bout of fisticuffs in Jackson's Boxing Saloon. The trainer had been required to step in and call a halt to it, before his sparring partner got hurt.

He withdrew the receipt he'd found among his father's papers from the bag and stabbed a finger at it. 'The proof lies before you, madam. Signed by H Godfrey. Either you or your father signed this.'

'It was not me.' She picked the receipt up in trembling fingers, her white knuckles clearly indicating she was more nervous than she wanted him to think. She peered at it closely. Setting it on the counter, she raised her gaze to meet his. 'Let me check that it is genuine.'

Seething at her ridiculous implication that he might have created a fraudulent receipt, he glared at her.

She went around behind the counter. As she moved away, he was fascinated by the sensuality of her walk and the curves of her figure. While she was nowhere near as tall as him, she was substantially taller than the average woman. She bent down behind the counter and pulled out an enormous ledger.

'What is that?' he asked.

'If my father sold this item, it will be recorded in this book.'

'If?' Ice ran through his veins. 'If? Are you saying you do not believe the evidence of your own eyes? That this is not a receipt from this shop?' He pointed to the heading on the receipt. 'Are you telling me that is not the owner's signature?'

She winced. 'It certainly looks like my father's writing, but there is no need to shout.'

He lowered his voice to slightly above a whisper. 'I can assure you, I am not shouting. If I were to shout, the people in the shop across the street would hear.'

Her eyes widened. Her lips parted on a gasp. Such inviting lips. Full and soft and rosy red. He shook the thought off. Now was not the time to notice a female's allure.

'Someone could have forged the receipt, the same way they forged the statue,' she said calmly.

So that was her game. Well, he wasn't going to put up with it. 'Fiddlesticks. That article was bought in this shop. And you very well know it. For all I know, you father could have neglected to record it in his book.'

She looked at the receipt again. 'November 1802...' She opened the ledger and riffled the pages until she found what she was looking for.

She ran a neatly manicured nail down the line of entries, turned the page and...and frowned.

'Well?' he said.

'I don't understand.' Her voice was rough around the edges.

He leaned over, pulled the ledger to his side of the counter and turned it around. There was the evidence, scrawled in the same handwriting as on his receipt.

Sold to the Earl of Westram, one Isis statue for the sum of one thousand guineas.

'I told you.' He picked up the receipt and tucked it in his pocket.

She leaned over, pointing at the entry, inadvertently giving him an unimpeded view of the rise of her breasts beneath the modest fichu tucked in the neckline of her gown. Good God what was he thinking? He was betrothed. Or he would be again, once he had sorted this out. He forced himself to look at her pointing finger, not the swell of that delicate flesh. As he focused, he realised she was not pointing at the entry he had read, but at the one above.

An entry indicating the purchase of the same item.

'Clearly, he bought it from someone else. There is nothing surprising in that,' he said.

'Yes, but look at the date and the price. My father bought it for nine hundred and eighty-five guineas and sold it for one thousand all on the same day. It looks to me as if he was acting as some sort of intermediary for a small finder's fee.' She frowned at the name of the seller. 'Mr Maxwell Clark. I have never heard of him, but he is the man you want. He is the man who committed the fraud. Ask him for your money.'

He stepped back, startled by her gall. 'Oh, no. Your father vouched for this item. He was the seller. If this Maxwell fellow is the fraudster, then it is you who must chase down your money from him. Besides, how do I know your father and this Maxwell chap were not in it together?'

Her eyes widened.

Oh, yes, he had her on the ropes. Now he was going to get his money, and everything would go back to normal. His wedding to Eugenie would go on and all would be right with the world.

She sank down on to what must have been a stool on the other side of the counter, staring up at him, shaking her head. 'Even if it was true, we do not have that sort of money.'

We? Red frowned. 'Who is this we you speak of.'

'My mother and I.' She glanced about her. 'Look for yourself. If I sold every item in this shop, I would not raise one thousand pounds.'

He grimaced. The place was full of knick-knacks, many of which were of a most lurid sort. The kind that appealed to youths and ladies of a certain ilk. There were a few nicer pieces, small figurines, the sort of thing one might find at a fairground, and some paintings by unknown artists, but the bulk of what crowded the shelves and hung on the walls was rubbish. Like his father's statue.

Damn it all! She had to pay him back.

The woman, whom he judged to be in her early to mid-twenties, was watching him intently.

'How do I know you do not have thousands of pounds tucked away somewhere?' he asked. 'No. You owe me this money. If need be, I will swear out a warrant and have you arrested for debt. You and your mother.' Then Featherstone would know he had at least brought the fraudster to account. But only a refund would satisfy the other man. And what would Eugenie say? He could not help but wish she had taken his part in this matter.

Miss Godfrey shot him a look of dislike tinged with a healthy dose of worry. Her hands curled into fists.

She let go a long sigh and flattened her hands on the highly polished but battered counter. 'Then you must give me time.'

'I do not have time.'

'Nonsense. You cannot tell me that your need is so urgent that you cannot wait for me to get to the bottom of this matter.' Her gaze sharpened. 'Unless you have foolishly gambled away your fortune. I gather that is what men of your ilk like to do.'

'Men of my ilk?' He looked down his nose. 'What do women like you know of men of my ilk, I should like to know.'

She stiffened. 'I read the newspapers. I see the way members of the nobility flee the country because of their debts, rather than go to prison. Hah! Some don't even have to go to prison because they have a title, leaving poor honest tradesmen to rot in the Fleet because the debts owed to them are not paid.'

'Let me assure you, I have always paid the tradesmen with whom I do business.' Though, dammit it, he had paid late on occasion, when the harvest was bad, or his cattle did not achieve the price he had hoped for.

Devil take it, now he was getting into a war of words with the wench. Worse yet, what she said made sense. And he had wangled a bit of time from Featherstone.

'Very well. I will give you a week.'

She frowned. 'Two.'

Two weeks was all the time he had to get Featherstone his money. 'Why two?'

'Because if I am to find this Mr Maxwell Clark, it will mean travelling to Bristol and back.'

A suspicion reared its ugly head. 'Oh, no! If you think I would let you leave London and disappear, you must think me a complete flat.'

Chapter Two

The man was impossible. Bad tempered. Suspicious. Grasping. Cruel. And stupidly handsome despite his obvious anger. Bother! Where had that last thought come from?

Was she ready for Bedlam, noticing his looks when he wanted to throw her and Mother in prison?

She inhaled a deep steadying breath. It would do no good to shout and rail, she had to find a way out of this mess. What on earth could Papa have been thinking? She could not recall him speaking of this transaction and he had always told her everything. Or so she had thought. Her stomach churned. He always had been too soft-hearted. She glanced at the date in the ledger. It had been some ten years ago. The year they were locked up in the Fleet.

Desperate times.

Oh, Papa, what did you do? She had to find this Clark person. He was the one who had reaped the profit. She must try to resolve the issue somehow.

'If you do not want me to go alone, then come with me.' The words popped out of her mouth before she thought about them.

Westram's jaw dropped. His pretty green eyes widened. 'What?'

Despite beginning to wonder if she really had run mad, she brazened it out. 'If you do not trust me out of your sight, then come with me. Help me track down this Mr Clark. When we find him, you can decide on whom to exact your vengeance.'

'Vengeance?'

He was raising his voice again.

She pressed her lips together and shrugged. 'What is debtors' prison, other than vengeance? Locked up, I cannot earn any money to repay the debt, not even piecemeal. It is a punishment. Nothing more.'

'What about relatives? Is there no one who can loan you the money?'

Why was he, a nobleman, so desperate for money? Yes, it was a vast sum and a great loss. But a man like he had far more resources than she. And she could easily imagine her grandfather's reaction if she went to him for help. He'd kick her out of the door, or have her flung into the street without ceremony, the same way he had tossed her father out. 'I have no relatives. Other than my mother.'

His expression tightened. 'I don't believe you. Everyone has relatives.'

'Then let us say, I have none with that sort of money at their disposal.'

That he appeared to believe because he hissed out a breath of frustration.

'If I go to Bristol, I could at least discover the real criminal.'

The arrogant nobleman straightened to his full height. My word, he really was tall. She forced herself not to shrink back from the threatening size and breadth of him and kept her gaze steady on his face.

He glared down his nose. 'Very well, I will give you two weeks to locate Clark and get my money back.'

She breathed a sigh of relief.

'And I will accompany you to Bristol.'

That he would take her up on her suggestion she had not expected. Not really. The idea of travelling anywhere with this man made her heart stutter and stumble, because he was furious at her and made her feel uncomfortable. Not because he was so lovely to look at. And, having proposed he accompany her, she could hardly turn around and now refuse to allow it.

Not to mention she and Mother were at his mercy. No judge in the whole of London would believe her word, or her evidence, against the Earl of Westram's demand she be incarcerated. She had to convince him her father was not to blame.

Because, although Father had never really had a good head for business, he had been an honourable man. As honest as the day was long. Everyone said so. Certainly, it was not fair that she and Mother should be punished for a crime she was sure Father did not commit. Almost sure. Around the time of the transaction, their situation had been dire and she pushed the niggling doubt aside. She must find the real criminal.

'We cannot go until tomorrow,' she said, hoping he did not hear the tremble in her voice. 'The coach departs from the Swan with Two Necks at eight in the morning, arriving late in the evening.'

He gave her a hard look. 'How is it you are so familiar with the timetable?'

Blast his suspicious mind. 'Bristol is a port, I go there seeking items to sell in my shop, Your Lordship. As you may have noticed, I am in trade.'

His eyes narrowed. 'I see.' He pulled a magnificent gold watch from his waistcoat pocket. 'You are right, it is too late to set out this evening. Therefore, so I can be sure you will not disappear overnight, you, my dear, will accompany me home where I can keep an eye on you.'

Spend the night at some nobleman's house? Alone? A terribly attractive nobleman at that? She'd heard about noblemen who took advantage of maids and shop girls, making promises they had no intention of keeping. Heart pounding, with… What? Anticipation? Surely not? She shot to her feet. 'Oh, no.' She shook her head. 'That I will not do.'

They stared at each other across the counter.

Red narrowed his gaze on the adamant young woman. What right she had to be furious, he did not know. He was the victim here. On the other hand, suggesting she spend the night at his home was far beyond the pale. Damn it! Then what? Even if she was not part of the plot to defraud his father, as she declared, he was not going to give her a chance to slip through his fingers.

At the very least, she was going to admit to her father's part in the scheme to Featherstone. It was the least she could do.

'Very well. I shall spend the night here.'

'You most certainly will not.'

He folded his arms across his chest. 'Then I shall call the constable and have you arrested. Let the courts decide the matter. Your choice.'

Her lovely eyes blazed fury. 'You think just because you are a man, you can bully me. You have no right to simply announce you will spend the night in my home. I have informed you I will go with you to Bristol and so I shall, sir. I am a woman of my word.'

Despite her femininity, she held her ground like a square of British infantry. Her anger seemed so genuine he could not help wondering if he was completely mistaken. *All right, Red, behave the way you did with your sisters. Give in to feminine pleadings and deal with the consequences.*

Not this time. There could be no doubt that his father had bought the statue in this shop, she had admitted it. She must know about what had gone on. He hardened his heart against this beauty's obvious distress. He would not be cajoled by a pretty face, no matter how appealing.

'A woman of your word, as your father was a man of his, I suppose.'

She recoiled. 'I—well—'

Having taken the wind out of her sails, he looked about him. 'Where are your private apartments?'

She frowned. 'My mother and I live above the shop. But you are not coming up there, so do not think it.'

'And there is a back door to the alley, no doubt.'

She nodded.

'Is there more than one set of stairs to your apartments?'

She stiffened. 'What business is it of yours?'

'Since you object to my company, I will spend the night down here, while you retire to your rooms. I simply want to be sure you cannot sneak out without my knowing.'

'Sneak out?' She gave a bitter laugh. 'What sort of person do you think I am?'

'The sort of person who would defraud someone of a thousand pounds.'

She flushed red. 'There is only one set of stairs up to the rooms above the shop.'

'Very well. Give me your keys.'

'Certainly not.' Fear shadowed her gaze.

His gut twisted. He pushed the uncomfortable sensation aside. He was not a pigeon for the plucking, like his father. Anyway, she would soon learn she had nothing to fear from him. He was a gentleman.

'I assume there is a bolt on the inside of the door to your rooms. Throw it. I will lock you in from the other side and we will both have peace of mind for the night.'

'And what am I supposed to tell my mother?'

He gave an unconcerned shrug. 'The truth.'

'Mother would worry herself silly.' A thoughtful expression crossed her face. 'I—'

What scheme was she cooking up now? 'Out with it.'

'Well, perhaps you could pretend to be a watchman. There has been a string of robberies here about and many of the shopkeepers are employing men to guard their wares.' She shook her head. 'No, that will not work. Not if we take off for Bristol tomorrow and leave Mother to fend for herself. You really have to leave. Trust me. I will be here in the morning. I want to clear this matter up as much as you do.'

Trust. He had trusted his father to know what he was doing with the statue. And he had, he realised with a twinge of annoyance, trusted Eugenie to stand up for him to her father. He was through with being a trusting fool. He shook his head.

Her shoulders slumped. Her eyes darted hither and yon as if searching for something, some solution to her problem. And stupidly he felt sympathy for her plight.

He sighed. 'I will have one of my employees organise watchmen for the duration of our absence. I will send for him now to give him his instructions. Your shop will be perfectly safe. Will that satisfy you?'

Her lovely eyes widened. 'You would do that?'

'I will.' Fool that he was. 'He will also be instructed to ensure that your mother does not leave the premises before our return.'

Her expression of gratitude changed to one of cynical amusement. 'How like a man to turn it to his own advantage.'

Scornful little wench. Ire sent heat along his veins.

With practised ease he tamped it down and spoke calmly. 'Well, do you accept my terms or not?'

While she continued to look doubtful, she removed a key from a drawer in the counter and flung it down. 'Very well. It seems I have no choice.'

Too easy.

'I will take your mother's key, also.'

She glared at him, her full lips tightened in anger.

He raised his eyebrows.

She huffed out a breath. 'One moment.'

Stiff-backed, she turned, pulled aside the curtain behind the counter and whisked out of sight. He followed her.

A small area full of clutter gave on to the foot of a narrow set of stairs lit by a small high window and a heavy wooden door that must lead outside. Miss Godfrey was already at the top of the stairs as he set foot on the bottom.

Had she told him the truth when she said there was only one door to the rooms above? He could not see how it could be otherwise. Sandwiched between two other establishments, there could be only two entrances, one out on to the street from the shop and the one in this hallway out to the alley behind.

A few moments later, her footsteps sounded on the landing above. When she saw him waiting at the bottom of the stairs, she gave a little toss of her head. A defiant gesture of disgust. Clearly, she did not like it that he did not trust her, but honestly, he didn't give a fig what she liked. One way or another, he was either going to get his money back, or he was going to bring the guilty person to justice and clear his name in the eyes of Featherstone.

And Eugenie.

How could she have thought he might have tried to cheat her father?

But Eugenie was a dutiful daughter…and full of notions of propriety. She simply wasn't strong enough to stand against her papa. Was she?

And…well…yes, he had felt some doubt about their arranged marriage when he'd seen the *love* matches his sisters had made this past year. But an hour in Eugenie's company on his return from his older sister's wedding had convinced him he was being foolish.

Eugenie had been most complimentary about his sisters' second marriages, pointing out the advantages of their matches and congratulating him on finally bringing everything to such a successful conclusion.

She had been condescension itself in her forgiveness of his sisters' foray into commerce, which if it had become known would have been a stain on his family's name. He had been grateful for her discretion. Not one word about his sisters' mistake had she ever uttered in public.

He should count himself lucky.

When Miss Godfrey reached the bottom step, he stepped back and held out his hand. She slapped a key into his palm. He matched it against the other and nodded.

'Now I suppose you will spend the rest of the evening getting underfoot?' she snapped. 'Or will you leave me to go about my business?'

He winced inwardly. 'What time do you close?'

'At nine.'

Another two hours.

Thank goodness he had walked here. 'I will find a corner out of the way. Do you know of a lad who can deliver a message to my butler for me?'

She looked as if she wanted to tell him to find his own lad, but she opened the shop door and gestured to someone in the street. A moment later a lad of about twelve sauntered in.

'Wot does ye want, missus?' he asked.

'That gentleman there requires your assistance.'

Red tore a leaf from his notebook and wrote concise instructions for his secretary. 'Take this to Number Nine Grosvenor Square,' he instructed the lad. 'Hand it to the porter who opens the door. Here is thruppence. I will give you another when you bring the reply.'

The lad touched his cap and shot off.

'Sixpence for taking a message,' Miss Godfrey said, sounding scandalised. 'You'll ruin him. He would have been happy with a penny.'

There was no pleasing her. 'I might have need of him again later.' And he wanted to make sure the lad returned.

She turned her back on him and began dusting one of the shelves.

Lord Westram was as good as his word. He tucked himself in the alcove behind the curtain and stayed out of her way. The only interruption was when a middle-aged good-looking man with grey hair and warm brown eyes arrived, looking intrigued, and asked for him. Westram introduced him as John Preston, the man who would look after the safety of the shop until their return from Bristol.

The two men took their discussions outside. So annoying. She would like to have heard what Westram was saying. After several minutes, the Earl returned alone and returned to his place in the alcove without telling her anything, blast him.

A trickle of customers came in over the course of the next two hours, keeping Harriet busy enough to not let panic overwhelm her, but it was there, nevertheless, sitting low in her stomach, rising each time her thoughts wandered to the spectre of prison. Sometimes, when she couldn't sleep, she could remember the chill of that awful place, the smell of damp coming from the walls and the sounds of people coughing. They had been fortunate. They had not had to share accommodations, yet they had been crammed into one small room with the few belongings they had been permitted. The lack of fuel for a fire had been the worst part. Mother and Father had done their best to keep her away from other residents, but even so some of the male inmates were clearly not debtors, but unrepentant criminals.

She still had nightmares about them.

What if she did not find this Maxwell Clark? How could she ever repay the Earl? It might take years. Even if he would allow her to try. He seemed more interested in sending her to prison than getting his money back.

Her knees suddenly felt weak. She sank down on to

her little stool. To be locked up in such a place again, it didn't bear thinking about.

'Oh!' Mother said from behind the curtain. 'Who are you? What are you doing here?'

Dash it. She'd been so busy with her grim thoughts she had forgotten to let Mother know about their supposed watchman. She jumped up and went through the curtain.

Lord Westram was already on his feet and bowing over Mother's hand—not exactly how a hired guard would behave.

'West—'

'Mother, I meant to tell you,' she said, interrupting his introduction. 'Mr… West happened to come by having heard about the robberies and offered the services of him and his employees as watchmen. I…er… I hired him immediately. Mr West, this is my mother, Mrs Godfrey.'

Both the Earl and her mother stared at her open-mouthed.

'Oh,' Mother said. She pulled her hand out of his grasp. 'Pleased to meet you, I am sure.' She looked at Harriet. 'Did you get references?'

Westram frowned.

'Oh, yes,' Harriet said airily before he said something stupid. 'He is also providing watchmen for Mr Trotter, the jeweller. He vouched for him.' A bit of wickedness popped into her head and she grinned at the Earl. 'Besides, he used to be a Bow Street Runner, didn't you, Mr West?'

Those glittering green eyes widened for a second,

then a small reluctant smile curved the corners of his mouth—such a lovely mouth when he smiled. 'Indeed, ma'am,' he said and bowed again.

'Oh, I see,' Mother said. She leaned closer to Harriet and lowered her voice. 'Is he terribly expensive?'

'Terribly,' Harriet said drily.

'But worth every penny,' Westram shot back. 'I will stay tonight, Mrs Godfrey, and one of my men will take over tomorrow. You can be assured of your safety.'

Mother nodded. 'I just came down to tell you the stew is on the hob, Daughter, and will be ready whenever you are. Will you join us, Mr West?'

He looked surprised. 'I—'

Harriet glared at him. The man was threatening to throw them in prison—was he going to eat what little food they had, too? Besides, his presence would make her too nervous to eat a bite.

He caught her glance and frowned. 'It is kind of you, ma'am, but I have already ordered my supper from the chop house across the street.'

Harriet breathed a sigh of relief. 'Perhaps you would like to see the mechanism for locking the door before I go upstairs?' she said.

'Good idea,' he agreed with his charming, but completely false smile. So why on earth did it make her want to smile back?

'Don't be too long, lovey, or dinner will be cold,' Mother chirped and haltingly made her way back upstairs.

Chapter Three

Red could not believe the way the lies tripped off this young woman's tongue. Nor could he quite believe he had participated in her prevarications. Honestly, when was the last time he had had so much fun?

Fun? With his future father-in-law threatening a scandal and his bride-to-be practically accusing him of theft, how could he possibly be enjoying himself?

Yet there was a lightness in his chest he did not understand. As he followed Miss Godfrey to the shop door, he could not but help notice the gentle sway of her hips and her neatly turned ankles. She was, when she wasn't glaring at him, a most attractive female.

Curse it. He was disappointed that she had not wanted him to join her for dinner, too, but likely it was better that he kept his distance. His only reason for remaining here was to make sure she did not give him the slip.

She opened the door and called over the boy who had run his errand earlier. 'Jimmy, Mr West has need of you.' She turned back to him. 'He'll fetch your dinner if you do not want to go yourself.'

He gave his order to the boy and the requisite coin.

Miss Godfrey gestured to the door. 'There are three bolts as I am sure you can see. One at the top, one at the bottom and one here just above the keyhole.'

He frowned. 'How can you possibly reach that one at the top?' It would be a stretch for him and he was nigh on six foot tall.

She gave him a glance full of derision and pulled out a stool he had not noticed, hopped up and threw the bolt. She turned to him with a triumphant smile. 'Like that.'

Without thinking, he put his hands around her waist to help her down. Such a tiny waist. So deliciously curved.

He gazed up into her face and her lips parted. His lips tingled. His body heated. He fell into the deep blue of her eyes for what felt like for ever.

She gasped.

He blinked and lifted her down, allowing himself, for one brief moment, to savour the weight of her body, before her feet touched the floor.

He stepped back. 'I see.'

She looked puzzled, perhaps even a little dazed, and her breathing was a little quicker than before. Had she felt the same pull of attraction? How very odd.

'I see how you manage to lock the door,' he said.

She lingered.

'Do not fear, I will see it locked up tight once my meal is delivered.' He reached up and unbolted it. He certainly did not need a stool.

When he turned back to her, she was rearranging little ornaments on a small table near the entrance. All shapes and sizes of female breasts.

'What the devil?' he said.

'Snuffboxes,' she replied. 'Men seem to like them.'

Well, he had seen some titillating snuffboxes in his time, usually made of silver, or ormolu, and delicately handpainted, but these were crude affairs.

'Not the men I know,' he said repressively.

'No, these are not very expensive. I do have some better ones in the glass case over there. I do not put them out, in case they are stolen. They are for my more discerning customers.'

'Good Lord,' he muttered. Now he looked closer there were all sorts of erotic objects mingled among the everyday figurines of shepherdesses and beer mugs. What sort of woman was she?

She whirled around. 'How am I to explain going to Bristol with you to Mother?'

Really? 'I am sure you will think of something. You do not seem to have been at a loss for a handy lie, so far.'

She shook her head. 'Mother will think it very odd the two of us going off together.' She pursed her kissable lips, her fertile imagination clearly at work. She made an odd face. 'She might approve if we told her who you really are and said we were betrothed.'

He reared back. 'Oh, no, young lady. I am not falling for that one. Next, you'll be having me in court for breach of promise. Besides, I am already betrothed.' Or he would be again once he had this matter resolved.

'Then you will leave first and I will follow you a

short time later and we can meet at the bottom of the hill.'

'Leaving you free to disappear?'

'You will have to trust me.'

Trust her. She must think him brainless. 'I have a better idea. I will offer to carry your bag to the coaching inn before I go about my own business.'

Her eyes sparkled. 'Well, well. It seems I am not the only one who is good at making up stories.'

'Needs must, Miss Godfrey. Besides, it is not a lie. Going with you is going about my business.'

The muscles in her jaw flickered as if she was gritting her teeth so as not to say something rude.

A handbell tinkled somewhere above their heads.

She sighed. 'Dinner time. I will see you in the morning, my lord.'

He had an odd urge to turn her back towards him and…kiss her senseless?

Instead, he stood looking out into the street, watching for his dinner to arrive.

It did not take long. Mindful of Miss Godfrey's earlier admonition, he gave the boy a penny for his troubles and took the tray to the counter where he perched on the stool where Miss Godfrey had sat earlier.

Beef stew. His chef would have called it an abomination, but Red found it and the mug of beer he had ordered reasonable and satisfying. What would it be like to be an ordinary fellow who went to labour every day as a…what? Shopkeeper? Blacksmith? Ostler at an inn? The idea of working for someone else seemed remarkably appealing. He'd been responsible for his sisters, the estate, the honour of the family name for many years now. Sometimes he felt as if a millstone hung around his neck.

Light female voices drifted down from above. No words, simply a murmur. The sound reminded him of home before his father died, when his sisters were in the schoolroom and there was laughter at Westram Hall.

He missed laughter in his home. And female company. He gazed at the beef congealing on his plate. Eugenie wasn't much of a one for laughter, she was too serious, but their children would fill an empty house. Wouldn't they?

He shook himself free of his maudlin thoughts. Of course he would marry Eugenie as soon as he found a way to convince her father he had not committed some sort of trickery. He tore of a hunk of bread and dipped it in the gravy, but found he had lost his appetite. He covered the plate and pushed it away, then took his mug of ale and retired to the chair in the alcove.

Light footsteps on the stairs brought him to his feet. Miss Godfrey appeared around the corner.

'Are you sure you want to stay?' she said. 'There is no bed down here.'

'Do not worry about me, my dear Miss Godfrey. I will be perfectly comfortable in this chair.'

'I am not your dear anything,' she shot back. 'I wish you a pleasant night.' She swung around and marched upstairs.

'Goodnight, Miss Godfrey.'

The upper door closed with a decided bang.

* * *

'The poor man has been guarding our property all night, lovey,' Mother said. 'The least we can do is offer him a cup of tea and a bite of breakfast.'

Breakfast consisted of a slab of ham, scrambled eggs and homemade bread when they usually ate toast and preserves. Mother would not be so happy to entertain *Mr West* so royally if she knew he was practically the devil incarnate.

Harriet had hardly slept a wink all night, knowing he was only a few feet below her. Every time she closed her eyes, his image floated in her mind, his lovely green eyes, his large manly physique, his charming smile. Bah! She was having nightmares because she feared what he might do if they were not able to recover his money.

Harriet sighed. 'Very well. I will take it down to him.'

The bells on the shop door tinkled.

Was he leaving?

Her heart picked up speed. Perhaps he had decided to go out for breakfast. For a moment, she considered running down and locking the door behind him. Her stomach sank. He'd be back with the constables in a trice. No. She would have to see this through, hoping and praying Mr Clark would be the answer to the problem.

The sound of male voices let her know that Westram had not gone out. He had let someone in.

It was barely half past six in the morning, so it wasn't a customer. She added another mug to the tray and carried it down. Mr Preston had arrived and he and

Westram were engaged in a low-voiced conversation. Westram broke off from what he was saying and smiled. 'Good morning, Miss Godfrey.'

Oh, good Lord, the scruff of beard darkening his jaw and upper lip along with that smile made him look like every girl's dream of a handsome pirate.

She banged the tray down on the counter. 'Good day, my lord. Mr Preston. Would you care to break your fast?'

Mr Preston put up a hand. 'I ate already, thank you, Miss Godfrey, but a cup of tea would not go amiss.'

'Is that for me?' Westram asked, looking at the tray.

'It is.'

'Thank you. It is most welcome.' He bowed and lay the napkin on his lap. 'Mr Preston will remain here until it is time for us to leave. I have some business to take care of, but I shall return in time to walk you to the coach.'

It seemed as if he had been spending his time planning how things were to be managed.

She nodded and left him to eat, while she set up a stool for Mr Preston by the door and went upstairs to finish packing.

Mother hovered in the doorway of her tiny little room.

'Do not try to open the shop in my absence.' Mother could not see well enough any more to serve customers. 'I will put a sign in the window saying we are temporarily closed. You do not need to feed the watchmen, they will come and go in shifts.'

Mother nodded, but she had an odd expression on her face.

'What?' Harriet asked.

'It is all a bit sudden, dearie. One minute we cannot afford a watchman, now we have a guard twenty-four hours a day and off you go to Bristol.'

'I told you, I received word of an important auction. Items perfect for the shop.'

Mother did not look convinced. Indeed, she looked worried. 'Mr West is a very handsome gentleman. But handsome is as handsome does.'

Harriet hated lying to her mother, but she did not want her to worry needlessly. Unfortunately, Mother sometimes saw more than Harriet wished. 'My departure is nothing to do with Mr West.'

She picked up her valise. 'I will be back before you know it.'

When she got downstairs, Westram had returned and was waiting beside the door. In the light from the oil lamp nearby, she could see evidence of fatigue.

He would be even more tired after the trip to the West Country.

Narrow-eyed, he looked her up and down. 'What on earth? Has there been a death in the family?'

Startled, she stared at him, then realised what he was talking about.

'I find, when travelling, people leave widowed ladies in peace.' Men, in particular. Particularly when she hid behind the veil draped over her plain black bonnet.

He shook his head. 'I do not think you need fear any interference if you are travelling with me.'

Her heart gave an odd little skip. Apparently, it was not other people she had to fear. It was herself.

He opened the door for her and they stepped out into the street. Clouds dashed across the sun every now and then and she pulled her cloak tighter around her against the chilly wind. At first, she had difficulty keeping up with his lengthy stride, but then he shortened it somewhat.

A gentlemanly thing to do. Respectful. It made her feel warm inside. Which was foolish, because he was the sort of man who would be polite to any woman.

Surprising thought. But he had been mostly polite, once his temper had settled.

The Swan with Two Necks when they arrived bustled with coachmen, ostlers, horses and passengers. The coach had not yet arrived and luggage was piled up outside the ticket office. Harriet usually bought her ticket in advance. Hopefully there was still room.

She strode to the ticket window.

Westram caught her arm. 'Where are you going?'

She looked at him askance. 'To buy my ticket.'

He shook his head. 'There is no need to be travelling by public conveyance. We will take my coach.' He gestured to a handsome black carriage with matching horses waiting outside the coffee shop.

Her jaw dropped and she gasped in shock. 'I cannot travel in that.'

'Why not? What is wrong with it.'

Really? 'I cannot travel in a gentleman's private

coach. If anyone sees me...why, they will think... Well, it is simply not suitable.'

He frowned. 'Who is going to see you? And why should they think anything?'

She glared at him. 'I do not know how things are done in your circles, but in mine, respectable unmarried females do not travel in closed carriages with single gentlemen. I travel to Bristol regularly. Any one of a number of people I know might see me. Besides, it will take days, for you cannot tell me you will risk your horses travelling all that distance in one day?'

'Certainly not.'

'Well, the stage takes fourteen hours. We will arrive in Bristol at ten tonight. I do not intend for this journey to take a moment longer than is needful.' He opened his mouth. 'No, I do not care what you say. I am going on the stage.' She pulled her arm free and marched up to the ticket window.

'Bristol,' she said and plunked down her coins.

'Good day, ma'am. Should have a good run today, weather looking to be fine.'

'I am glad to hear it.' She took her ticket.

Westram, who was looking puzzled rather than annoyed, followed suit, then left her standing, waiting with the other passengers, and crossed to his carriage to have a word with the coachman. He returned with his valise in hand, a smart black leather one, so different to her own made of canvas.

The mail bowled into the courtyard and with much pushing and shoving the passengers climbed aboard.

Somehow, Westram managed to get them each a seat

in opposite corners, the most prized position of all. One of the other passengers looked rather disgruntled since he had been the first to get on and had still ended up jammed between Westram and a farmer who had a bag of what smelled like onions on his knee. The elderly lady beside Harriet gave her an encouraging nod and a gentle smile. 'Right sorry for your loss, my dear.'

Feeling guilty, Harriet murmured her thanks. She did not dare look at Westram, since likely he would be very disapproving.

In no time at all the coach was off.

The best thing to do on such a long journey was to try to rest as much as possible. It certainly wouldn't do to spend her time gazing at the handsome young man opposite. Instead, she closed her eyes and imagined what it would be like to kiss his lovely mouth.

In the dim light inside the coach, Red watched Miss Godfrey, her head resting against the squabs, her eyes closed, her breathing even. In sleep, she looked sweeter, younger, than when she was wide awake and issuing orders. Her face was heart shaped and her lashes like blackbirds' wings against the pale skin beneath her eyes. Dressed fashionably, the *ton* would consider her a diamond of the first water. Not that a shopkeeper would be admissible to society, especially considering the sort of items she sold.

Eugenie would be horrified to see him travelling in such low company. The thought of Eugenie's horror gave him a flash of something uncomfortable. Irritation? Why would that be? Eugenie was a well-bred young woman, why should she not be horrified at the thought of him making a journey on a common stage?

Miss Godfrey, on the other hand, took it all in her stride. Yet oddly, though she lived in the meanest of circumstances, she seemed to be just as well-bred as his intended…but with a great deal more spirit.

He leaned forward and gently eased the veil over her face. She looked far too vulnerable and lovely. Though how she could sleep in such awkward circumstances, he could not imagine. The fellow beside him had knobby elbows and every time the coach jolted over a rut or took a corner one of those elbows found its way beneath his ribs.

What on earth had possessed him to allow Miss Godfrey her way and travel in this ridiculous manner, anyway? As a lad, he might have enjoyed it. He had often watched the stagecoaches go through the town near Westram and thought it would be a fine lark to ride on top or grab the ribbons from the coachman and drive himself. Older and wiser, he knew better. More than one accident had occurred because some wag had driven into a ditch.

The coach stopped at coaching inns every few miles to let passengers alight and climb aboard while they changed horses. Despite the jolting and the noise, Miss Godfrey did not stir. Was she asleep or merely pretending? He stared at her. Her posture was not as relaxed as one might expect if she was truly asleep.

A slender young woman with a basket full of mewling kittens took the place of the farmer which gave everyone on his side a bit more room. She inspected each of her travelling companions in turn and smiled broadly, revealing a mouth full of rotting teeth. 'Taking them to market. Their mother be a good mouser. Only asking a penny each.'

'Stupid girl,' said the thin man with the enormous moustache. 'Should have drowned 'em. No one *buys* cats when you can pick 'em up off the street.'

The girl hugged her basket closer. 'These be good kittens, sir. Mousers.' She peered up at Red appealingly.

No doubt this was why Miss Godfrey feigned sleep. He shook his head. 'I wish you good fortune finding them a new home.'

As the girl alighted at the next stop, he slipped a penny in her hand. 'Keep one for yourself,' he said.

She was still staring at him, mouth agape, as the coach rumbled out of the inn yard.

Hours passed. The names of the villages became a blur. Red found he, too, dozed and barely noticed as people came and went, though he was always aware of Miss Godfrey each time she stirred.

At six when they stopped, a waiter opened the door and shouted. 'Dine in the coffee room, ladies and gents, be you so inclined. Meat pies. Best ales in the West Country. This way, ladies and gents. This way, if you please.'

Miss Godfrey flipped back her veil and bolted.

Red leaped down after her. But she did not make her way to the coffee room, or try to disappear in the crowd, but instead headed in the same direction as the two other women from the coach.

Right. Needs must. He took care of his own needs and went to the coffee room, which was full of jostling passengers, and, by way of his greater height, managed to purchase a mug of ale, two pasties and a glass of water in short order.

He commandeered a bench against a wall in the courtyard sheltered from the wind and beneath a lantern and called out to Miss Godfrey as she, too, headed for the coffee room.

He held out the meat pie.

'My word,' she said. 'I rarely get time to buy food when we stop here. Thank you.'

'I am glad to be of assistance.'

She shot him a considering glance as if wondering if he meant what he said, then nibbled delicately on the pasty and sipped at her water, while keeping an eye on the progress of the change of horses and the coachman's own meal.

She did have lovely manners. Too bad she was not a member of society, she would make a lovely wife. What? No, no, he was not thinking about himself, it was simply an observation. He had a prospective bride.

She brushed crumbs off her skirts and, wiping her hands on her handkerchief, rose from the bench. 'We should reclaim our seats.'

Indeed, they should. Red took her arm and escorted her to the passengers milling about beside the coach. Only two of them were previous occupants: the thin man with the moustache and the elderly lady who had been sitting next to Miss Godfrey. The other two were men boarding for the first time.

When the guard opened the door Westram smiled politely at the others in the queue and they drew back a little. He helped the elderly lady through the door first. She beamed up at him as she mounted the steps 'Nice to meet a real gent.' She shot a backwards glance at the men pressing forward.

Red helped Miss Godfrey aboard and hopped in. They settled into the seats they'd held before. The rest of the passengers squeezed in and there was a bit of pushing and shoving to claim space and settle personal items.

A young man in a flashy bright green-and-red-striped satin waistcoat with frayed edges eyed Red up and down as the coach jerked and trundled out of the inn yard. 'Bit of a ladies' man, are ye?' He grinned, looking around as if expected some sort of congratulations for a witty remark.

''e's more gent in his little finger than you'll ever be,' the elderly lady said with a sniff.

''is *little* finger, is it?' The young man cracked a laugh. He jabbed an elbow in the side of the man sitting next to him, a portly gentleman with a bulging stomach and wearing old-fashioned buckskin knee-breeches. The man returned the elbow jab with interest.

One of the others muttered, 'Shut your pie hole', and the would-be dandy subsided into silence. The lights of the inn faded and now the only light on the world outside was the swinging lanterns either side of the driver.

Red took a leaf out of Miss Godfrey's book. He feigned a doze, while remaining fully aware of Miss Godfrey and his fellow passengers.

Chapter Four

Harriet slowly came to her senses to the sound of a child's piping tones. Surely she had not actually fallen asleep? While she always pretended sleep to avoid conversation with her fellow passengers, avoiding awkward questions about her mourning, she was usually too cautious to actually drift off. And now she had done so twice. Daylight illuminating the inside of the coach must have woken her.

Somehow the presence of Lord Westram gave her a sense of security she would be an absolute fool to trust. She sat upright and stretched her back as much as she could in the confines of the seat. She took in her fellow passengers. The old woman had also nodded off, her chin resting on her chest, and her lips puffing in and out with each breath. The young man in the bright green waistcoat looked to be asleep also, yet there was an odd tension about him.

At some point a mother with a small boy child on her knee had replaced one of the male passengers and she hadn't even noticed. They were seated beside Lord Westram and it was he to whom the boy was talking. 'Let me see it again, please, sir.'

'Don't you be a-troubling the gentleman, Georgie,' the mother said. 'I do beg your pardon, sir, but he do like anything mechanical.'

Lord Westram glanced at Harriet and raised an eyebrow. So, he was aware that she had woken. He smiled at the boy. 'One more time, then I expect we will reach your stop and we will bid each other farewell.'

The young mother nodded. 'We will indeed.'

The boy looked at Harriet. 'We are going to visit my grandfather. Mother has baked him a pie and some bread. We go every month.'

What a charming little boy.

He looked expectantly at Westram. Not at his face, but at the region of his waist. Westram pulled out his watch. A beautiful gold timepiece on a chain. Far too rich looking for a person travelling on a public conveyance.

The dandy's eyes opened, then closed, instantly, as if he had taken note of the handsome watch.

Westram flicked open the back of the watch and the boy gazed at the workings with a look of wonder on his face.

'The large gear is called the fly wheel,' Westram said.

The boy nodded. 'Yes, and that one there is the escapement wheel. And those are jewels. But how does it keep going for such a long time?'

Westram ruffled the lad's hair. 'You are a curious young fellow, aren't you?'

'Don't be troubling the gentleman any more, Georgie,' his mother said.

'He's not troubling me, ma'am. I am glad to see that he has such curiosity. You might want to apprentice him to a watchmaker when he is older. It is a good trade.'

'His pa wants him to be an ostler, same as he is,' the woman said.

'I want to be an inventor,' the lad said. 'I invented a way to pull up our water bucket with only one twist of the handle,' he said proudly.

His mother nodded. 'That you did. Till the string got in a tangle.'

'I needed better twine. If only Papa would have bought better twine—'

'Papa can't be spending money on string when there is food needs to be bought. You know that, Georgie.'

The boy nodded reluctantly. 'So, what makes it keep moving, sir?' He frowned. 'Does it have something to do with that there metal coil?'

'Yes, George,' Westram said. 'You have spotted it. That is the mainspring and, when I turn this little knob, it tightens the spring and it makes the wheels turn and they make the hands move and then I can tell the time.'

The two of them had their heads together, peering into the depths of the watch, and Harriet became aware of a strangely soft feeling in the region of her heart. A warm soft feeling. The man would make a wonderful husband and father.

She brushed away a tiny drop of moisture that

seemed to have formed on her lashes. What? Was she regretting that she would never have children? Or a husband? Nonsense. Had she not learned to value her independence, her self-reliance? If *she* made a mistake, then she would accept the consequences. What galled her was being forced to accept the consequences of folly committed by others. A husband or a father, for example.

The young flash in the green waistcoat shifted position and while his eyes seemed to be closed, his expression was intent and Harriet was sure his interest was focused on the watch.

The carriage began to slow.

The boy glanced up at his mother. 'Oh, no. Are we here already? I wanted to wait until the watch needed winding so I could see how the spring tightened.'

Westram chuckled. 'That won't be for a day or so, I am afraid. I tell you what. If you are still of a mind to be an inventor when you are older, come and see me.' He pulled a calling card from his pocket as the coach halted. He pressed it into the boy's hand.

The woman and the lad got out and the last Harriet saw of them was the young mother standing beneath the lamp beside the coaching inn door, staring at the card with her mouth open. The old lady also departed.

The young man in the green waistcoat shifted along the seat so he was now sitting next to Westram, watching him tuck his watch in his waistcoat pocket.

Harriet glared at him. 'Are you sure that timepiece is secure, Cousin? There are a great many rogues and cutpurses to be found travelling by stagecoach.'

Westram shot her a glance of surprise. He ran a slow glance around his fellow passengers, allowing it to linger on the fellow beside him before giving her an easy smile. 'I doubt there is anyone here who would care to tackle me for the privilege of relieving me of my possessions.'

The scrawny little fellow pretended to be oblivious of the look and the remark. 'Together, are ye?' he said. 'I am sorry for your loss, ma'am. You are fortunate to have a family to care for you at such a time. Going to visit relatives in Bath, are ye? Take the waters to pick up your spirits?'

'We travel on to Bristol,' Westram said, leaning back into his corner.

A couple of women boarded the carriage and squeezed in beside Harriet.

The green-waistcoated fellow gave them a speculative glance, then clearly dismissed them as being of no account. He turned his attention back to Westram. He nudged him with an elbow and Westram opened one eye. 'Your cousin is right, though, sir. The highway ain't no place to be displaying such finery for all to see, though I wouldn't say no to a closer look at that watch meself. Even from a distance, I made it out as a mighty fine piece.'

'A gift from my father,' Westram said quietly, 'and primarily of sentimental value.'

'Ah well, not all that glistens be gold, I suppose.' The fellow leaned back against the squabs and closed his eyes. They popped open again. 'Bristol, did ye say?'

But Westram's eyes remained firmly closed and he

did not answer. From behind her veil, Harriet determined to keep a close eye on their companion, and did so for a good few miles, until the guard's voice calling out the next stop had her jerking awake.

A scuffle opposite elicited a squawk from the woman beside her. Lord Westram had a fistful of green waistcoat in one hand and the fellow's other hand twisted up his back. 'I think not,' he said softly.

Green waistcoat struggled, then gave up. 'Can't blame a fellow for trying.' He tossed Westram his prize. Westram released him to catch it and green waistcoat made a dive for the door being held open by the guard, He was neatly propelled on his way by a large shiny boot to his rear end. He ended up an indignant heap on the mucky cobbles. He glared at Westram, but a growl from the guard who seemed to take his hasty departure from the carriage as some sort of personal insult caused him to scurry off. Passengers waiting to board crowded around and soon the young man in the green waistcoat was nowhere to be seen.

'Good riddance,' Westram said.

'Oh, my word, yes,' the lady beside Harriet said. She fluttered her eyelashes. 'How nobly you dealt with the rogue, sir. I declare that your very presence in this coach makes me feel easy in my mind. I am sure I shall have nothing to fear from highwaymen or any other sort of rogue we may meet upon the road. Isn't that right, Rose?'

Her companion nodded her assent. 'Heroic, I would call it.'

Harriet rolled her eyes. It seemed that Westram could

not travel quietly on a stagecoach. No. He had to attract all kinds of attention to himself. First the girl with kittens, then the boy. Then a common thief, no less. And now a couple of spinsters who looked as if they would like to eat him for breakfast.

'You are so brave, sir,' the first woman said, leaning forward as if about to throw her arms around Westram's neck. Harriet stifled the urge to yank her backwards. 'You are clearly a man of action. May we count on you for our safety until we reach Bath? I am Miss Ann Perry, by the way. Very pleased to make your acquaintance.'

'West,' he said and shook her proffered hand. He gestured in her direction. 'My cousin's widow, Mrs Godfrey.'

Harriet nodded.

'And this is my sister Rose,' Miss Perry said.

'Miss Rose,' Westram said, smiling. Somehow, he managed an elegant bow in the other lady's direction.

Both women giggled.

Really? Now he was flirting? Harriet wanted to bash him over the head. 'Since we have but a distance of twelve miles left to travel,' Harriet said, 'I should hardly think we are likely to run into another rogue like that one. Besides, he was a weedy little fellow. I'm surprised he had the nerve to attempt such a trick.'

Lord Westram made a sound that Harriet interpreted as a laugh cut short. 'He likely thought I was asleep,' he offered as if by way of an excuse for the fellow's foolhardiness.

Miss Perry turned her gaze on Harriet, clearly trying

to get a glimpse of her face. 'But one cannot be sure, can one? Being able to rely on a man ready to come to one's defence, a man of action… It must be a great comfort. I could only wish I were so fortunate.'

Westram's shoulders shook slightly. The wretch was enjoying the attention.

'My dear young lady,' said the male passenger who looked like a clerk, 'I can assure you I would be more than happy to come to the aid of any lady in distress. However, I would like to point out that Mr West here was doing what any man would do under the circumstances. He was protecting his property from a light-fingered thief. Property he unwisely flaunted under the fellow's nose.'

Harriet gave the speaker a nod of approval.

'As my cousin so wisely pointed out,' Westram acknowledged. 'One might almost say it was my fault he was tempted to try his luck.'

'Cousin?' Miss Perry said. She narrowed her eyes on Harriet. 'How delightful.' She fished in her reticule and handed a card to Harriet. 'Perhaps you and Mr West would do us the honour of calling on us if you ever visit Bath.'

Harriet took the card. 'I thank you, Miss Perry,' she said, 'but unfortunately that is highly unlikely.' She tried to hand back the card.

'Oh, no, please. Keep it. One never knows, does one. Be assured you and Mr West will be most welcome, even if you only have time to take a dish of tea.' She beamed at Westram, making it perfectly clear with whom her hopes rested.

Well, Westram could do as he pleased. Harriet was only interested in one thing. Getting out of his clutches.

'Have you always lived in Bath, Miss Perry?' Westram asked.

'Not always. Father used to be a clerk at the Customs House in Bristol. I can assure you, if you ever visit Bath, our father would give you his thanks for offering your strong arm as protection after such a dreadful incident.'

Harriet's jaw dropped. Good heavens, the woman was making it sound as if she was the one who had been the thief's victim.

Westram beamed at them. 'As my cousin says, it is unlikely, but I am happy to be of service.'

He was a wolf in sheep's clothing, was what he was. Harriet folded her arms across her chest and comforted herself with the thought that they would soon be rid of the Misses Perry and could return to the matter at hand.

The matter of discovering who was responsible for cheating Westram's father.

'Did you number a Mr Maxwell Clark among your acquaintances in Bristol?' Red enquired since it had occurred to him that these garrulous ladies might be of some assistance in their quest and the receipt Miss Godfrey had provided showed no street address for the man.

'Maxwell Clark,' Miss Perry mused. 'The name does not sound familiar. Does it to you, Sister?' The younger sister shook her head.

Disappointing. 'He imports antiquities, I believe,' Red added.

'Then our father must surely have heard of him,'

Miss Perry offered with a bright beguiling smile. 'Anyone importing anything into England through Bristol must pay duties. Father knew everyone. Perhaps you should stop in Bath after all and ask him.'

'Thank you for your kind offer, but we shall enquire at the post office. We shall certainly find an address for him there,' Miss Godfrey said in that prosaic way she had.

Miss Perry looked disappointed. 'Well, if you do not find him that way, then perhaps you will return to Bath and seek out my father.'

He smiled. 'Perhaps I shall.'

The coach slowed to a walk and turned into an inn courtyard. 'Bath,' the guard shouted. ''Next stop Bristol.'

Westram stepped down and helped the Perry sisters to alight to a chorus of effusive farewells.

When he returned to his seat, Harriet shook her head at him. 'You know you have no intention of calling on her papa. Why get her hopes up?'

'I was simply being polite.'

'You were flirting unashamedly. Just the sort of thing you men about town think you can do with impunity, never realising that the poor woman will probably dream of your arrival with hope in her heart for the next two days and be terribly cut up when you don't.'

'I had no thought of causing her pain.'

'Of course you didn't. You were simply enjoying yourself at her expense.'

The accusation left him speechless—and more curious about Miss Godfrey than ever.

* * *

When they arrived at their final destination, the Rummer, on High Street, an ostler yanked the door open. Typically, Miss Godfrey was out of the door before Red could offer assistance, blast her.

Once away from the press of people, she paused. 'Our first order of business is to find accommodations and a meal. I usually stay at a boarding house nearby. It's run by a respectable woman and reasonably priced with breakfast and supper included.'

'And how do you intend to explain my presence as your escort to this respectable woman?'

She threw her veil back. 'Well I suppose you could stay elsewhere.'

Once more she was trying to be rid of him. 'Why not take rooms here?' The Rummer would, like all coaching inns, be a hive of activity at all hours of the day and night and would accept their presence without question. 'We will set out first thing tomorrow to find this Maxwell Clark and be on our way back to London by evening, our quest accomplished.'

She looked up at the inn with an expression of doubt. 'I do not think I can afford anything as fine as this.'

Red frowned. The house was neither fine nor did it look terribly expensive in his book. 'I have no intention of staying where I am likely to encounter bad food, bad wine and bed bugs, Miss Godfrey.'

She shuddered and did not demur when he led her inside the inn where the landlord was waiting to greet them. 'Two rooms, please, and a sitting room, if you have it,' Lord Westram said, removing his gloves.

The landlord glanced down at the register. He frowned. 'I have but one room with a parlour, Mr...'

'West,' he answered unhesitatingly. 'And my cousin Mrs Godfrey.' He glanced at her and winked. The wretch. Was he enjoying this adventure? Had he forgotten her whole life hung in the balance?

The landlord smirked as if he did not believe a word of it, then shrugged. 'It is all I have available.'

Westram hesitated, clearly weighing the proprieties. He turned to her. 'What do you think, my dear Cousin? Can we manage? It will be but for one night, after all.'

She should tell him no and go to the boarding house where she usually stayed, but then, as he had remarked earlier, how would she explain his presence? She would likely never be able to stay there again. 'For one night, then,' she said.

The landlord looked relieved. He turned back to Westram. 'If you would care to leave your bags with me, sir, I will have them sent up. Do you have servants who require accommodation?' Once more he looked concerned. 'I might be able to find a corner in the commons, or in the hayloft.'

Westram shook his head. 'My cousin will require a maid. I will do for myself. We will take our supper in the private parlour.'

A maid. She didn't need a maid. She glared at Westram, but he seemed oblivious to her disapproval.

The landlord led them upstairs and to the back of the house. He opened a door to a nice little apartment. 'I do hope you find everything to your satisfaction.' He handed over the key to Lord Westram. 'Your bags will be sent up shortly. Supper will be served in an hour.'

The rooms looked out over the streets at the back of the house rather than the bustling courtyard.

Westram opened the door to the adjoining bedroom and gestured for her to enter. 'You can sleep in here,' he said. 'I will use the couch.'

Relief flooded through her, tinged with a smidgeon of disappointment. What? Had she thought he might share her bed? Or at least make the suggestion, so she could refuse? Was she such an antidote that the thought didn't even occur to him?

Good heavens! What a highly inappropriate thought. What was the matter with her? First, she had felt a twinge of jealousy when he had flirted with the ageing Misses Perry and now she wanted him to at least notice her as a woman. Even if he was too much the gentleman to do anything about it.

'Thank you,' she said, walking past him and into the bedroom as if it was the most commonplace thing in the world. 'I will refresh myself before dinner.'

He closed the door behind her and she collapsed on to the bed, fanning her suddenly hot cheeks.

The bedroom was a luxurious affair compared to her usual lodgings, with a four-poster bed on one side of the window and an escritoire, washstand and dressing table on the other. This suite of rooms was going to cost a fortune. And she was going to have to pay her share. Not to do so would be unseemly and put her under an obligation.

Harriet availed herself of the necessary facilities and

bathed her face and hands in the water on the washstand, then sat down on the edge of the bed, tipped
out her purse and counted her precious store of coins.
It had seemed like a goodly sum when she left home,
but now she wondered if there would be enough left to
cover her ticket home, once they found Mr Clark and
Lord Westram was satisfied that neither she nor her father were criminals.

She gathered up her crowns and shillings and pennies and replaced them in the little leather pouch. Since
Father's death, she had become adept at dealing with the
household finances. She never went into debt. Would
she be forced to borrow from His Lordship to pay her
way? Heaven forbid. No. When they got to the bottom of who had defrauded Westram's father, she would
insist on being recompensed for her expenses as was
only right.

After removing her nightgown and her washing kit
from her valise, she hid the purse in the bottom of it and
tucked it under the bed. On second thought it would be
better if she kept in on her person. She hauled the valise out again and, taking the ribbon from the neck of
her nightgown, tied the purse around her waist under
her skirts. Fortunately, they were not the flimsy narrow
skirts worn by fashionable ladies and their fullness hid
its presence quite nicely.

A scratch at the door and a maid entered. She glanced
around. 'Is there anything I can do for you, ma'am?'
she said.

With a sigh Harriet added to her list of expenses. In a
place like this the servants would expect to be rewarded

handsomely for any small service they performed. If she did not find Mr Maxwell Clark soon she would be ruined. 'Not at the moment, thank you.'

The girl dipped a curtsy. 'Ring the bell when you are ready to retire and I will come and take your gown and freshen it for the morning.'

'That will not be necessary,' Harriet said firmly. She was going to have a word with His Lordship and request him not to spend her hard-earned income on such frivolities.

The maid looked surprised, but nodded. 'I am to tell you that dinner will be served in about fifteen minutes.' She bobbed a curtsy and left.

When Harriet returned to the parlour His Lordship was lounging in a chair by the hearth with a glass of red wine. The moment he saw her he leapt to his feet.

Such nice manners. Her father had been like that. Always the gentleman. No matter how poor they were, he never failed to observe the niceties.

'Miss Godfrey. May I pour you a glass of wine or water?' Westram asked.

'Nothing for me, thank you.'

She eyed his wine with some misgivings. Would he become drunk and forget his gentlemanly manners? Men often became amorous in their cups she had noticed during the stops at various coaching inns over the years when she travelled.

Good Lord, was that a flutter of anticipation rather than fear hopping around in her stomach? What had come over her? Whatever it was, it needed to stop. This man had made it very clear he would not hesitate to bring her to ruin if he did not get his money back.

Red was glad to see that Miss Godfrey had exchanged her ugly bonnet for a small lacy cap and her shapeless spencer for a shawl, though both were black. Perhaps she did not realise that, despite her drab and old-fashioned clothing, she was an exceedingly attractive woman. Dressed in silks and feathers with her glossy black hair styled in something less severe than a tight knot at her nape, she would be stunning.

Whether it was her feminine curves, her heart-shaped face or her dark blue eyes so luminous and expressive of her feelings that made her so attractive, he wasn't sure. Certainly, she was as unlike Eugenie as any woman could be.

And he liked her spirit.

She had a mind of her own. Unlike Eugenie, who was concerned only with what other people thought and what she thought of them.

Good Lord, where had these disloyal thoughts come from? Eugenie was the standard to which ladies in society should aspire. He wasn't marrying her for anything so mundane as her looks or her spirit. Quite the opposite. He was marrying her to bring them both advantage. She, the advantage of his title, And he, the restoration of the Westram title to its former glory as he had promised his father.

If not for the action of this woman's parent, he would have been preparing for his nuptials right now. Once more he felt a twinge of misgiving at Eugenie so easily backing out of their arrangement.

Nonsense. She was obeying her father. And she would be a good and dutiful wife, just as she was a good and dutiful daughter. Though he could not help wishing she had taken his part rather than her father's on this particular occasion. He could not deny her lack of loyalty to him had stung. But Eugenie was a stickler for duty. And so was Red. It was the reason he had always been sure they would do well together.

As the heir to the title, duty and honour had been drummed into him from the day he was born. Sometimes, growing up, he'd felt a twinge of envy for his siblings' freer existences, but they, too, had had their duties and responsibilities. Besides, no honourable gentleman ever went back on his word, once given.

Meanwhile, he had allowed himself to be convinced to go on a wild goose chase with Miss Godfrey, but not because he felt sorry for the young woman or because she was attractive. His decision had been practical and rational. If there was the faintest chance to get the money back, then it was his duty to try.

'I hope your bedchamber is to your liking?' he asked to fill what had become an uncomfortably long pause.

'It is far too expensive. One night is all I can afford, so we must hope we find Mr Maxwell in short order on the morrow.'

He frowned. 'I beg your pardon, but while I, too, hope we may accomplish our mission quickly, I had no intention of asking you to pay for rooms which I engaged.'

She glared at him. 'You cannot think I would let you pay for my accommodations. What must people think should they discover...?' She made an all-encompassing gesture. 'It is simply not appropriate.'

There was an edge of censure in her voice.

A censure he did not deserve. Despite very trying circumstances he had behaved with the utmost forbearance. It was she, challenging him at every turn, who had brought them to Bristol and to this inn in the first place.

He looked down his nose. 'Perhaps you would prefer that we bed down in the commons with the servants?'

An odd expression crossed her face. Her expression lightened. 'Very well, since the hiring of these rooms is entirely for your convenience, I shall have no objection to your paying the shot, just as long as you remain on this side of that bedroom door.'

She gave him a challenging look.

A trickle of heat ran along his veins. Desire. A powerful longing. He liked a challenge.

Angry at his responses to the woman whose father had tricked his family out of a fortune, he strode to the console and poured himself another glass of wine. When he turned back to her, she was eyeing his glass with disapproval. Or was it trepidation?

Did she think that after two glasses of wine he would forget he was a gentleman?

Red took a deep breath. He really had had enough of people impugning his honour. But this woman was not a member of society. She did not know that he had been brought up with strict standards with regard to the proper treatment of women. After all, there were many men who would take advantage of the circumstances in which they found themselves. But he was not one of them.

Which he would have to prove by actions, not words.

A rap at the door heralded the entry of a couple of waiters with their supper on trays.

They stood in silence while the waiters set up a table for two beside the window and delivered several courses of what looked like a very fine dinner including soup.

'Would you like us to serve you, sir?' the waiter asked. 'Or would you and the lady prefer to be alone?' He gave Miss Godfrey a sly glance.

Miss Godfrey stiffened.

Red's hands curled into fists at the innuendo. Damn the man. 'Yes, you may serve us.'

The waiter looked disgruntled, but seated Miss Godfrey and they started with the soup. It was hearty and delicious.

Next came the roast beef accompanied by buttered parsnips, boiled potatoes and peas.

Miss Godfrey ate well, he noticed, and conversed with admirable calmness throughout the meal, on whatever subject matter was raised. She had a good mind and was clearly well read. Something he had not expected. There was so much more to this woman than met the eye.

Dinner finished, he leaned back in his chair. The waiter refilled his glass.

'Let us hope we quickly find Mr Maxwell upon the morrow,' he said.

She toasted him with her water. 'Indeed. The sooner the better.'

She sounded so convincing, he was tempted to take her word for her and her father's innocence.

But that would be foolish. He wanted proof of the truth. And he wanted his money back.

Chapter Five

Harriet eyed the bedroom door. Did she just leave the table and go to her room?

Should she ring for the maid from here and then retire? It was going to be very strange removing her clothes and putting on her nightdress, knowing he was on the other side of the door and would be for the rest of the night.

The less time she spent in this disturbing man's presence, the better. He seemed to be constantly weighing and measuring her words and her person—looking for signs of guilt, no doubt.

Worry gnawed at her insides. Why had Father not spotted the idol was a fraud? Yes, it was a good one, but surely not that good. Perhaps once they found this Mr Clark she would have more understanding of what had happened.

'I think I will retire now,' she said.

He glanced up from his wine. 'Good idea. It has been a long and tiring day. I imagine you must be exhausted.'

It wasn't the travel that had exhausted her, it was being around him. 'I am indeed tired.' She rose to her feet and he followed suit.

'I think I will visit the taproom, for a bit,' he said. 'See if any of the locals might give us word of the man.' He reached in his pocket and she expected him to pull out his watch, though there was a perfectly good clock on the mantel. But, no. What he brought forth was a key. He put it down on the table in front of her. 'So you can lock your chamber door. I will let our host know he can clear away the meal.' He strode out.

She rang the bell for the maid, who arrived looking red-faced and harried.

'I am sorry, ma'am, I do not have long. A party of five arrived seeking lodging and a meal and Mr Derby do be in a taking given that one of them be a duke. He's had to move other guests around to accommodate him.'

A duke? Oh, good heavens, no doubt he would be someone Lord Westram would know. Would Westram have enough sense to avoid him? It would certainly look very odd if the said duke was to discover Lord Westram had used a pseudonym and was travelling incognito with a woman. Should she warn him?

'Is something wrong, ma'am?' the maid asked.

'I—no. I mean I need to get a message to Mr West at once. I believe you will find him in the taproom.' She dashed to the escritoire and scribbled a note.

'But, mum,' the maid said, sounding distraught, 'I has to help you to bed and get back to help out in the kitchen.'

'That's fine. Deliver the message and return to your

other duties. I can manage to undress without help. It is important that Mr West get this note as soon as possible.' Imperative. Though why she should care if this unknown duke caught him out in a lie, she wasn't sure. Westram should have known better than to have stayed at the main coaching house in Bristol.

Yet for some strange reason she did care. Perhaps it was because, despite all of his suspicions, he had been perfectly gentlemanly to her and then there was his kindness to the people they had met along the way. The girl with the kittens and the little boy. And, when it had come to the man in the green waistcoat, he'd been truly magnificent. So she might have told him, if not for the Misses Perry hanging on his every word.

'If you are sure, mum.' The girl grabbed the note and the penny Harriet held out to her and bustled off.

Harriet paced the small chamber.

Time passed and no sign came that Lord Westram had received her message. Perhaps she had been too late.

Perhaps he had met the duke and the two of them were carousing in the bar.

At the end of an hour, she decided she was worrying needlessly. Whereas she had always taken charge where her father was concerned once she realised he had no more sense than a baby when it came to money, Lord Westram could no doubt take care of himself.

And so what if the duke discovered he was travelling with a lady who was not his wife? It wasn't as if she was a known society miss whose whole life depended on her maintaining a spotless reputation. No, indeed. She was an independent business woman who could do exactly as she pleased.

Her only worry at the moment was to get to the bottom of how this fraud had been perpetrated on both Westram's father and her own. Because no matter how badly Father had let her and Mother down, she would not, could not believe he would ever knowingly stoop to criminal activity.

Having come to her decision, she readied herself for bed and slipped beneath the covers. In the quiet, the sound of male voices and the clink of glasses floated up through the floorboards. From time to time, the shouts in the courtyard heralded the arrival of another coach full of noisy passengers.

Tomorrow they would find Mr Clark and get to the bottom of the mystery. They must. Otherwise what would become of her and Mother? Gentlemanly he might be, but Westram had shown he had a ruthless streak.

She shot up in bed. What? A loud thump from the adjoining parlour had her swinging her feet over the side of the bed, her heart racing. Then she recalled where she was. She must have fallen asleep and His Lordship's return must have awoken her.

It must be him. Mustn't it?

Who else could it be?

What if some stranger had wandered into the parlour by mistake? She slipped out of bed and padded across the room to the door. She hesitated. She dropped silently to her knees and peered through the keyhole.

It was Westram, wearing nothing but a shirt. He stood before the fire sipping a glass of wine. In addition to the clear view she had of the backs of his naked knees, well-muscled calves and large male feet, the outline of his form from wide shoulders to narrow flanks created dark shadows beneath the translucent material. It really was the most enticing thing she had ever seen. Her mouth dried. Her heart seemed to pound in her ears.

The figures of naked men she sold in her shop left her mostly unmoved, but this view of a large vibrant male staring into the fire, feet planted wide, muscular legs softened by the fuzz of hair that gleamed red in the flickering flames, left her breathless. Heat travelled up from her belly.

She gasped at the shock of the visceral reaction.

He seemed to still, as if listening. Had he heard? She leaned back, covering her mouth with a hand.

She should creep back to her bed and pretend to sleep, after one quick look to make sure he was unaware of her peeking.

Her heart thundered. No. It was all very well to make sure it was His Lordship who was moving around in the room beside hers, but it was not all right to spy on him.

She swallowed. But what if he had heard her and was even now making his way to her door? She leaned forward and looked again.

Sadly, he had moved away from the fire and was in the process of rearranging the pillows on the sofa. As he leaned over, the shirt rode up and offered her a brief glimpse of a beautifully formed firm and slender buttock gilded by firelight. So smooth, like fine marble, yet warm and alive. Her palm tingled with the desire to touch, to stroke, to— She curled her hands into fists. This really would not do. While he was handsome and desirable, he had made it perfectly clear that he thought her a criminal.

With a sigh he lay down on the sofa on his back and put his hands behind his head. His feet hung over the arm at the opposite end and bony knees filled her view. It looked most uncomfortable, to be sure. And he didn't even have a blanket.

Oh, how unkind that she had not thought to leave him some sort of cover.

Red gazed up at the ceiling and shifted, trying to get comfortable. He doubted he was going to get much sleep for the second night in a row. It was hard not to resent the comfortable bed occupied by Miss Godfrey.

The note she had sent him had stopped him from running into an old friend and sent him, instead, to a nearby tavern frequented mostly by seamen. It was odd how the worst of all scenarios could result in the desired outcome. If he had not left the inn—

The chamber door creaked. He lifted his head.

The object of his thoughts stood framed in the doorway with a candle in her hand and something over her arm. A cloak. Was she trying to sneak out in the middle of the night?

He sat up. 'Miss Godfrey?'

Her gaze skittered away from him and fixed upon the hearth. The light of the candle in her hand cast her features into planes and shadows. She looked ethereal.

Quite lovely. She wore a robe over a nightgown that was high about her throat. Her black hair fell in a thick braid that lay over one shoulder and hung down almost to her waist. How would it look if it was loose? Like a river at night?

Curse it. That was none of his business.

He set his feet on the floor and stood. 'I beg your pardon, did I disturb you? May I be of assistance?' For example, assist her to return to her comfortable bed with a warning not to try to leave.

'I—no, not really. Actually, since you are paying for this room, I thought perhaps I should take the sofa and you the bed.'

She held out the item slung over her arm and he now saw that it was not a cloak at all, but a blanket.

A flash of guilt at his uncharitable thought tightened his chest. 'That is most kind of you, but I assure you I am quite comfortable.'

She looked doubtful.

He took the blanket from over her arm and flung it over the back of the sofa. 'This will make it perfect. I thank you for your message, by the by. It turned out that the duke's arrival was most fortuitous.'

She held the candle higher as if to see his expression.

He offered her a smile. 'I left the inn and discovered word of your Mr Clark.'

Surprise, or some other emotion, caused her hand to shake and wax spilled on to her knuckles. She hissed in a breath.

He snatched the candle and set it on the table. He

caught her wrist and lifted her trembling hand to the light. 'Let me see.'

She tried to pull away. 'It is nothing.'

He held her fast. 'Let me be the judge of that, Miss Godfrey.' He flicked off the now cool drip of wax. The delicate skin beneath had reddened.

'Sit,' he commanded.

When she did not move, he pressed down on her shoulder and she sank into the chair. He brought an ewer of water on the console by the window over to the table. He knelt at her side and used his handkerchief to bathe the burn. 'That should take some of the heat out of it.'

'You said you have word of Mr Clark?'

'I do. Apparently, he trades in curios and knick-knacks from the Orient and is known to several of the ship's captains.'

Her shoulders relaxed slightly. 'That makes sense. And you have his direction?'

'He owns a warehouse near the docks. The men I spoke to were vague about the address, but a few enquiries should lead us to him in the morning.' He dipped his handkerchief in the water, wrung it out and once more laid it over the burn.

She bit her lip, as if she still felt some pain. 'This is good news.'

'Yes. It is now a simple matter of finding the gentleman at his place of business.'

Her shoulders slumped.

He was surprised by her reaction. He had expected her to be pleased. 'Come now, Miss Godfrey, no need to be anxious. We have proof of this gentleman's existence, something, I have to say, I rather doubted when we set out on this venture. We shall get to the bottom of this matter within a day or so, I am sure.' Good Lord, was he actually trying to comfort the woman? Since when had he begun to believe her story that she was as much of a victim in this as he was? Besides, whether she knew about it or not, her father had profited from this fraud.

'To be honest,' she said softly, 'I worry about my mother. I never leave her alone for more than two nights.'

'She is not exactly alone. My men will ensure her safety.'

She inspected the burn on her hand. 'Thank you. That feels much better.'

'You are welcome.' He stood up and looked down at her. 'What really troubles you, Miss Godfrey? Up until now, you seemed so sure that once we located Mr Clark everything would be explained, and my money would be refunded. Now, when we almost have the man in our grasp, you seem to have doubts.'

'What if Mr Clark denies any knowledge of the artefact? If he is indeed responsible for the fraud perpetrated on your father, he is quite likely to do so, is he not?'

'We have your father's ledger and the receipt. Enough proof to swear out a warrant against him, should he not own to his crime and make restitution.'

She rose to her feet. 'You think it enough?'

He hated that she sounded so uncertain and put an arm about her shoulders and gave her a light squeeze. A gesture of comfort. Yet once he felt her curvaceous form aligned down his side, he was loath to release her. 'We will get to the bottom of this, I promise.' He tilted her chin with his other hand and gazed down into her lovely face. 'No matter the outcome of our investigation, Miss Godfrey, I do believe that neither you nor your mother were in anyway involved.'

'But you are not convinced of my father's innocence.'

'No. Are you?'

'I never knew him to be dishonest in his dealings. But...' her eyes, so deep and dark in the dim candlelight, met his with a quiet sort of desperation '...now we are close to discovering the truth, I find myself less sure. The transaction took place at a time of great difficulty for my family. He might have been led astray by our dreadful circumstances.'

Her slight body shook and he could not help himself. His arms went around her and he held her close. 'Please, Miss Godfrey, Harriet, do not let your courage desert you. We have come so far. Your fears may be groundless. Let us not imagine the worst until it happens.'

Without thinking, he bent his head and brushed her mouth with his. Her lips were velvet soft, pliant and warm, and for a brief instant she responded to his light touch with a melding of her mouth to his. A soft yielding that left him wanting more.

The beat of her heart through his shirt set his blood coursing hot through his veins. He'd been attracted to her the moment he saw her in her shop. The anger he harboured with regard to the circumstance of their meeting had tainted his opinion. In all of their conversations, she had been open and honest. He felt sorry for her. That was all this was, surely?

Eugenie had always admonished him for being too soft-hearted with his sisters and it seemed they weren't the only ones who could pull at his heartstrings. He could not allow himself to be diverted from his need to get to the bottom of this fraud and to clear his family name. Not to mention reinstate his betrothal, as he had promised Eugenie he would.

He stepped back. 'I think perhaps you should return to your chamber. Thank you for the blanket. I will put it to good use.' He bowed. 'Goodnight, Miss Godfrey.'

She stared at him for a long moment, swallowed, and turned and fled. Cursing himself for a quixotic fool— after all, what man would not have seen just where the sort of kiss they had shared could lead?—he stretched out on the sofa.

That kiss had been lovely. Unlike anything Harriet had ever experienced. As she dressed the following morning, she touched a fingertip to her lips. She had only been kissed once before and it had been nothing like the gentle touch of Lord Westram's lips upon hers. Rodney Stover had been more intent on convincing her that now he'd kissed her, she was honour bound to wed and thus he would get his hands on her father's premises.

The moment Rodney had realised her father had run into debt and would lose the premises, he had turned as cold as the north wind in January. Thankfully, since that time she had built up a nice clientele and now she and Mother could be sure of their futures.

Then Lord Westram had come along and burst her bubble. What if she was wrong about Father? The idea that Lord Westram would see her as complicit in a crime against his family was mortifying. She did not want him to despise her. Not to mention that it might land her in prison.

She pulled out the ledger and the receipt from her valise. The name, Mr Maxwell Clark in bold flowing script at the bottom of the receipt, once more bolstered her belief that he was the guilty party.

The date was the year prior to their incarceration, thus was not related to her father's need to pay off the debt that had resulted in imprisonment, though his debts had been mounting for a long time. She had assumed they had been paid off by selling the stock they had in the shop at the time. But he would have been trying to find the money long before then. Why had he never mentioned having sold something to the Earl of Westram? A noble client like that would have been a feather in his cap. When Harriet had questioned her mother, she said she had heard nothing about it, which seemed strange.

Apparently, Harriet was about to discover the truth.

A knock sounded at her chamber door. 'Breakfast has arrived,' Lord Westram announced.

She pinned a smile on her face and stepped out into the parlour. The blanket she had brought him the previous evening lay neatly folded at one end of the sofa. He was already seated at the table and rose as she entered.

He pulled out a chair and seated her. 'I hope you slept well?' he said in that lovely, deep, rich voice.

'Yes, thank you.' Well, there was no point in complaining about feeling restless and anxious, was there?

'And your hand?'

She glanced down at her knuckle. 'How kind of you to remember. Completely healed, thank you.'

'I am glad.'

The sincerity in his voice strummed a little chord low in her belly. She felt cared for. Which was nonsense. His only care was the return of his money. Once that occurred, she would never see him again.

Her heart gave a painful squeeze. Why should it matter so much? Was it that brief kiss playing with her emotions? Surely not. She was far too sensible to make it into more than it was. A bit of nonsense.

Fortunately for her, he had drawn back before she made a complete and utter fool of herself.

She would certainly not let it happen again.

'May I pour you a cup of tea?' he asked. 'Or do you prefer coffee?'

If only he were not so considerate. It would be so much easier not to fall under his spell. But then she had just as easily fallen under Rodney's spell, had she not? At the age of seventeen she had been flattered by his attention. He had made her feel like an adult woman whereas Father always treated her as his little girl. At least, until she'd insisted he see her otherwise.

In those days, Rodney quite often came in when Father was busy with a customer and would ask her about the items for sale, as if her opinion mattered.

Sometimes when she went shopping, he would offer his escort. On those occasions he'd made her giggle and feel giddy when he complimented her hair or her gown. She'd found herself trying new styles, in case she met him on the street. When he asked her to secretly walk out with him, because he did not want her father putting a stop to their friendship, she had thought he actually cared for her.

Fortunately, his real interest was revealed before she let him do more than kiss her. It hadn't been her he was interested in, it was the shop. Knowing she could never be more than a passing fancy for Westram, she would be an idiot to fall for his charm. 'Tea would be lovely, thank you.'

The breakfast he had ordered was far more substantial than the tea and toast she was used to at home and she tucked into the scrambled eggs and the generous slice of ham with relish. He picked up his newspaper and scanned the headlines.

How oddly comfortable she felt sitting here across the table from him. She could almost imagine... She blinked the vision away. They were here on business and the sooner it was completed the sooner her life would return to normal.

'If you are finished eating, I think we should set out.' She must have sounded a little waspish, because he glanced up swiftly with a frown.

'I was waiting for you, Miss Godfrey.'

'Then I will fetch my coat and we will depart.'

It was not many minutes before they were setting out to find Mr Maxwell Clark.

Though Harriet had visited Bristol several times before in search of items for her shop, she had never visited the docks. The importer she dealt with always displayed the items he had set aside for her at the back of his emporium. He primarily dealt in objets d'art, but when he came across things he thought she might like he would set them aside until he had enough to make her journey worthwhile.

Some of her most successful trinkets had come through him.

This time, they walked down to the docks themselves, to the new floating harbour designed by Mr William Jessop. Built only a few years before, it allowed ships to remain afloat at low tide, instead of sitting in the mud. Warehouses, tall and grimy, crowded close to the edge of the wharves and sailors and dockworkers hustled about their business.

The warehouse they sought did not front on to the water, but rather was reached by way of a dingy alley. Harriet tried not to breathe too deeply or to think about exactly what caused the appalling aroma.

Westram rapped hard on a narrow door with a peeling sign that read 'Farge's Imports'. It creaked open. An elderly man, with white hair straggling over his bent shoulders and droopy moustaches, peered up at them with dark rheumy eyes.

'We seek Mr Maxwell Clark,' Westram announced and held out his calling card.

The old man looked at it as if it might bite. He shook his head. 'Not here.'

Westram glared at him. 'Do you mean you do not know him, or that he is not here at the moment?'

'Not here. Why does ye want him?'

Harriet's heart stilled. It seems they had indeed found the man they sought.

'I do not see why you need to know. I am a customer of his.'

The old fellow squinted. 'Then ye should know where to find him.'

'Perhaps I should speak to the owner of this establishment. Mr Farge, is it?'

The man cackled. 'Farge be dead this many a year. If ye wants the owner it be Maxwell Clark.'

Harriet pushed forward. 'If you would be so good as to give us Mr Clark's direction, we will not need to trouble you any further.'

The old fellow chewed on the edges of his moustache for a moment, then shrugged. 'I suppose it ain't no secret. I suppose as 'ow I could tell ye.' He looked expectantly at Westram, who sighed.

He dug in his waistcoat pocket and tossed a coin into the old man's waiting palm. 'Where, then, may I find him?'

'Mr Maxwell lives in Queen Square, sir, but you won't find him there. Not this week.'

'Where will I find him?'

'Bath, sir. His wife has the ague and they went to partake of the waters. He be back in a week, mebbe sooner.'

A week? They could not wait here for a week. Harriet exchanged a glance with Lord Westram. He nodded at the old man. 'Thank you for the information.'

He took her arm and they left.

Once more out on the street, Westram looked grim. 'Well, it looks like we will be kicking our heels here for a few more days.'

Chapter Six

'Certainly not,' Harriet said. 'I'm going to Bath.'

Here she went, trying to rule the roost again. 'Don't be ridiculous. For all you know, you might pass him on the road.'

'His man said he'd be gone a week.'

'At most. Besides, we will go all the way to Bath, only to have to return to Bristol.'

'It is twelve miles. We can walk there before dinner time.'

He had a vision of her marching down the road, carrying her valise. 'Dash it, woman. I am not walking. If we must go, we will rent a post-chaise.'

She shook her head. 'Too expensive.'

He glared. 'Did I ask you to pay?'

'No, but it is not right that you should have to bear the expense—'

'A post-chaise costs the same whether there are two passengers or one.'

'Oh. I did not know. Still, it would be cheaper to go by mail or the stage.'

'I have had enough of travelling by stage to last me the rest of my life.'

She laughed.

When he glared at her, she gave a little shrug. 'I am sorry, but you looked so disgruntled I could not help it. I thought you enjoyed yourself during the journey.'

He could not resist a grin. 'It was an experience, I must admit. But once was quite enough. I am not so nip cheese as to begrudge a pound or two on the hiring of a carriage.' He caught her frown. 'I do, however, resent being defrauded of vast sums of money. Especially when I am also implicated in the scheme. My family's name and reputation are at risk.'

'As is mine,' she said, 'which is why I am so anxious to get to the truth of the matter as soon as possible.'

'Very well. We travel to Bath in search of Clark, but let us hope it will bring this wild goose chase to a conclusion.'

Having returned Miss Godfrey to the inn and set her to packing, Red went off to arrange for a post-chaise. He also took the time to visit Mr Clark's abode. The knocker was off the door, indicating the owner was not at home, but the retainer who answered the door was a great deal more forthcoming than the warehouse man had been.

Miss Godfrey was right to want to follow Mr Clark to Bath. The family was not expected back in Bristol for at least a fortnight. Not that he planned to tell her she was right. It would make her bossier than she was already.

The thought made him smile.

He arranged for a post-chaise to pick them up at the inn and returned there to find Miss Godfrey seated in the coffee shop, waiting for him.

Good Lord, she could have wandered off without a word and he might never have seen her again. He had not given it a thought. Indeed, he had fully expected her to be waiting for him and she was. It seemed that, somewhere over the past two days, he had begun to trust her.

'I will get my bag and pay the shot,' he said. 'The post-chaise will be here momentarily.'

The ride to Bath was a great deal more pleasant than the journey by stage. First, they had a good view of the road ahead, secondly the vehicle was well sprung and comfortable and the journey only took an hour and a half.

'Oh, what a splendid view,' Miss Godfrey said as they drove down the hill towards the centre of the town. 'One never sees such a vista when travelling by stage.'

'I have only been here once before,' Red said. 'When the family came to visit my grandmother. She came here for a few weeks every summer. She used to swear by the healing properties of the waters and somehow persuaded my father to try the cure for his gout. I was quite young and don't recall much about it.'

'I have only ever passed through on the stage,' Miss Godfrey said. 'One gets to see very little apart from the coaching inns.'

They pulled up at the posting inn and climbed down. 'Now what?' Harriet asked, looking about her.

'I suggest we try the Pump Room at this time of day. That is where people go to take the cure.'

'Very well,' Miss Godfrey said.

'I will get directions.' Inside the inn, he was encouraged to purchase a guidebook to all the pleasures to be had in Bath which also included a map.

'The Pump Room and baths are in the lower part of the town,' Red informed Miss Godfrey. 'Fortunately for us, according to the book, the fashionable time of year for visitors has not yet started, so we should easily run our quarry to earth.'

Miss Godfrey winced. 'Even so, are you likely to run into anyone you know?'

'It is always possible, I suppose.'

'And how will you explain me?'

He hadn't thought about it. He certainly didn't want it getting back to Eugenie that he was escorting a young and attractive widow around the countryside not two weeks after she had ended their betrothal. Eugenie would not be pleased. And nor should she be. It would show a remarkable unsteadiness of character. Something Eugenie would deplore.

As he would himself for that matter. Wouldn't he?

'We shall explain that you are the widow of a distant cousin of mine, taken suddenly. As an old family friend, I am escorting you to stay with relatives, but you felt the need to take the waters. Not feeling quite the thing, you know.'

She lowered her veil. 'I suppose it will suffice.'

'Well, it would,' he said, realising the flaw in his suggestion, 'if you had a maid or a female companion.

Otherwise, it looks a little odd.' More than odd. It would look most particular and start a whole round of gossip should anyone he knew happen to meet him.

'Perhaps we can say my maid was taken ill with a cold and so you have kindly agreed to accompany me to the Pump Room?'

No one would believe it for a moment. Respectable females did not trot around on the arms of single gentlemen. It would leave her open to insult. 'Or perhaps I should go alone. I could rent us a room for the night and leave you there and bring back word of Clark.'

'Yes,' she said. 'It might be for the best.'

She sounded disappointed.

'But you do not like the idea?'

She waved a dismissive hand. 'It is not that. It is that I have heard of the Pump Room in Bath and I was quite looking forward to seeing it for myself. Never mind. Perhaps I shall have the opportunity some other time.'

'Very well, let us see if we can find lodgings for one night before I set out to find Clark.'

They found quiet yet respectable lodgings not far from the Assembly Rooms. Their landlady was quick to tell them that they were fortunate to find a vacancy, that in the height of the season she was usually fully booked.

This time, Lord Westram registered himself under his real name and Harriet as Mrs Godfrey, mentioning to the landlady that she was the widow of his cousin hoping to benefit from the waters. The landlady accepted the explanation without demure. They took a suite of two bedrooms and a parlour.

* * *

As soon as they had refreshed themselves and enjoyed a luncheon of cold meats and cheeses, they set off walking down the hill to the Pump Room.

The city's white stone buildings gleamed despite the sky being overcast. There was an air of calm about the place and cleanliness. No wonder members of the aristocracy came here in droves. It was unlike any town she had ever visited.

Perhaps, when her shop had made enough money, she would bring Mother here and they could explore it together. Mother's rheumatism would surely benefit from the waters.

The Pump Room near the baths was surprisingly busy with patrons of all ages and walks of life in the great room. In one of the alcoves a plump middle-aged woman dispensed cups of curative waters from a spigot. Patrons paraded around the octagonal room or sat on stone benches, sipping their medicine with expressions on their faces which made one think of the face a child made when tasting a lemon. Most of those present were exceedingly elderly, several of them leaning on canes or being pushed in wheeled chairs by servants or relatives. There was even an elderly woman in what must be her own private sedan chair being waited upon by a footman.

'How will we ever identify the Clarks in this crowd?' Harriet murmured to Westram.

'Like finding a needle in a haystack,' he replied. 'Good Lord, look at that old woman in purple and orange stripes. Did you ever see such a quiz?'

The woman in question was dressed in the fashions of the last century and sported an enormous powdered wig.

'I suppose we should try the cure,' Harriet said doubtfully, gesturing to the woman pouring the water into tin cups from a dipper.

Westram escorted her to a bench. 'Wait here and I will bring it to you.'

The stone bench was one of several grouped down the centre of the room and along the sides, with urns of rather straggly potted palms creating little pockets of privacy.

Westram chatted to the woman at the pump and, while she dispensed the water, Harriet guessed he was making enquiries about their quarry.

'Any luck?' she asked him when he returned to her side.

Handing her the cup, he shook his head. 'She has no knowledge of anyone's names, but suggested I seek out Mr King, the Master of Ceremonies for the Upper Rooms. To be honest, I had hoped to avoid any formal sort of presence here. But it looks as if that will not be possible.'

Harriet lifted the cup he had brought her to her lips beneath her veil. The smell was so appalling she thought she might gag and she shuddered. She could not bear to even wet her lips. 'This is nasty.'

'It smells pretty awful, doesn't it, but people swear by its restorative properties. Drink up.' He grinned.

She glared at him, but the effect was lost given her veil. 'You drink it.'

A dapper gentleman approached them. 'Are you newly arrived in Bath?' he enquired. 'Allow me to introduce myself. King, Master of Ceremonies of the Upper Assembly Rooms.' He bowed.

It seemed they did not need to seek him out.

'Westram, at your service. And this is the widow of a cousin of mine. Mrs Godfrey. She is here to take the waters.'

Mr King bowed deeply. 'My condolences, ma'am.'

Harriet inclined her head.

King turned back to Westram. 'Welcome to Bath, my lord. While the season is not yet in full swing, I am sure you will find entertainments to please you. I imagine the lady would not be interested in balls and such, but I should point out that afternoon tea is offered daily in the Upper Rooms and we have a concert planned for tonight that may be of interest. Of course, the card rooms are open to subscribers every day except Sunday.' King beamed. 'Let me show you the visitors' book, my lord, and get you signed in.'

'I am not sure how long we will stay, to be honest,' Westram said.

'It doesn't matter,' King insisted gently but firmly, propelling Westram towards a table upon which rested a large register.

Harriet remained on her bench, staring at the still-full cup of water. If she tried to drink it, she was sure she would be ill. She glanced around at the other people clutching their little tin cups. Apparently, they were braver than she. When she was sure no one was looking her way, she tipped the water into the plant beside the bench. The poor thing looked none too healthy—perhaps she wasn't the first to dispose of the water that way.

Well, if it made a plant shrivel up, heaven knew what it would do to her insides.

Westram strolled back to her side, looking pleased with himself.

'The Clarks are listed in the guest book?' she guessed.

'They are. Along with their address.'

She breathed a sigh of relief.

He glanced down at the cup. 'Well done. You finished it.'

She grinned beneath her veil. 'Not me. I watered the plant.'

He chuckled. 'You are nothing if not resourceful, Mrs Godfrey. Well, if you are done taking the waters, I suppose we should pay a call on Mr Clark. He has taken lodgings in Gay Street.'

'Yes, indeed. Let us call on him at once. And believe me when I tell you, I shall never again set foot in this place.'

He took the cup, left it with the woman in charge and escorted her out into the street.

The clouds had rolled away and they were met with bright sunshine.

'Oh, my goodness me, how very dazzling the buildings are, when the sun is out,' she exclaimed. 'They almost blind one.'

Westram pulled his hat brim lower. 'Indeed. Though I doubt they will stay so for long, given the way the smoke lingers in this valley. They will soon be as grimy as those in London, I shouldn't wonder.'

The stroll up the hill to the address on Gay Street might have taxed a more delicate female, but Miss Godfrey seemed to enjoy the walk. She was a woman with a great deal of energy. Red liked that about her. He liked a great many things about her. Good Lord, he had actually found her attractive enough to steal a kiss.

Not the sort of thing a gentleman should do when the lady was under his protection. And she was a lady. Despite the shop she kept, she was as genteel as any lady he had ever met and far more sensible than most.

She reminded him of his sisters, whom, as a new earl, he had always found annoying in the extreme. They had been far too independent-minded when he had been struggling to find his feet as the head of the family. In contrast, Eugenie had been a haven of peace. She never argued or threw a temper tantrum, though her notions of propriety had been particularly strict. He recalled with a wince her horror when she had learned his sisters had decided to take up residence at a cottage in Kent rather than reside under his roof.

He had a feeling that part of his sisters' decision had been their dislike of Eugenie. Well, it had all worked out for the best in the end and, against all odds, all three of them had made very suitable matches. Though Eugenie had not been exactly complimentary about them, had she?

'Here we are!' Miss Godfrey announced.

He had been so busy with his thoughts he had not

noticed. He rapped on the door with the head of his cane. The footman who opened the door looked them up and down and properly assessed them as worthy of his notice.

'Is Mr Clark at home?' Red asked, offering his calling card.

The footman glanced at the card and started slightly. 'No, my lord. Mr and Mrs Clark have gone to Wells to visit friends. They are expected home the day after tomorrow.'

Dammit. 'What time are they expected?'

'Early evening, my lord.'

'Do you have an address?' Harriet asked. 'Of their friends?'

The footman shook his head. 'I do not, ma'am. The housekeeper might know?'

'Do not trouble her,' Red said firmly. 'Please tell Mr Clark we called and will call on him again in two days' time. I will be obliged.'

The footman bowed.

They turned to their lodgings.

'Why would you not seek their address?' Miss Godfrey asked, clearly annoyed. 'Wells is hardly any distance from here.'

'By the time I organise a carriage, we will arrive too late in the day to visit, and who knows whether we would find them at home or out on some jaunt or other. Two more days won't make much of a difference.'

'Not to you, perhaps, but my shop will have been closed for nearly a week by the time I get back. My customers will begin to think I have gone out of business and look elsewhere. Not to mention my mother will be worried.'

He had not thought of that.

'Can your mother not manage the shop in your absence?'

She sighed. 'Her eyesight is too poor now. She gets quite flustered. And once or twice she has broken some valuable items. We agreed she would take care of domestic matters and I would be responsible for the shop. That way there are no upsets.'

'It is a big responsibility for one of your age.'

'I am not a child and I enjoy the challenge. But some months we barely make enough to pay the rent.'

They entered the front door of their lodgings and climbed the stairs to their suite. She removed her bonnet and her coat.

'I had hoped we would locate Mr Clark today,' she said sounding less resilient than usual. He did not like that she sounded so dispirited.

'I also. Would you like to go to the concert Mr King spoke of?'

She looked surprised. 'You want to take me to a concert?'

She had looked so forlorn, he wanted to cheer her up. Now he saw the hope in her expression, he was determined he would do so. 'Why not? Otherwise we will be sitting here twiddling our thumbs. Not to mention I had no choice but to pay the subscription demanded by King.'

She looked horrified. 'Yet more expense.'

He shrugged. 'It is expected.'

'It does seem a shame to be here and not take advantage of the entertainments you have paid for.' She sounded wistful.

'I agree. We shall go. I will order us an early dinner.'

She glanced at her bonnet and veil. 'What if you meet an acquaintance? Someone who knows you do not have any cousins by the name of Godfrey?'

'I can assure you, I do not know the name of every relative of every peer of the realm. And nor will they. If you wish, we could say you are a cousin twice removed. Besides, there wasn't a single name I recognised in the guest book, so I doubt we will run into any of my acquaintances.'

If he did, they would likely think Mrs Godfrey was his mistress, given that she did not have a female companion or a maid. Let them think what they would. It was no one's business but his own.

And if word got back to Eugenie?

Well, she had ended their engagement, had she not? He wouldn't be the first man to have sought solace in the arms of another woman after his suit was rejected. The shred of the anger he had felt bubbled up. The anger that she would believe, even for a moment, that he had deliberately set out to cheat her father.

The thought gave him pause. It was not so much that his heart had been hurt, given that their marriage was a matter of family advancement, as was usual among their set. It had rather been a case of a stab to his pride. On the other hand, as his future wife, did he not have the right to expect a modicum of loyalty?

Up until the moment the fraud was discovered, he

* * *

It was almost two hours before he returned and, having made up her mind, Harriet was ready for him.

He tossed his hat and gloves on the table by the door and glanced around. 'Did they bring the tea tray?'

'They did and collected it again some time ago. Would you like me to ring for another?'

'No, thank you. I stopped at a coffee shop.'

The pause that ensued made her feel strangely ill at ease. 'Did you enjoy your walk?'

'I did. I needed time to think.'

'If you were thinking about your offer to take me to the concert,' she said stiffly, 'I have changed my mind. I do not wish to go.'

He gave her a long considering stare, his lovely green eyes perusing her face as if he could read the truth there. 'Why?'

She had not expected him to question her, merely to be relieved that she had given him a graceful out. 'I do not think it appropriate.'

'Why?'

Heaven help her, she had not expected this to be so difficult. 'I am here under false pretences. I am neither your cousin, nor a widow. It is nonsense for us to go about in society. I cannot like it at all.'

'I see.'

There. It was done. No drama. No argument. 'I am glad you understand.'

'I stopped at an employment agency and hired a lady's maid-cum-companion.'

For a moment she could not believe her ears. 'What?'

had assumed their mutual respect was firm ground on which to base a marriage. Now he was not quite so sure.

He needed to clear his head. 'I think I will take a walk.'

Miss Godfrey stared at him. 'We only just came in from a walk.'

'I require something more energetic. I will order a tea tray for you on the way so we may attend the concert on time.'

He bowed and left.

Chapter Seven

Was it something she had said that had made him depart so suddenly?

Perhaps he had regretted his invitation the moment she'd accepted. Men. There was no understanding them. Rodney had more than once told her she should curb her tendency to frankness. Perhaps His Lordship felt the same way.

Indeed, she should not have accepted his invitation. She wasn't here to enjoy herself at his expense. Only… she had never gone to a concert apart from those she had attended in one of London's parks on a Sunday afternoon.

Clearly, upon his return, she must tell him that she had changed her mind. Inform him that she was perfectly happy to read a book in her room if he wanted to join the gentlemen playing cards in the Assembly Rooms this evening.

The tea tray arrived and she sat in the bay window, watching the passing pedestrians and traffic. She was

certainly not watching for His Lordship's return. She did wish she had brought some embroidery or her knitting. She had begun a pair of mittens for Mother which she planned to give her as a Christmas gift. It would have been a far better use of her time rather than staring out of the window waiting for Lord Westram to return.

What had she been thinking? Accepting an invitation to go to a concert. She had nothing to wear. But then a widow needed nothing beside her weeds and her black bonnet.

Resolutely she got up and took a seat as far from the window as possible. She refused to gaze outside like some besotted fool. Unfortunately, she had the odd sensation of becoming dependent on Westram. On the way he took charge and organised things that were far above her normal level of luxury. And he made her feel feminine and cared for, when she really needed to care for herself. Besides, he was a gentleman. Why could she not remember that these nice manners of his were simply pro forma. It was the way he behaved to all women. It meant nothing.

When she thought back to the day they met, she could not help but think she was fortunate that he had not brought a constable along. He could easily have had her arrested then and there.

And yet…she could not help the way he made her feel inside. All warm and fluttery. No matter how much she tried to resist. And that kiss… She really must not think about that kiss.

'It seemed to me you could hardly go about with only me for an escort. It isn't seemly. Our landlady has room for her in the servants' quarters. She will arrive here within the hour and will accompany us to the concert this evening.'

'But I said—'

'That was before you knew I had hired Miss Pomfret.'

'Well, it is very kind of you, but—'

'Nonsense. I wish to attend the concert. You wish to attend the concert. Why should we not enjoy it together?'

Put like that it seemed silly to argue. Yet she did not like the sense that he assumed he had the right to make decisions on her behalf. 'I cannot afford to hire a maid, let alone a companion. I will not put myself under such an obligation when you have already laid out a considerable sum on our accommodations.'

His eyes narrowed. 'Simply because I am demanding the return of the enormous amount my father paid for the idol does not mean I am without means. My fortune is tied up in property, but my rents are adequate for everyday living. You are under no obligation, when it is for my entertainment. But if you do not wish to go to the concert there is no more to be said.'

'So you will tell this Miss Pomfret her services are not required, after all.'

'There would be no point. I am required to pay her a month's salary, so she may as well earn her wages while we are here.'

'In which case, it makes no sense not to attend the concert,' she snapped.

'Exactly.' He grinned. 'I knew you would come around eventually. You are too sensible a woman not to.'

The gleam of triumph in his eyes made her want to hit him over the head.

'You are impossible.'

'That is what my sisters always said.'

'That accounts for it.'

He tilted his head. 'Accounts for what?'

'Your ability to get your own way. You must have driven your sisters mad.'

He laughed out loud. 'Very true. But you know, before I became head of my household, they used to spoil me dreadfully.'

She could not help smiling back. He looked like a naughty boy caught in some mischief. 'Then what will you do about Miss Pomfret when we are finished our business here?'

'She knows it is a temporary assignment.'

Red could not have been better pleased with the way the evening had gone. Miss Pomfret clearly understood her role as a lady's companion and had been quite content to remain in the background during the concert and afterwards when they had taken tea in the antechamber.

Now as they strolled back to their lodgings, she trailed along behind at a discreet distance. But his greatest pleasure had been watching Miss Godfrey's enjoyment of the music. The orchestra had, given the parochial nature of the town and the thinness of company, been excellent. They had played selections from Bach, Haydn and Mozart and, for once, Miss Godfrey had not covered her pretty face with the veil. She had clearly enjoyed the experience. The thought warmed him.

They strolled along arm in arm, the street lamps lighting their way.

'Thank you,' she said, looking up at him as they approached their lodgings. 'I have never heard such beautiful music.'

He frowned. Music was something he took for granted. 'Really?'

'I have listened to bands playing in the park from time to time and of course the choir in church, but the complexity of the music we heard this evening—it defies description. I am so glad you convinced me to go with you.'

'I was glad to have your company.' More than glad. He could not remember when he had enjoyed an evening more.

They climbed the stairs to their suite. Miss Godfrey turned and smiled at Miss Pomfret who had followed them up. 'I am sure you must be tired. I shall not need you any more this evening, thank you.'

'Very well, ma'am.' The woman curtsied and returned downstairs.

Red was surprised that she would not avail herself of the woman's assistance, but Miss Godfrey was a woman who enjoyed her independence, so he said nothing.

Inside the parlour she removed her bonnet and spencer with a sigh. Her black hair was neatly pinned at her nape as usual. He had the urge to remove the pins and run his fingers through the dark tresses.

'Would you care for a nightcap?' he asked. 'A nip of brandy, perhaps? It will help you sleep.'

'Yes,' she said. 'A little brandy with water, if you please.' At his glance of surprise, she smiled, something she did only rarely. It lit her whole face and made her eyes sparkle. She looked so pretty. And younger.

'Mother and I sometimes indulge in a nightcap, after a particularly trying day.'

He poured them each a drink, cutting hers with a splash of water. 'To a most pleasant evening,' he toasted. 'Thank you.' He sat beside her on the sofa.

They sipped their drinks in silence, but somehow he knew her brain was busy.

'What shall we do if Mr Clark denies any knowledge of the statue?' she finally said.

He recalled his threats the first day he had walked into her shop. 'If he does, we have other means at our disposal.'

'Prison, you mean. If you will give me time, I will pay you back, though I deny my father was in any way part of a scheme to defraud your family.'

He took a deep breath. 'Even if your father was part of it, I do not see how I can hold you responsible.'

She shifted to face him, her expression full of incredulity. 'That is not what you said two days ago.'

Was it only two days ago? He felt as if he had known her for most of his life.

'It seems that this is a case of the sins of the fathers being visited upon the children. I hold you blameless.'

Her posture relaxed, but she frowned. 'Children?'

He had not intended to give so much away. 'I sold the

idol to someone else. It is that person who discovered the fraud. He is insisting I return his money.'

Her eyes widened. 'My goodness. I had no idea.'

'My future father-in-law. He is not pleased.'

'Oh, dear.'

'Unless I return his money, he will drag my family name through the mud.'

'That doesn't make sense, surely, if you are to marry his daughter.'

'Was. She broke off our engagement.'

'She surely does not think you were complicit in the scheme?'

'I think she obeyed her father's instructions.'

'How very poor spirited.'

Dammit, he'd thought so, too, but he would never admit it. 'She is a dutiful daughter.'

Harriet made a face. 'And I am sure she will make a dutiful wife.'

That was what he wanted, wasn't it? That and financial security for his heirs.

His shoulders stiffened as he recalled how unhappy his sisters had been prior to their current marriages. Marriages approved of by his father. Was that to be his fate with Eugenie? He'd been so focused on the needs of the title and had always seen their match as the perfect union of two estates. And before this, Eugenie and he had never disagreed.

Unlike in his conversations with Miss Godfrey. They barely agreed on anything.

She gave him an odd look. 'So you are no longer betrothed.'

'It is a temporary setback. I have no doubt once this matter is sorted out everything will be back to normal.'

She nodded. 'I see. Well, I am sorry that this business has the potential of affecting your future and I thank you for seeing that, whatever the case with my father, I am not at fault.'

'If it wasn't such a huge sum of money—'

She rose from her chair and he came to his feet, assuming she was about to retire. Instead, she took his hand and gazed up into his face. 'For your sake, I hope tomorrow you will have the answer you need.'

Her small fingers curled around his, offering comfort. Warmth emanated from her touch and tingles travelled up his arm. His heart beat faster.

He gazed down at her and her sincere expression of sympathy, her lovely face, and for the first time in a long time felt as if he wasn't completely alone.

He'd been the head of his household since he was a boy. He'd been required to make the decisions for his siblings and bear the consequences of their actions. He had accepted that as his duty and responsibility, but in that brief moment, he felt as if, by sharing his worries, the burden of them had lightened.

As if she, of anyone, understood.

He traced a finger along her jaw, revelling in the feel of her soft skin, sensing the quickening of her breathing as her lips parted on a quick indrawn breath.

His hand trembled.

Harriet gazed up into his handsome face with a longing for things that could never be. His future was set in stone, as was hers. Then why this sense of a missed opportunity? She had intended to offer sympathy and gratitude for his generosity. But there was so much more in her heart. Indeed, her heart seemed almost too small to contain all she felt.

He was a great deal kinder and sweeter than he appeared at first sight. The knowledge that his father and perhaps hers had been engaged in some sort of nefarious business together, possibly, a business that had blighted his hopes for marriage, seemed too, too cruel.

She wished desperately that there was more she could do.

He dropped his hand and her skin felt cold from the loss of his touch.

'I—'

He stepped back. 'I beg your pardon, Miss Godfrey.'

'Harriet,' she said softly. 'Please. Call me Harriet.'

'Harriet,' he murmured. 'You know, I cannot help wishing we had met under other circumstances.'

She laughed, albeit it a little breathlessly. 'If not for these circumstances, I do not believe we should have met at all.'

An expression of regret crossed his face. 'I suppose not.'

It might have been better that they had not met, for she had the feeling she would always recall this visit to Bath with a deep longing for what might have been. 'I am going to miss you.' She started when she realised she had spoken out loud. 'I should not have said that.'

He touched a finger to her lips. 'Strangely, I also,' he murmured, 'will miss you.'

'Strangely?'

He chuckled. 'I shall miss our spirited discussions.'

'Our arguments, you mean.'

He grinned. Such a charming grin. His eyes danced with amusement. His face seemed more youthful, his smile infectious.

She was going to miss this smile. And his kindness.

As a girl she had dreamed of love and marriage, what girl did not? But as time progressed, her experience of the world had taught her that women, once married, had no rights at all. A man made all the decisions and their wives and daughters suffered the consequences. Even now, even after her father's death, she was at his mercy. And to think she had thought she would be happy marrying Rodney. She shivered. What a mistake that would have been.

On the other hand, she had never imagined she would be lonely, or alone. She had Mother and the business and neighbours. Her life was full. So why now did the future seem so empty?

And look at the subterfuge she was forced to engage in when travelling. She could not travel as herself. She travelled as a widow. A woman who had been married. It gave her an aura of respectability she did not have as a single lady and added protection. What did the future hold once she was past a marriageable age? She would be viewed as an old maid. Unwanted. Rejected. The butt of jests.

Sometimes she had daydreamed of meeting a man who would introduce her to the pleasures of married life without any need to tie the knot. She was aware that some married gentlemen took mistresses. Those gentlemen quite often visited her shop. She had overheard their talk with their friends. She had found their ribald conversations rather sordid.

Her dream lover was nothing like them. Indeed, if there was an ideal man, he would be a lot more like Westram. He was honourable and had principles, which was why he was out of reach.

'Were you sorry when your engagement ended?' she asked.

He turned away. 'I was shocked, to be honest.'

'I am so sorry.' She sat down on the sofa. He sank down beside her.

'Eugenie and I were betrothed when we were children. We were destined to marry from childhood. It was our parents' fondest wish.'

She frowned. 'Why?'

'Our estates march alongside each other, with Eugenie inheriting a good portion of it by way of her mother. Uniting the families makes sense. And Featherstone was taken with the idea of a title for his daughter.'

'So it is really what they call a marriage of convenience. An arranged match? Did neither of you resent not having a choice?'

He smiled grimly. 'I am an earl, Harriet. With that comes a great many responsibilities. To the country. To the estate. To my siblings. To my family name. One does one's duty. Eugenie feels the same way, I know.'

The way he put it made it sound awfully cold and calculating. To Harriet it sounded a bit like a lucky escape, except for the having to pay back the money part.

She could see how he would feel honour bound to return it. 'I see.'

He shrugged. 'It will all get sorted out when we find Maxwell Clark.'

He was not betrothed. Nor was he in love. Her heart picked up speed. A strange fluttering set up residence in her stomach. A sort of do-or-die feeling. Like taking the chance to leap over a fast-flowing river to find the very best blackberries on the other side.

Intent green eyes gazed back at her as if seeking to read her mind.

The sensation of falling into those bright emerald depths overwhelmed her. Unthinking, she reached for his shoulder for stability.

He hissed in a breath as if her touch shocked.

He reached up and curled his fingers around hers, bringing her hand to his mouth. The warm brush of his lips, the tickle of his breath sent tingles from the tips of her fingers up her arm and across her shoulders. Her breathing shallowed as the storm-tossed depths of his gaze held her captive. Yet she had no desire to escape.

Instead she turned towards him, without reason or thought, only the longing to touch guiding her action. Se combed her fingers through the dark red waves at his temples. Silky locks caressed her skin.

A smile pulled at her lips. 'I have wanted to do that since the first time I saw you.'

His gaze dropped to her mouth. 'And I have wanted to kiss you for the past two days. You are a beautiful and enticing woman, Harriet. I find myself tempted beyond reason.'

She sighed. Her eyelids felt heavy, her body languid, while her heart pounded wildly. 'No more tempted than I.'

The truth set her free.

Unable to bear even the smallest distance between them any longer, she slid her arm around his neck, leaned in and pressed her lips to his lovely mouth.

For a brief moment he hesitated.

Had she gone too far?

Then his mouth melded with hers and he folded her in his arms.

Chapter Eight

Red's mind darkened. All of his awareness narrowed to the feel of her soft lips against his and the stroke of her fingers through his hair.

He deepened the kiss, swept her mouth with his tongue, tasted her sweetness, felt her lush breasts pressed against his chest and all thoughts fled. All that remained was the sound of his heartbeat, their mingled breaths and the wonderful sensation of being kissed by a warm, willing woman.

Breaking the kiss, he swept her up in his arms and headed for her chamber. As he opened the door, he glanced down at her. Her eyes were hazy, her lips full and rosy from his kiss. Yet there was an innocence in her expression, a wonder that he had not expected.

'Are you sure?' he asked, surprising himself, because if she changed her mind he was going to be very disappointed indeed.

She nodded.

But she did not look as confident as he would have expected.

Instead of doing what his body urged, tossing her on the bed and falling on her like a ravening wolf, he deposited her gently on its edge and sat beside her, stroking her palm with his thumb. 'You seem worried.' Against every instinct, every muscle straining in his body, he was stupidly giving her a chance to change her mind.

She closed her fingers around his thumb, staring down at where their hands joined, his large one, hers small in comparison.

'I am not very knowledgeable about this sort of thing,' she whispered so quietly he had to lean closer, Even so he heard the nervous shake in her voice.

He stilled.

'Are you saying I would be your first?' His voice was strangely hoarse, his throat dry.

She nodded and quickly looked away.

She had seemed so bold, so confident and so matter of fact around the erotic items she sold in her shops that he had not considered that she might yet be innocent. Yet now he thought about it, the signs had all been there—her lack of artifice, her obliviousness to her charm. Instead he'd focused on the self-assuredness, her competence.

He took a deep breath and raised her hand to his mouth, turning it over to kiss the inside of her wrist, and felt the frantic beating of her pulse against his lips. She was terrified.

'We can call a halt to things, right now if you wish,'

he said, knowing if she accepted his offer, he was about to spend a very uncomfortable night.

'Would you be terribly angry?' she asked.

He frowned. 'No. Not angry. Certainly disappointed.'

She sighed. 'Me, too.'

Warmth and a strange, sharp twist of pain in his chest caused him to hiss in a breath.

She glanced up at his face. 'I was almost engaged once. He was most ardent for a time, but my mother guarded my virtue like a dragon.' She gave a rueful laugh. 'I was most indignant that the best he could do was steal a kiss when we escaped for a walk in the park. I was mad for him, but he eventually decided he preferred a wealthy widow whom he had been courting while he had been making up to me. Hedging his bets, Father said.'

'The blackguard.'

She shook her head. 'The only thing he cared for was getting his hands on our shop. If my mother had not been so vigilant, I might have found myself ruined by an unscrupulous fortune hunter. And to think, I actually believed he loved me.'

Inwardly, she winced. Perhaps he would think she was criticising his decision to marry for money.

'Love,' he said with a grimace. 'It makes people do things beyond comprehension and regret them for the rest of their lives. My grandfather is a perfect example. He made a complete fool of himself over my grandmother for years and she walked all over him.' Not to mention he had ruined the fortunes of those who came after him. 'My father despised him.'

'I do not believe my father ever regretted marrying my mother, whereas I am quite content to be single. But…'

'But—'

'I am not without longings and desires. I know there is pleasure to be found between a man and a woman—I have only to look at the figurines in my shop.'

His body heated. 'And you wish to experience those pleasures?'

She drew a circle with her free hand. 'I thought so.'

'But now you have doubts.'

'I am embarrassed by my lack of practical knowledge. I have seen pictures and many of the items in my shop leave little to the imagination, but after that kiss, the sensations that sent my head spinning, I did not feel like myself at all.'

'You were overwhelmed.'

'Completely.'

'Would it surprise you to know I felt exactly the same way?'

'You did?'

'Of course. Though I am not inexperienced and am knowledgeable enough to control my animal passions.' He hoped. 'I, too, felt as if I could easily lose control. If I allowed it.'

She inhaled a shuddering breath, as if those words strummed a chord of pleasure within her, and his ballocks tightened. Without doubt she was a woman of passion, despite her innocence.

'What if we were to make a child?' To have a child out of wedlock would be dreadful.

'There are ways to try to prevent such an occurrence, though it cannot be guaranteed. Certainly, were I to have a child under such circumstances, I would take responsibility for its upbringing. So far, I have not.'

'Not as far as you know.'

'I do know. I ceased sowing my wild oats many years ago and I have no illegitimate children. I know this, because my past lovers remain my friends.'

Her eyes widened. 'We live in such completely different worlds.'

Oh, yes, she was definitely going to call a halt to their dalliance. She was having second thoughts and so she should.

'Not so very different. We both take our responsibilities seriously. We both care for our families. Whatever your decision, it will not alter my respect for you.'

And if she decided she did not want to continue he was going to regret it, heartily.

Harriet's heart squeezed. He spoke only of them becoming lovers. But she appreciated his honesty. How could she not? Besides, even if she did find him hugely attractive and even if her heart longed to keep him, she knew it was not possible. The difference in their circumstances made it impossible.

She had seen what her father had suffered with regard to his family as a result of his marriage to her mother. His family had cast him out. While he had done his best to hide his pain, whenever he spoke of them, which was rarely, she had sensed a raw open wound.

For an earl, like Westram, it would be even worse.

Not only would his family turn up their noses, so would the rest of the nobility.

But she wasn't talking about marriage any more than he was. Once this quest of theirs was complete they would go their separate ways. Perhaps she would never meet a man she liked as well as she liked him.

'Can you teach me?' she asked hesitantly. 'How to be a good lover? And how to avoid becoming with child?'

His jaw dropped. 'Teach you to... Good Lord.'

She frowned. 'Is it such a terrible thing to ask?'

He grimaced. 'Terrible. No, I suppose not. But it is highly unusual.'

'Then how do women learn?'

'The same way men do, I suppose. Trial and error. Most women learn from their husbands, who may or may not have learned from other ladies.'

She recalled some of the conversations between her mother's friends. 'I have heard that it is simply a case of lying still and waiting for it to be over.'

He grimaced. 'I can assure you those ladies are missing out.'

'That is how I feel,' she blurted. 'As if I am missing out. But I want someone I can trust to teach me the way of it. The right way. So that if I ever should meet a man I wanted to be with, I would know what I was doing.'

He raised his eyebrows and there was a strange little smile on his lips. 'I don't believe there really is a right way or a wrong way.'

'But how does one know?'

His eyes danced with amusement. He was laughing at her. She was making a fool of herself.

She jumped up from the bed. 'It doesn't matter. I am never going to marry anyway.'

He leaped up and caught her by the shoulders, looking down into her face with a sympathetic expression. 'I'm sorry, Harriet. You took me by surprise. Of course there are things a woman can learn. Ways to give a man great pleasure and to ensure that she receives the same—as she deserves.'

'But it is not something you wish to teach me.'

'That is so far from the truth it is laughable. I simply do not want to take advantage of your innocence. It would not be honourable.'

'And I suppose my innocence makes me a less than desirable partner.'

He frowned. 'It would give me very great pleasure to instruct you in the ways of love. To be honest, it is one of the most erotic suggestions I have ever heard. So erotic I can hardly think straight, but I am doing my best to maintain some veneer of civility.'

Her insides tightened at the hoarseness in his voice and the tension that caused his hand on her shoulder to shake.

He did want this. But she must make her intentions clear at the outset. 'And when the lessons are over, you will go your way and I will go mine.'

He hesitated. 'Unless a child should result. Certainly, I shall do my very best to ensure it does not, for both our sakes, but should things turn out otherwise, you will promise to inform me. I will not neglect my responsibilities.'

Which was not to say he would marry her. But he

would support his child. It was the way of the nobility. Or at least it should be.

She nodded briskly. Her heart picked up speed. She swallowed, surprised to discover her tongue cleaving to the roof of her mouth as if parched. 'Very well. Let us get started.' She was proud of how calm, how matter of fact, she sounded.

But if she was ever going to do this, he really was the only man she had ever met that she would trust enough to do it with her.

Trust. Was it trust? Or something deeper? She pushed the thought away.

He guided her back to his bed, one arm around her waist, the other still holding her hand.

They sat side by side on the bed, looking at each other.

Heat from his gaze scorched her face. Oh, heavens above, she was really going to do this?

'Relax,' he murmured softly, his deep voice strumming a chord deep within her. 'There is no rush. We can take all the time in the world. If there is anything I do that you find you do not like, tell me.'

'What should I say?'

'No. Or stop.'

'Shall I take my clothes off now?'

He touched the warm pad of his thumb to her bottom lip, stilling her words. 'Harriet, dearest girl, stop trying to rush things. There is more pleasure in delayed gratification, than there is in rushing to finish.'

The words made no sense, but she stored them away to study later.

Then his head dipped and his lips replaced his finger. Gently, softly, they brushed her mouth. And, once more, heady dizzying sensations that started low in her belly rose up to engulf her until she could scarcely think at all.

Of their own accord, her hands traced their way up the fine fabric of his coat, the feel of the wool against her palms a sensual stroke of softness, until they reached his strong wide shoulders and his lovely column of throat. Her fingers sifted through the silky waves of his hair.

Her lips parted on a sigh and his tongue slipped into her mouth.

A jolt of something hot sliced through her body all the way to her core.

She gasped. Drew back. He was gazing into her face. A rueful smile crossed his lips. 'Too much? Too soon?'

'I—I wasn't expecting it. It was nice.'

'Only nice? I must do better, then.'

She stroked his lovely cheekbones with her thumbs. 'It was lovely,' she admitted. 'Surprising.'

'Ah. For a moment there I thought I had lost my touch.'

She frowned at the amused smile on his lips. 'You are teasing me.'

'A little,' he admitted. 'This is not such a serious business, you know.' He kissed the tip of her nose, then nipped at her chin. 'It is supposed to be fun.'

Fun. Did she even remember how to have fun? After their incarceration, she had spent all her time in the shop, making sure Father never let them get into debt. Perhaps it was time she had a little fun.

She took a deep breath and smiled. 'I'm sorry. I suppose I am trying to be a good student.'

He beamed. 'Let me assure you that, so far, you are proving a very apt pupil, my sweet.'

His sweet. How very nice that sounded.

Red had been telling the absolute truth when he said that her proposition was the most erotic thing he had ever heard. He was rock hard and barely lucid. Despite her innocence, her melting kisses and responses to the most nuanced touches of his tongue told him she was one of the most passionate females he had ever come across.

The man who had abandoned her must have been a fool to let a woman like this slip through his fingers. Clearly, he had not deserved her.

And yet she was innocent. Which meant no matter how much he wanted her beneath him, he had to take his time. He had to make sure that everything they did gave her pleasure, even at the cost of his own. The fact that she would trust him to be her very first lover was a huge responsibility. He was determined not to let her down.

He had the feeling that if he let her, she would rush things and be thoroughly disappointed. To boot, she would never realise just how lovely and desirable she really was. He kissed her briefly on the lips.

Her eyes closed, then popped open when she realised he was gazing down at her.

'Since the moment I met you,' he said softly when he knew he had her full attention, 'I have wanted to see your hair unbound.'

She touched her bun with a self-conscious little gesture. 'My hair?'

'It is such a glossy black. I long to see it loose about your shoulders.'

'Really?' She sounded pleased and began to pull at the pins.

'Allow me,' he said, catching her hand and bringing the knuckles to his lips.

'Oh, yes,' she said, her voice breathless. 'If you wish.'

One by one, slowly and carefully he removed the pins from the bun at her nape, taking the time to kiss her cheek and the soft delicate place, beneath her ear.

Although she was no longer quite so rigid, he could still feel her anxiety, her need to do things correctly. And he could understand that need, for had he not tried most of his adult life, to do the right thing for his siblings and for his family name?

Look how well that had turned out.

When the last lock uncoiled, he leaned back and admired his handiwork, gleaming black tresses falling down her back and streaming over her breasts. 'Like a midnight sky on a moonless night.'

She shrugged self-consciously. 'The colour runs in my father's family, so he said.'

He sifted his fingers through the long silky strands. 'It is quite lovely. Like you.'

She blushed.

'I thought so the moment I saw you in your shop.'

She chuckled. 'I would never have guessed.'

He gazed deep into her eyes. 'I apologise. I was

angry. Sometimes my temper gets the better of me. Can you forgive me?'

'Yes. Of course. I was not exactly nice to you either.'

'We got off on the wrong foot. But that is all in the past.' He kissed her, and she kissed him back with enthusiasm, her tongue tangling with his and tentatively touching his lips and dipping into his mouth with tiny little flicks which almost drove him insane.

He needed her closer.

He lifted her off the bed and sat her on his lap. She made a small sound of surprise and gazed up at him shyly.

'I thought we should be a little more cosy.'

She twined her arms around his neck and resumed her explorations with her tongue. He folded his arms around her, her breasts pressed against his chest, yet it was nowhere near close enough.

He drew in a steadying breath and reminded himself there was no need to rush.

Her kiss was heavenly, as if their mouths were designed to fit, and his tongue roamed her mouth while his hands wandered her slender back and tangled with her mane of hair. For long moments, he became lost in sensation.

Unsteadily, he drew back and gazed into her lovely face. She was flushed and breathing hard, as was he.

'Oh, my goodness,' she muttered when she could speak. She snuggled her cheek against his chest. 'That was…'

'Was?'

'Like a storm. Wild. Breathtaking.'

God, every word out of her mouth left him hard and wanting. He quelled his animal urges. If they were going to do this, and he still had some doubts about the wisdom of it, he was going to make sure it was perfect.

He stroked her beautiful hair. 'What is your favourite colour?'

She stilled. 'What?'

'I have only ever seen you in grey or black. I was wondering what colours you like to wear?'

'Oh? I like pale blue, or green, anything really, except pink, it does not suit me at all. I mostly wear grey, because it is best for working in the shop. It doesn't show the dirt.'

The idea annoyed him. Her beauty deserved more than drab grey.

'What is your favourite colour?' she asked him.

'Green, though when I was younger I had a passion for purple.' He chuckled at the recollection. 'I had a purple waistcoat with green fleur-de-lis embroidered on it. It cost me a fortune. With my shirt points above my ears, I thought I was top of the trees. My father almost had an apoplexy when I came home from university in that get up.'

'I nagged Father into buying me a peacock-blue-and-black-striped coat. I felt so grown up in it when I went out walking with him and Mother, until someone asked me if I was from the circus.'

He heard the hurt in her voice and gave her a hug. 'People can be cruel to our feelings when we are young.'

She sighed. 'Indeed.'

He picked her up and swung her over on to the bed.

She moved up on to the pillows and he stretched out alongside her, propping himself on one arm in order to see her expression.

'Did you have a happy childhood?' he asked.

She frowned. 'Yes. Mostly. I did not go to school and we could not afford a governess, but my father tutored me when he wasn't busy in the shop. He had been provided with a good education and was a good teacher. He also liked to talk about the places he had visited which made geography more interesting.'

'He travelled a great deal, then.'

'In his youth. To Europe and Africa. He was an expert on their antiquities. Unfortunately, he often bought things he could not really afford and had to sell them at a loss to pay the rent on the shop.'

'That must have been worrying.'

She made a face. 'I try not to think about it. Father was fun when the dibs were in tune. We were happy.'

It almost sounded as if she was trying to convince herself.

Chapter Nine

Harriet could not believe how much she was telling him, or how comfortable she felt doing so. But why had he stopped…? Did he not like kissing her as much as she liked being kissed?

She rolled on her side and propped her head on her palm, to better see his expression.

He smiled at her, a sweet boyish smile, leaned forward and kissed the tip of her nose.

How was she to ask? What did she say? What if he really did not want to continue? A pain seized her chest. This was a terrible mistake.

'Have we concluded our lessons?' She sounded so stiff, when she had meant to sound light-hearted, uncaring.

His gaze narrowed. 'I thought we should get to know each other a little. While we have spent a good deal of time in each other's company these past few days, we have kept our distance. If we are to be lovers, then we should also be friends, or we are not lovers at all. It will be something very different.'

He was watching her intently and she felt heat rise to her cheeks. 'I am sorry, I do not quite understand your meaning.'

'I do not deny I am attracted to you. You are a beautiful woman, but physical attraction is only part of the equation—there needs to be more if we are to enjoy each other to the full.'

'You want to know me as a person.' Her heart squeezed. She wanted to know more about him, too. Of course she did. But if she got to know him, would it not be harder to say goodbye when this quest of theirs was over? Already, she knew she was going to miss him.

'Very well. What else would you like to know?' she said.

He laughed softly. 'You do not make this easy, do you?'

'I am not trying to be difficult, I assure you.'

'It comes naturally, then.'

Outraged, she glared at him, then saw the teasing light in his gaze. 'I think you know too much about me already.' She punched him lightly on the shoulder. 'You know exactly how to make me rise to your bait.'

He grinned. 'I only jest, my love.'

My love. No one had ever called her that before. Her heart gave an odd little pulse.

Followed swiftly by a suspicion. 'Tell me about your family?'

He lay back on the pillow, tucked one hand behind his head and looked up. There was a sudden tension about him she had not expected to see. 'A brother and two sisters, one sister is older, one younger. I have a sister-in-law, though now that she has also married again, I am not sure that we are related any longer.'

'Also?'

'My sisters lost their husbands and have since re-married.'

'And your brother?'

He turned his head to look at her and there was pain in his expression. 'It is an old story now, but at the time it caused a great deal of gossip. My younger brother and my two brothers-in-law left their wives and went off to join Wellington on the Peninsula apparently for the sake of a bet. They were all killed in battle shortly thereafter.'

'How dreadful.'

'It was. Particularly for my sisters. Fortunately, they are now happily married, and all is well with the world.'

He sounded a little bitter.

'You are angry.'

'I was angry at those idiot boys who thought they were men. They left me with three women to support and a number of debts to repay. It meant I had to put off my wedding until I had cleared up their mess. Not to mention the unhappiness their irresponsibility caused to their wives.' He let go a sigh. 'Though, in truth, it was not a wager that took them abroad, but a far more serious matter. My older sister's husband was abusing her and Jonathan and Harry chased him all the way to Spain, intending to punish him. The end result was the same, though.' He looked sad.

'You blame yourself?' she hazarded.

'Perhaps if I had been a better head of household, they might have come to me, instead of going off half-cocked. They should have come to me.'

'It was a heat of the moment thing, I presume.'

'It was.' He sighed. 'Mind you, with my temper, I might have gone with them, knowing what they knew, and be equally as dead.'

'Then perhaps it was well you did not. Your sisters needed you.'

He nodded slowly. 'You are right. It is water under the bridge now. But I still miss my brother. I used to think him a nuisance when he was small, but he was a great go when I used to get him into mischief. When we got older we grew apart. I wish I had not let that happen.' He had found Jonathan and his friends too frivolous and Jonathan had accused him of being stuffy.

She put her arm around his waist and kissed him. It was a sweet tender kiss and she slowly felt him relax. Warmth swelled in her heart as she felt she had brought him some comfort.

He groaned and brought her body flush with his, holding her tight. She loved the way his lean hard length felt against her, and when he rolled her over and covered her with his body, her heart beat so fast she thought it might fly right out of her chest.

One large hand came to her breast and the weight of it was delicious. Heat slowly permeated the layers of her gown. Her insides tightened strangely, yet her limbs felt lax and heavy. She arched into him, wanting more.

'I feel as if I might fly apart at any moment,' she said in a gasping whisper against his mouth.

He raised himself up on one hand and looked down into her face. 'You are a beautiful, passionate woman, Harriet Godfrey, and I find myself quite undone.'

To her disappointment, his hand left her breast, stroking its way over her stomach and down her thigh almost to her knee. He bent his head and kissed her while gently, slowly, easing her skirt upwards above her knees. He dipped his hand between her thighs and she gasped at the feel of rough male skin on the bare flesh above her stockings. Instinctively, she closed her legs, holding his hand fast.

'Do you want me to stop?' he whispered against her mouth. 'Tell me and I will.'

Did she? 'No,' she muttered and let her thighs fall apart.

His fingers stroked the inside of her thighs, slow, gentle little circles. The sensation was tantalising and exciting. She could scarcely breathe and her blood raced hot through her veins.

He combed through the curls at the apex of her thighs.

She froze. Her mouth dried. Was she really going to do this?

He gently stroked her and slowly she became used to the feel of his touch. As he did so, he rocked against her hip in gentle nudges.

He moved his hand and cupped her mons, increasing the pressure, and little pulses of exquisite pleasure radiated outwards from her core.

She gasped.

'Is that nice?' he asked.

'Lovely. I think.'

'You are lovely,' he whispered. His warm breath tickled her skin.

The pressure eased, then she became aware of a new sensation, a delicate touch at first, then the pleasure changed into something quite unbearable. Her body went taut. She could not breathe.

'There it is,' he murmured. And the movement against her inner flesh quickened and became so unbearably pleasurable, her hips rose to meet his hand and her fingers clenched on his shoulders and...

She flew apart. Waves of heat washed over her. She collapsed against the pillows.

After a moment or two she was able to open her eyes and look at him.

'What—what happened?'

He smiled and there was a good deal of male pride in his expression. 'Why, my dear sweet Harriet, I do believe you experienced your first petit mort.' At her blank look, he chuckled. 'Little death. It is what every lover hopes to bring to his partner.'

'Did you experience—'

He kissed her briefly and silenced her question. 'Do not worry about me, my dear. Now it is time for you to sleep. Come, let me help ready you for bed. We will have another lesson tomorrow if you are still of a mind.'

The strange warm lassitude in her limbs and her mind seemed to rob her of all propriety. And when he started helping her undress, it seemed like the most natural thing in the world.

* * *

Red's hands were shaking so badly, he could hardly get the ties of her gown undone. The brief glimpse he had of her high pert breasts and the black glossy curls at the apex of her thighs as he helped her out of her stays and shift nearly sent him to his knees, but with a Herculean effort he dropped her nightgown over her head and tucked her up in bed.

'Sleep,' he managed to say, though it was more of a growl than a word. 'I will see you in the morning.'

Right before he blew out the candle, he glanced at her face and she smiled sweetly. Something in his chest twisted painfully.

He strode for his own chamber and as he put out the fire in his loins all he could see was that beautiful soft look on her face.

To his chagrin, he wanted her as much the next morning as he had the previous night. He felt like an adolescent all over again, more light-hearted than he had been in years, as if some great weight had been lifted from his shoulders.

The chink of china in the room next door told him that breakfast had arrived.

He strolled into the parlour and found Harriet seated at the table behind the teapot. The smile she sent him, half-shy, half-knowing, stopped him in his tracks. She was just so beautiful.

He smiled back. 'Good morning, my dear.'

She blushed. 'I thought we might go for a walk, if

the weather is fine. Which it is. I hear the Sydney Gardens are quite something to behold.'

'We could also visit the Pump Room again, if you wish,' he said, inspecting the buffet where a feast had been laid out. There were scrambled eggs and ham and toast as well as assorted cheeses and sweet rolls and crispy apples.

She shuddered. 'It seems my one taste yesterday has cured all my ills, so I have no need.'

He chuckled. 'A walk sounds like a fine idea.'

'Would you like tea?' she asked.

'I would indeed. May I prepare you a plate?' He gestured to the food.

'Thank you.'

He brought two plates to the table and she handed him his cup of tea.

He could not help but watch her as she ate. It seemed she had a good appetite. 'I would love to see you in something other than black,' he said.

She winced. 'It is not very flattering, is it? But it shields me from all sorts of unpleasantness.'

He frowned. He wanted to please her, not make her uncomfortable. 'Perhaps it is time for Mrs Godfrey to put off her mourning. Since you will likely not come to Bath again, who is to know?'

She blushed. 'I cannot afford new clothes which I will likely never wear again.'

He had never met a woman who did not like the idea of new clothes. And, despite her words, he could see the longing in her eyes. 'You must allow me. After all, you are doing it at my request.'

She looked worried. 'I should not think you have money to waste either.'

Pride reared its head. 'Because I cannot put my hands on a thousand pounds at a moment's notice does not mean I am indigent, Harriet. The cost of a ready-made gown won't set me back more than a few shillings.' And he could likely sell them again afterwards if she no longer wanted them.

'I cannot allow you to spend money on me. It would not be right.'

He admired her scruples and her independence, he really did. 'It would please me a good deal if you would allow me to make you a gift.'

Her expression softened. 'Very well. If it would please you.'

'Good. Then if you are finished breaking your fast, let us go shopping.'

According to the landlady, all the best shops were on Milsom Street, but Miss Pomfret, who knew Bath since she had worked there all her life, was able to direct them to a shop in a less fashionable part of town where one could buy ready-made gowns for a few shillings, mostly those sold by ladies' maids who had received them as a gift from their mistresses.

It did not take Harriet long to discover two gowns she liked, a pretty blue gown of figured muslin trimmed with burgundy ribbons that she thought would fit and a burgundy taffeta which needed alteration. The shopkeeper produced a burgundy coat to go over them, along with a navy bonnet. Either outfit would be perfect for a walk in the park. Harriet went behind the curtain with Miss Pomfret to try them on.

While he waited, a pale turquoise evening dress, with festoons of silk roses, caught his eye. The shopkeeper was quick to show him how it could be altered to fit his *cousin*. He arranged for it to be delivered later in the day. He was likely to get the edge of her tongue for that purchase, too, but devil take it, he'd done nothing but count pennies since he inherited the title. He deserved to engage in a bit of extravagance for once.

When Harriet came out of the dressing area in the blue gown, she looked lovely. But it was the glow of pleasure on her face that filled his chest with warmth.

'Do you like it?' she asked shyly. 'This one fits really well. It might have been made for me. The other is too big.'

'I like it very much,' he said. 'Shall we purchase them both?'

'Both? I do not think I need two.'

He looked a little haughty. 'Naturally. My cousin cannot be seen in the same gown two days in a row.'

A look of longing crossed her expression, followed swiftly by doubt. 'Are you sure it is not too expensive?'

'It is but a trifle.' If she knew what he had spent on clothes for his sisters when they were under his roof, she would realise he was getting a bargain. The sum of all three gowns amounted to pin money.

'What if we meet the lady who owned them? It would be embarrassing.'

This time the shopkeeper came to his rescue. 'Oh, no, madam. You need not worry about that. Even if you should meet the former owner, she would never recognise it as her own. I often have ladies who are invited to events at the last minute and find themselves unprepared. I always change the trim. Give it a fresh look.'

'Excellent,' he said. 'The lady will wear this one now and you will send the remainder to our lodgings along with her own gown.'

If the shopkeeper was surprised at his request that she wear their purchase, she did not show it. He paid the bill and gave her their address.

They strolled along the street side by side. 'Thank you, Lord Westram,' she said softly. 'I have never owned anything so fine.'

'Please, call me Red. All my friends do.'

She frowned. 'Your real name is Redford, is it not? May I call you that?'

Surprised and, well…pleased, he stared at her. 'You would be the only one who calls me by my full name. And, yes. I would like it very much.'

'Good. And I will accept the gowns, Redford, if you will agree that, before we leave for London, we sell them back. You will not get all your money, but you will get some of it.'

'I would prefer you keep them,' he said. 'It is a gift.'

She turned her face up to him and her smile was sweet. 'Very well. Thank you. I will keep one and wear it to church on Sundays. It will remind me of you and this adventure of ours. I really hope it turns out for the best.'

He had almost forgotten about the real purpose for being here. 'I also.' He leaned closer and gave her a conspiratorial smile. 'Do you think we need Miss Pomfret's company on our walk?'

'I suppose not.' She turned back. 'Miss Pomfret, perhaps you would return to our lodgings and receive the delivery from the dressmaker.'

The woman nodded. 'Will you require luncheon, madam?'

'I presume so,' Red said. 'Though I am not sure what time we shall return.'

Miss Pomfret nodded. 'I will tell the landlady to expect you. Sydney Gardens is a treat you won't want to miss, my lord, madam.' She dipped a curtsy and headed back up the hill.

They walked down Great Pulteney Street and went into the Sydney Hotel where they paid their sixpence and received a guide to all the gardens had to offer. They walked through the lobby and out of the loggia flanking a paved square with a bandstand at its centre.

Harriet opened her parasol to shade her face. The pretty frilly edge rippled in the light breeze. She had never felt quite so elegant in her life.

It was almost as if she had gone from a nightmare, where prison loomed in her future, to a world where dreams actually came true.

She would be wise to be wary of such dreams.

Beneath the loggia people were breakfasting to the accompaniment of an orchestra and they wandered along a winding walk beneath shady trees. It opened out at a charming cascade and the mechanical depiction of a neat little village.

'One can almost forget one is in the middle of a city,' Harriet said.

'Indeed, it is a remarkable place. It very nearly rivals Vauxhall. Let us partake of breakfast here tomorrow.'

Tomorrow would be their last day in Bath. 'I would like that very much.'

The walk took them over an iron bridge and they were surprised by the sight of a canal. Barges and small rowing boats passed beneath them.

'How pretty this is,' Harriet said.

'Would you care to sit for a while?' He gestured to a strategically placed bench beneath a willow tree that provided an excellent view of an open grassy area bordered by late blooming roses and the treed walkway beyond.

She sat and he joined her.

'Thank you for bringing me here. I would never have thought to enter a pleasure gardens by myself.'

'I am glad of your company. I doubt if I would have bothered had I been alone. Indeed, to be honest, most of my acquaintances would consider Bath a dreadfully dull place, full of geriatrics.'

She chuckled as an elderly gentleman in a Bath chair, pushed by a sweating footman, passed them by. 'It is, rather. But there are others like us, here to enjoy the delights the gardens have to offer. The guide mentions something about a most complicated maze.'

He gave her a quizzical look. 'Would you like to experience it?'

'Do you think we dare? I should not like to be lost for hours.'

He laughed. 'It will not be as bad as that. I am sure there will be someone there to rescue us if need be.' He consulted the guide. 'If we continue along this path, we should come to it quite soon.'

Two ladies were walking towards them as they strolled onwards.

'Oh, no!' Harriet said.

Red glanced at her. 'Do you know them.'

'It is the Misses Perry. From the stagecoach.'

'By Jove, so it is.'

'Oh, my goodness, what will they think, seeing us walking together like this?'

He frowned. 'Why would we care? We don't know them. We can give them the cut direct, if you wish.'

Shocked, she stared at him. 'That would be dreadfully unkind.'

Anyway, it was too late. The elder Miss Perry had recognised Lord Westram as the man she knew as Mr West and her face was wreathed in smiles. The smile faltered as her gaze took in Harriet.

Red bowed. 'Well met, ladies,' he said. 'You remember my cousin, Mrs Godfrey.'

Miss Perry's eyes widened. 'I must admit, I would not have recognised you, ma'am. I see you have put off your mourning. I understood you to say you would not be visiting Bath, Mr West.'

'A change of plan,' Red said. 'Our business brought us here after all.'

'Our offer of tea still stands,' the younger Miss Perry chirped.

'Regretfully, I do not think there will be time,' Harriet said firmly, not liking the way the elder sister had somehow managed to insert herself between Harriet and Redford.

'How are you liking Sydney Gardens?' the younger sister asked Harriet.

'Very well. I hear they are a close rival to Vauxhall, though I have never been there myself.'

Before Harriet realised what was happening, Miss Perry was walking with Red and she was relegated to bringing up the rear with Miss Rose.

'We were on our way to the maze,' Redford said. 'Mrs Godfrey had a hankering to get lost.'

'Oh, you will love it,' Miss Perry said, turning to look at Harriet with a rather triumphant expression on her face. 'And you must try Merlin's Medical Swing when you reach the centre, it is of great benefit to one's health.'

'My health is perfectly sound,' Harriet said, but Miss Perry had already turned back to Redford, extolling the virtues of swinging at great length.

'I am surprised to see you here, Miss Rose,' Harriet said.

'We take a turn about the gardens every day, when the weather is fine,' she said. 'Everyone does. We are sure to see someone we know.'

It would be wonderful if they did meet an acquaintance, then she and Redford could continue their walk in peace.

A richly dressed elderly lady and gentleman tottered towards them, both leaning on canes and each other.

'Why, it is Lord Godfrey and his wife.' Miss Perry

exclaimed. 'They must be recently arrived. I did not see their names in the register at the Pump Room when I was there the other day.'

Harriet turned cold all over. Red had introduced himself to Mr King as Lord Westram and must have signed the register as such. Oh, this was not good. Their subterfuge was about to be revealed.

'Admiral!' Miss Perry called out. 'Welcome back to Bath. It is good to see you here again. Are you in your usual lodgings in Laura Place?'

The Admiral bowed and his wife dipped a stiff curtsy. 'The delightful Misses Perry. How are you? Is your father well?'

'In excellent health, sir. May I introduce Mr West and his cousin, Mrs Godfrey, who has only recently put off mourning. Sir, Mrs Godfrey, this is Admiral Lord Godfrey of the Blue.' Miss Perry cast Harriet an arch smile. 'No relation, I assume?'

Harriet nearly fainted, she suddenly felt so light-headed. No relation? If she wasn't mistaken, this was her grandfather, though she had never met him. There could not be two Admirals named Godfrey, now could there? Oh, what a foolish mistake it was to go about in public while here in Bath. And oh, heavens above, Lady Godfrey was staring at Harriet with a puzzled look on her face.

'No relation at all, I am sure,' Harriet said in a hoarse voice.

'Retired now,' the Admiral said, sticking out a hand.

Redford shook hands with Lord Godfrey. 'It is Westram, not West.'

Miss Perry's eyes widened. "Oh my word, I do apologize, I must have misheard."

'Miss Perry, tell your papa I shall expect to see him in the card room tomorrow night,' the Admiral said. 'I owe him a trouncing.'

'I will indeed,' Miss Perry said. 'Will you be attending the ball tomorrow night, Lady Godfrey?'

'I will,' the lady said, but she was looking at Harriet. 'Shall I see you there, Mrs Godfrey?'

'No,' Harriet said.

'Perhaps,' Redford said at the same moment.

'Oh, you must,' Miss Rose said eagerly. 'The ball is the highlight of the week and we are so thin of company at the moment.'

Nonplussed, Harriet did not know what to say.

'We shall see,' Redford replied.

Thank goodness he had not made a commitment.

The crunch of gravel beneath rapid footfalls and a shout caused them all to turn around. A small slender fellow barrelled into them. He narrowly missed colliding with Harriet, but rebounded off Redford and hurtled into the trees.

'Devil take it!' Redford said. 'My watch!'

He set off at a run.

'Oh, do be careful,' Miss Perry called after him. She turned to Harriet, 'The fellow might be armed.'

'These gardens are becoming plagued with pickpockets,' Lady Godfrey said. 'And in broad daylight, too. So brazen.'

'It is time they did something about it,' the Admiral said. 'I will have a word with Mr King.'

Lady Godfrey peered at Harriet. 'I know this sounds strange, but have we met somewhere before?'

Harriet froze. Since, according to her father, Harriet looked very much like the Admiral's sister, how could she be surprised that the woman thought she knew her? 'I do not believe so, your ladyship.'

'You look strangely familiar. I cannot put my finger on it.'

Hopefully she never would.

Redford strode across the grass towards them. In his hand was a shabby old coat. He tossed it over a bush and dusted off his hands.

'You didn't catch him,' Harriet said.

'No. He slipped out of the coat when I had him by the collar. The blighter dashed in front of a horse and hopped the fence into Sydney Place. He was nowhere to be seen by the time I got across.' He grinned and pulled his timepiece from his waistcoat pocket. 'I did, however, get my watch back.' He held it up in triumph.

'The fellow ought to be hanged,' the Admiral said.

'What he needs is proper work,' Harriet replied. 'Perhaps then he would not need to steal.'

The Admiral snorted. 'That sort don't want to work.'

Harriet held her tongue. Men never listened to a woman's opinion anyway.

'Wasn't that the same fellow who tried to steal your watch when we travelled on the stage?' Harriet said. 'I seem to recall that bilious green waistcoat.'

Redford nodded grimly. 'It was indeed.'

'Well, let us hope he is not third time lucky,' Miss

Rose trilled. 'I swear I will be too terrified to walk in these gardens ever again.'

'It is a disgrace. He comes from Avon Street, I have no doubt,' the Admiral declared. 'Nothing but a nest of rogues. In my day, we'd have had the rascals flogged around the fleet. I shall speak to the constable. What they need to do is clear all the criminals out of the area.'

'I must say,' Lady Godfrey said, 'one does wonder if one is safe going anywhere when that sort of thing happens in broad daylight.'

Redford looked grim. 'I certainly advise you not to walk unaccompanied.' He smiled at Harriet. 'I believe the maze is our next stop.' He turned to the others. 'Do you want to come along?'

'Can't,' the Admiral said. 'Due at the Pump Room.'

'No, thank you,' Miss Perry said. 'We have breakfast ordered.'

'Enjoy yourselves,' Redford said. 'We intend to partake tomorrow.'

'Their breakfasts are excellent,' Lady Godfrey said. 'Not to be missed.'

'Would you care to join us?' Red asked.

Harriet almost swallowed her tongue. 'We only ordered a table for two,' she managed to say.

Lady Godfrey frowned and stared at her hard.

Harriet wanted to shrivel up and dive under the nearest bush. She had been rude, but she could not imagine anything worse than having breakfast with her grandparents. She was bound to let something slip.

'We would love to,' Lady Godfrey said.

Harriet froze.

'But the Admiral has an appointment with my doctor tomorrow, so it will not be possible.'

She let go a sigh of relief.

Redford bowed. 'If you change your mind send round a note, we lodge on Green Street. I bid you good day, ladies, my lord. Come along, Cousin.'

He took Harriet's arm and they strolled away.

'Don't forget the ball tomorrow night,' Miss Rose called after them.

Inwardly Harriet groaned. Going about in public in Bath was the worst mistake of her life. And she was absolutely not going to any ball.

Chapter Ten

'Why are you so shaken, Harriet?' Red asked, seeing the tension in her shoulders. It was unlike her to look so anxious. 'I am sure pickpockets are a common occurrence in London. I feel fortunate to have recovered my watch.'

'I am not so hen-hearted as to be upset by a pickpocket,' she said. 'Though I would rather it had not happened.'

'Then what troubles you?'

'To be honest, I feel uncomfortable lying to these people. Telling them I am your cousin, when I am nothing of the sort.'

'What would you have me tell them?'

She made a sound of impatience. 'I would sooner not tell them anything. We should not be going about in public.'

'You mean we should remain locked up in our lodgings for two days, never setting foot out of doors?'

'You can go about, if you wish.'

He sighed. She wasn't wrong. He hadn't expected to meet anyone he knew in Bath. Not that he really knew the Perry sisters, any more than he knew Lord and Lady Godfrey, but he had no doubt they had acquaintances in common. He had simply wanted Harriet to have a bit of fun while they were here. And he enjoyed her company. Enjoyed seeing her pleasure at these novel experiences.

'If it does not trouble me, surely it should not trouble you?' he said. 'It is not as if you will be seeing any of them again, once we return to London.'

'Lying does not trouble you?' She sounded shocked.

The sign at the entrance to the maze proclaimed the benefits of the medical swing to be found at its heart.

He took her hand in his and gave it a little squeeze. 'You take things too seriously, Harriet. In a day or two, we will both go back to lives full of duty and responsibility. Why not have a little fun? We are not harming anyone. Are we?'

A reluctant smile curved her lips. 'I suppose not.' She tugged her hand free. 'I wager I beat you to the middle.' She dashed between the hedges and he easily caught her up.

'I think it better if we go together. I do not want you getting lost for hours.'

She laughed. 'We cannot. Look.' She pointed to a tall structure with a fellow sitting on top. 'He is there to direct us.'

'Good thing, too, I should think. Though I have a very good sense of direction and I am sure I can find the way.'

They passed a bench beneath the shade of a striped

awning, a place for the lost to rest, no doubt. The next corner they turned led them to a dead end.

Harriet giggled. 'So much for your sense of direction.'

He caught her by the shoulder, pulled her to him and kissed her thoroughly, until they were both out of breath.

Sweetly, she smiled up at him. 'I suppose you got lost on purpose.'

'Of course.'

Harriet giggled.

After a couple more wrong turns and stolen kisses, they found the grotto at the centre of the labyrinth.

The brightly painted swing in the shape of a boat held four persons, but since they were the only two in the grotto they climbed aboard and a young man pushed it into motion.

'This is fun,' Harriet said twirling her parasol. 'The motion makes my stomach dip most strangely.'

He wanted to kiss her again, but they were no longer private. Another couple had arrived. Laughing, they gave up their seats to the newcomers.

'I do feel as if it has done me some good.' Harriet gazed at the swing and it started off once more.

'Well, it has certainly put roses in your cheeks,' Red said. 'You look beautiful.'

She smiled at him and he felt heat trickle along his veins. He almost suggested they return to their apartments. As quickly as possible. He held his tongue. He had another treat in store.

An attendant guided them out of the maze by way of a hidden gate.

'Where now?' she asked.

There was really only one place he wanted to be right at that moment. But that was selfish. 'According to the guide, there are several other places not to be missed. Milsom Street has shops as fine as any on Bond Street, and the Royal Crescent is an architectural sight to behold.'

And so they spent the rest of the afternoon taking in the sights of Bath until Harriet confessed she had done enough walking for one day.

After delivering her back to their lodgings, Red had one more errand to run, but he waited until Harriet had gone to her chamber to freshen up before stepping out briefly.

Dinner at the lodgings was set for the early hour of five-thirty, something that would have horrified him in town, but, given all the walking they had done, was most welcome. The fare was excellent. Roast beef, a chicken pie, green beans and roasted potatoes, all cooked to perfection along with fresh fruit and a lemon tart. They talked about their day as they ate.

'Are you going to report the theft of your watch?' Harriet asked.

'Attempted theft.'

'For the second time.'

He sighed. 'I did visit the constable before dinner, but I did not swear out a warrant. I have the possible address for the man. An inn of ill repute in an alley off Avon Street.'

She stared at him. 'You do not intend to try to find him yourself?'

'Apparently, that quarter of the city is a den of iniquity well known to the police.'

'More or less as my—my Lord Godfrey said.' Her voice sounded oddly strange. There was a shadow of fear in her gaze.

Troubled, he shook his head. 'I think I will take the constable's advice and stay well away and I'll be sure to keep my watch tucked away.'

'You do not think he will try a third time, surely?'

'I think he is a bold, foolish fellow who might risk his neck to brag of his cleverness. But should he try again, I'll make sure he does not slip out of my grasp a second time.'

She gave him a long considering look. 'He would be a fool indeed to attempt to rob you a third time.'

'Indeed.'

After dinner, while Harriet mended a hole in the heel of one of her stockings, Red perused his newspaper and read aloud passages he thought she might find interesting.

It reminded him of when his sisters lived at home and they would gather around the hearth to sew and read books out loud. He'd thought it a dead bore in those days and chafed at being the head of the household. But now, with Harriet, he felt a deep sense of familiarity and comfort.

At nine-thirty he put aside his paper and rose to his feet. 'I hear Pomfret moving around in your room. I expect she wishes to ready you for bed. When she has left you, come back and we will enjoy a nightcap together.'

Gazing up at him, she visibly swallowed. 'More tutoring?'

Heat surged in his veins. 'Yes, my sweet.'

My sweet. How enchanting that sounded. And yet… Harriet's heart was thundering so loud in her chest, she felt as if she wanted to flee. She thought about telling him she was far too tired for lessons.

Coward. She was excited, but she was also scared. Well, there was no going back, after all this was her idea. A hot blush stole up her cheeks. How on earth she could ever have proposed such a thing she did not know. But the die was cast and, despite her nervousness, she was determined and not going to let the opportunity slip away.

She rose to her feet and offered up her lips for a kiss. He brushed his mouth across hers, a warm tender touch. 'Naughty little puss,' he murmured against her cheek. 'Go before your Miss Pomfret comes to find you.'

That would never do. She kissed the dimple at the point of his chin and walked calmly to her chamber door, when really she wanted to run.

Pomfret had laid out her nightgown and had warm water waiting in the wash bowl.

'Have you always lived in Bath?' Harriet asked while the woman undid the tapes of her gown.

'I have not, ma'am. My family were tenant farmers,

but when they couldn't afford the rent, they had to move to the city to find work.'

'I am sorry.'

'I'm not, ma'am. We have found good work here. I would like a permanent place, of course. But while I am waiting for a position to become vacant, I learn a great deal from the different ladies I serve during their visits to Bath.'

Harriet stepped out of her gown and petticoat and the maid undid her stays and slipped her nightgown over her head. Pomfret removed the pins from her hair and Harriet sat down at the dressing table so the woman could brush and braid her hair.

'What lovely hair you have, ma'am. So thick and soft.'

'It requires a great many pins to hold it in place,' she said.

'Perhaps if you cut it so it is shorter around the face and dressed it higher on your crown in a more fashionable style, it would require less pinning.'

Fashionable. That would go down well in her shop. 'I am quite happy with my bun.'

The woman pursed her lips. 'The ladies I have served have all complimented me on my hairstyles. I am sure you would be pleased.'

She seemed so eager, Harriet did not like to refuse her. 'Perhaps tomorrow. We are to breakfast at Sydney Gardens.'

'I hear the food is excellent, as is the entertainment. A new hairstyle will be just the thing.'

Pomfret swiftly braided her hair in two neat plaits, turned down the bed and left by the servants' door.

Harriet's mouth felt suddenly dry. She could not help but recall the heady sensations of yesterday, or the astonishing pleasure that had racked her body. It had been an otherworldly experience indeed. And Lord Westram had promised more. There was no way she would allow her cowardliness to cause her to miss such an opportunity.

She put on her dressing gown, tied it tightly at the waist and, after a deep breath, opened the door to the parlour.

Lord Westram was seated on the sofa in a silk dressing gown of royal blue. He smiled and her fears seemed to dissipate. She sat beside him.

He handed her a glass. 'Brandy.'

One sip and the raw liquid made her cough.

He took the glass before it spilled. 'I forgot that you prefer it with water. I apologise.'

Hot and still breathless, she chuckled. 'I wasn't expecting it to be so strong.'

'Perhaps you would prefer a glass of sherry?'

'Yes, I think that would be better.'

He got up and poured her a glass from the decanter on the console. They toasted each other and he sat beside her once more.

The silence seemed to stretch out between them, and the earlier comfortable feeling seeped away.

She took a deep breath, desperately seeking for something to say. Anything. 'Where is your home? I presume you have an estate somewhere in the country.'

He leaned back against the cushions and gazed up at the ceiling. 'I do indeed. Our family estate is in Gloucestershire.'

'Quite far from London, then.'

'Yes. I only come to London when I absolutely have to.'

Such as when he had to track down a criminal. She shivered.

He put his glass aside and put an arm around her shoulders. He stroked her cheek with his thumb and after a moment or two she rested her head upon his shoulder.

He gave her a little squeeze. 'That is better, sweet. You have nothing to fear from me. Nothing will happen that you do not want.'

How could she relax? Would he laugh at her clumsy attempts to please him? Would he find making love to her a chore?

He leaned down and kissed her. Her body hummed with contentment. All thought ceased. She gave herself up to the pleasure of his kiss and the delight of kissing him back.

It wasn't until he broke the kiss and gazed down into her face that she realised he had undone the tie at her waist.

She held her breath as his hand left her shoulder where it had rested throughout their kiss, and his fingers traced a trail across her collarbone and down to the rise of her breast, where it lingered.

She drew in a little breath. A shiver rippled across her shoulders.

Her breasts felt tight and when she glanced down, she could see the hard nub of her nipples pressing against the linen of her nightdress.

He cupped his hand beneath her breast, lifting as if testing its weight.

'I want to kiss you there,' he murmured softly. 'May I?'

The shadow of her breast beneath a prim and proper linen nightgown was one of the most enticing sights he had ever seen. The darker tone of the areola held his gaze.

But her shoulders were tense, her expression still a little nervous.

Gently, with one finger, he outlined the fullness of her breast in declining circles. Her indrawn breath and the tightening of her nipple to a hard point pleased him greatly. He brushed her nipple lightly with his thumb and she moaned softly.

Such a delight, this woman.

He lowered his head and drew her nipple into his mouth and flicked it with his tongue.

She gasped.

He drew back to observe her expression. She was looking decidedly startled and intrigued. He caressed her breast, feeling the little hard peak against his palm. It felt delicious. Arousing.

She went lax in his arms, shifting to give him better access. While he caressed her, he kissed her until his shaft was harder than granite and aching.

The desire to take her ran rampant through his veins,

but she was a maid and, while he had heard the talk, he had no first-hand knowledge of bedding a virgin. He would do everything in his power to make her first experience wonderful.

Her small hand, which up to now had been tightly clenched at his nape, gradually relaxed and began wandering across his shoulder and down to his chest. His dressing gown prevented him fully appreciating her touch, but when she palmed his nipple, it tightened and the hairs on the back of his neck rose to attention.

She was mimicking him.

He broke the kiss. 'That feels lovely.'

A blush stole up her cheeks. 'I like it, too.'

He rose with her in her arms. 'I think we will be more comfortable on your bed, don't you?'

'I thought you would never ask.' She sighed.

He strode for her chamber and set her on her feet beside the bed. 'May I?' he asked, tugging at the ribbon at the end of one of her plaits.

She smiled at him shyly and nodded. 'If you wish. I thought about leaving it unbound, but Pomfret would have wondered.'

He pressed a small kiss to her brow. 'I will plait it before I leave, so she will never know.'

Her forehead creased in a frown. Dismay filled her expression.

'What is it.'

She shook her head. 'Nothing.'

It wasn't nothing, but now was not the time for argument. He would deal with it later, when his brain was functioning rather than his male urges.

He pulled off the little blue ribbon and combed his fingers through the tightly twisted strands of hair until it fell free, then did the same with the other plait. The black hair fell in a curtain of soft ripples down her back to her waist. He lifted a section and watched it slide through his fingers like a dark waterfall.

'Beautiful,' he whispered. 'A crown of glory.'

She stroked a lock of his hair back from his forehead. 'Yours is beautiful, too.'

'Hardly. The colour is the bane of my life.'

'Is that why you are called Red?'

He continued lifting and letting fall the curtain of hair, fascinated by the way it glinted in the candlelight in ever-shifting patterns, like the sea at night.

'I am told my hair was black like yours at birth. Then it turned red. I was the butt of many jests growing up and it certainly didn't help that I had a temper.'

She narrowed her gaze on his face. 'You are quick to anger?'

'I have learned to control it, as everyone does. But there is no denying it burns hot, even if it burns slower than it did when I was a boy.'

She nodded. 'I felt its heat when you first walked into my shop.' She cast him a little glance askance. 'I did think you were frightfully handsome, though.'

He preened at the compliment. 'I thought you were the loveliest young woman I had seen in a long time.'

'Until we got to the reason for your visit.'

'Indeed. But you know it is a long time since I have thought badly of you.'

Her expression softened. 'I'm glad. I have long since stopped being annoyed at your threats.'

'Methinks you have a bit of a temper yourself.'

She laughed. 'Perhaps it is so.' She put her arms around his neck and kissed the point of his chin. She had done that before and he really liked it.

He swept her up in his arms and laid her down on the sheet. He climbed up beside her, leaning over her to gaze into her lovely face. 'You are not angry at me now,' he whispered.

Her eyes widened. 'Oh, no. Not the slightest bit angry.'

He nuzzled her neck, licking and tasting the delicate flesh before blowing gently in her ear. Her soft moans and shivers strummed at the hot desire running like a wildfire beneath his skin.

What red-blooded male would not enjoy such a responsive, sensual beauty in his bed, but somehow she was more than that. She was an intelligent, if outspoken, female who, despite her low beginnings, was also a lady.

She deserved respect as well as pleasure.

He nibbled at her earlobe and she giggled. 'That tickles.'

'In a good way, or a bad way?'

A little pause said she was thinking seriously about his question, so he did it again.

She pushed at his shoulder. 'A little of both, I think.'

'There can be pain with pleasure,' he acknowledged and, before she could guess what he was about, closed his mouth around her nipple once more and then scraped it very gently with his teeth. Her hips rose up from the bed. She made an odd sound in the back of her throat.

He rose up on one elbow to better see her face. 'Again?'

'No. I mean, yes. Maybe. Oh, you are teasing me.'

'Perhaps it would feel nicer if there was nothing between us.' He undid the ribbon at her neck and loosened the gown. 'I love the way this covers you from your neck to your toes.'

'You do?'

'Mmm. It is like getting a present, all wrapped up in paper and tied with string. The anticipation is almost as good as finding out what is inside.'

'Presents can be disappointing.'

She was smiling, but there was pain in the depths of her eyes. 'Is that the voice of experience speaking, my love?'

'Young people always have such high expectations, don't they? And my father was a great one for surprising us. He bought Mother the prettiest jewellery. On one occasion he took me for a ride in a hot air balloon for my birthday. Another year we took a boat ride to Greenwich. When I was seventeen, I could not wait to see what he would think of. I had not noticed that he was not his usual jovial self or that Mother appeared anxious. If I had been thinking less of myself, I might have realised something was wrong. It was the worst day of my life.'

She gave a small laugh as if to ward off the pain of the memory.

'What happened?' He imagined a carriage ride where it poured with rain, or a dress that did not fit.

She closed her eyes for a moment. When she opened them again they were full of hurt. 'He did not remember it was my birthday at all. He was too busy trying to avoid his creditors. On the morning of my birthday, we were evicted from our home and we all ended up in the King's Bench.'

He pulled her against him and held her close. She was shaking. 'You poor thing. I cannot imagine how awful that would be.'

Or perhaps he could. It would be something like the day that he was informed that all the male members of his family had been killed by the French in some minor skirmish in Spain.

'Did you remain there long?'

'A few months. It was horrible. We lost everything. I loved my father, but I never again trusted his judgement. After he paid his debts, we moved to the premises where we are now.' She took a deep breath and squared her shoulders. 'We have made the best of it, Mother and I.'

Even as he admired her strength after such an ordeal, guilt assailed him for the way he had marched into her life, threatening her with arrest. She must have been terrified. He would never have guessed.

'And you,' she asked. 'Were you ever disappointed in a gift?'

He felt the need to strike a lighter note, as he had so often felt the need to lift the spirits of his sisters. 'I did, though it does not add to my credit, I must say. One year, I was sure I was to get a horse for my birthday. I must have been five or six. Instead, I got my older sister Marguerite's pony. She got the horse. I was furious. With her. With my father.'

'Oh, dear. A horse. I could not imagine owning anything so expensive.'

'That is what Father's bailiff told me. He said if I wanted to own such a valuable animal, I had to show myself capable of caring for it and that so far I hadn't shown any great abilities in that direction.

'I then recalled all the hours Marguerite had spent in the stables, both learning and working with the head groom. I stormed into her bedroom and demanded to know why she hadn't let me into the secret. Poor Marguerite was most confused until I explained. Then she laughed at me. The only reason she had spent so much time in the stables was to get away from me and my younger brother, Jonathan. She had no idea it would result in her getting her own horse.'

She stroked his arm. 'You did get your own horse, though, I am sure.'

'Two years later, after a lot of mucking out and brushing and combing. But it was worth it. And of course, I let Jonathan in on the secret, so I had company in the barn. It was probably the happiest and most carefree time of my life.' He looked at her. 'Although this past couple of days comes close.'

He could not believe he had said that. And could not believe that he meant every word.

Besides, this evening was not about him, it was about her and her pleasure.

He cradled her face in his hands and kissed her,

until he stopped thinking altogether and let the pleasure of being with a warm, willing and highly desirable woman take control.

Chapter Eleven

His kisses seemed to rob Harriet of reason. She thought she would become used to it, but whenever his mouth melded with hers, as it was now, and his hands roved her body, stroking and shaping each curve and hollow, sensible thoughts slipped away.

All she wanted to do was to be closer to his long, lean, hard body, to feel his weight pressing her down into the mattress. This time, when he plucked at the hem of her nightdress, she had no trouble interpreting the meaning. Indeed, she felt as if she had on far too many clothes, her skin glowing and itching so much.

She raised her hips and then sat up so he could draw it up and off over her head.

For a long moment he gazed at her and she crossed her arms over her chest, feeling suddenly vulnerable.

'Do not hide from me, sweetheart,' he murmured. 'You are just so lovely, I want to gaze on you for ever and a day.'

She slipped a hand beneath the lapel of his dressing gown, feeling rough hair against her fingertips. It felt strange, but somehow exciting. 'Can I not see you, also?'

'Of course. If you want to.'

He went for the tie at his waist, but she brushed his hands aside. 'It is my turn to open a present.'

He made a rueful face. 'The male form is not nearly as beautiful as that of the female. Indeed, aroused as I am, it can be a little intimidating.'

'Aroused. What does it mean in this context? I know what it means when I say my curiosity is aroused.'

He closed his eyes. 'It means that my body is awakened and excited about the idea of making love to you.'

'My body is awakened, too,' she said.

'I am very glad to hear it.' Despite his amused tone, he sounded a little hoarse.

She untied the knot and pushed the silky soft material off his shoulders, then grabbed the sleeves and freed his arms and hands. His chest was broad and heavily muscled, his waist narrow. A triangle of crisp dark auburn curls formed a triangle on his chest that tapered to a narrow trail of hair that travelled downwards.

She parted the robe. She knew quite a bit about the male anatomy. She'd seen enough lewd statuettes of the intertwining of males and females to know what to expect. Yet his arrogant flesh standing proudly out from his hips, jutting from a nest of ginger-coloured hair and the soft round sacks beneath, was far more shocking than any statue. The head of it looked red and swollen and the stem was twisted about with ropey veins.

He was supposed to put all of that inside her body?

She'd always assumed that the statuettes and pictures were exaggerations, much as the cartoons she sold in her shop exaggerated noses and chins, and the size of women's breasts.

She swallowed. 'Oh.' She lay back on the pillows. It might be better to lie still and wait for him to be done. She closed her eyes.

A heavy weight descended on her thighs. Heavy. Warm. His leg. Shocked, she pressed her legs tightly together.

And winced inwardly. He was going to think her such a coward.

Teeth gritted, she forced her legs to relax.

He stroked her jaw with his fingertips. 'If you want me to stop, say so.'

A breath left her body in a rush. She hadn't realised she was holding it. She had wanted this. It wasn't anything terrible. Couples did this all the time. She opened her eyes. 'No. Go on.' It had the flavour of *Let us get this over with*.

The chuckle he gave made little sound, but his body shook. 'Yes, ma'am.'

Clearly, he had heard it, too. Mortified, she gazed into his eyes. They held no criticism. Only warmth. And, yes, a little amusement. But not the mockery she had half expected. She smiled.

The kiss he planted on her mouth was warm and wooing and tender. Her body heated, her limbs relaxed. She twined her arms around his neck and arched into him. She no longer felt fear. She trusted him not to hurt her. Her veins hummed with excitement.

When his knee pushed between her thighs, she welcomed him, parting her legs until he lay between them. His hand roved over her body and she revelled in his touch, caressing his back, learning the shape of him, narrow at the waist, rising to firm buttocks.

He broke the kiss and rose to his knees.

She gazed at him in wonder and awe. He looked better than any statue or picture, his wide chest defined by muscles that shifted when he moved, his strong arms and large hands that cupped her breasts, making them tingle and feel heavy. The hairs on his body glistened like polished copper when caught by the light of the candle.

Her mouth dried as she gazed at his phallus, so taut and erect.

He took her hand and guided it to him, curling her fingers around his shaft, showing her how to stroke him, setting the rhythm. It felt hard inside the hot velvety skin. So strange.

She lifted her gaze to his face and there was strain in his expression along with pleasure.

His hand left hers and he looked down, gazing at the apex of her thighs, then stroked and petted the dark curls. He was going to do that thing again.

Her body tensed. His thumbs gently parted her and he dipped a finger inside her. It felt strange. Intrusive. As he moved his hand the pleasure heightened again. Higher than before. The tension building.

He leaned forward, resting on one forearm while his other hand worked the magic that was lovely and yet not quite enough.

He kissed her lips, her chin, her throat, working his way down to the rise of her breast, and stroked her nipple with his tongue, then suckled.

Her core tightened unbearably.

'Ready, my sweet?' he murmured.

Ready for what? She could not speak she was so breathless, so awash in sensation. But, yes, she was ready for anything. She nodded.

His hand left her mons. And he pushed forward with his hips. He made a sound of pleasure that was also a groan of pain.

Instinctively, she hooked her legs around his waist and cradled him between her hips, and he thrust his phallus into her.

She squeezed her eyes shut.

'Look at me, darling.'

Gasping, she forced her eyes open and gazed into his face. He smiled down at her, his hips flexed and he moved faster and faster, all the while watching her face, stealing little kisses, stroking and caressing her breasts, until she felt she could bear it no longer.

'Let go, my darling,' he said, in guttural tones.

Her body remembered, even if she did not, as it reached for what it wanted. She cried out as something inside her flew apart, releasing her from the tension in a slow wave of bliss.

Her vision darkened and heat raced through her.

'Yes,' he groaned.

He withdrew from her and rocked against her stomach, his body shuddering.

She lay entwined in his arms, both panting and barely lucid.

His breathing deepened and his weight bore down on her, as if he had fallen asleep.

She had never felt so wonderful in her life. Or so womanly.

What she had experienced the day before was nothing compared to this. It was like the melding of two souls.

She snuggled up to him.

Might it have been better not to have known about this? For how could one not want to do it again?

The idea that she might never have the opportunity again gave her a feeling of loss.

The feel of a warm body cuddled up to his seeped into Red's awareness. The sense of closeness felt so right, he almost fell back to sleep.

The candle on the bedside guttered. Realisation of where he was, who she was, brought him fully awake.

He gazed at the beautiful woman lying in his arms. The black hair spread across the pillow and draped across the arm holding her close to his side. At some point, he must have pulled the covers over them, because all he could see of her was her shoulder and her face. He wanted to kiss that little rounded bone peeking out from the sheet. He wanted to kiss her all over, truth to tell.

If he could summon the energy.

He disentangled his fingers from her hair and rolled on his back. She stirred and moved closer. Beneath the covers, he tightened his hold and gave her a comforting squeeze. She sighed.

Devil take it.

He had expected to enjoy himself. He'd had no doubts that he could make her first dip into the waters of sensual play a delightful experience—for them both. He had not expected to lose all sense of himself in his efforts to please her. He'd almost lost control. He'd had to force himself to leave her body, a method he'd used for years as prevention of an unwanted child, until it had become second nature.

Until now. With her.

And already his body wanted to make love to her again, while his mind wanted to teach her all the ways known to man, how to enjoy her body and his. He wanted to see her above him, her black hair falling over him like a silky river of ink.

His heart wanted to make her his.

He froze. Not possible.

To let his heart rule his head was far too dangerous. It made a man weak. Look what had happened to his grandfather. Red never wanted to experience that sort of pain.

What the devil was he thinking? Harriet was a passing fancy. He had come to admire and respect her, and she had asked him to show her the way of it. And had decided it was better that it was he rather than anyone else.

The thought of anyone else touching her—

She was a shopkeeper. A woman of low birth. And he was betrothed. Or he would be again, once he found a way to repay Eugenie's father. He would insist that they call the banns right away. They had both waited long enough.

So why did the idea chill him to the bone? Dammit all. All he needed to do was put some distance between him and Harriet and everything would be back to normal.

He eased his arm out from beneath her, got up and shrugged into his dressing gown. He picked up the candle, now burnt down to a nub, and gazed down upon the bed.

The vision he saw there, the black hair tangled around her, the rosy lips relaxed in sleep, the dark lashes like half-moons against her pale skin, would be one he would not forget in a hurry.

Cursing himself for a weak fool, he strode from the chamber and poured himself a brandy before heading to his own chilly sheets and dark thoughts.

Red had left her some time in the night, Harriet remembered as she slowly became aware of daylight filtering through the bedchamber window. She had wanted to call him back, but hadn't fully awakened until she heard him closing the door behind him.

Beneath the covers she was warm and cosy, almost lethargic. And perfectly naked. He'd been right to leave, of course. It would not do for Pomfret to walk in on them. She stretched her arms over her head, feeling luxuriously lazy, and rolled on her side. The muscles in her thighs protested the movement, reminding her of the way she had cradled his large body. Last night had been wonderfully energetic. Oh, heaven help her, she hoped they got to do it again.

Hunger struck. She was starving. She threw the covers aside, clambered down from the bed and put on her nightgown and robe. As she pulled the bell to call the maid, she glanced around. Everything seemed in order.

Pomfret arrived within minutes. She was carrying a package folded over her arm. 'The package from the dressmaker, ma'am.' She laid it on the bed. 'It arrived a half hour ago.' She parted the brown paper to reveal the prettiest gown Harriet had ever seen.

'There must be some mistake,' Harriet said, fingering the silky fabric. 'We did not buy this. We ordered a walking gown.'

'Yes. That is here also.' She lifted the silky skirts to reveal the other gown beneath.

'Oh, dear, she must have made a mistake. This ball gown must be for another customer.'

'Oh, no,' Pomfret said. 'Your cousin bought it while you tried on the walking dresses. I assumed it was with your approval.'

He'd ordered it without asking her opinion. How could he do that? She had barely agreed to the purchase of the walking gowns. Did he not care what she thought about the matter? How typical of a man to barge ahead without any sort of consultation, assuming he knew best. Not to mention spending money rashly.

It was more than she could bear.

She wrapped her robe tighter about her and strode into the parlour where Redford was waiting.

* * *

'What is the meaning of this?'

Red lowered his newspaper. 'Good morning.' He glanced at the clock. 'Yes, it is still morning.' He kept his expression bland and raised a brow.

Harriet held up a turquoise froth of silk and lace. Her expression was grim as she shook the gown as if it was a rat. 'Good morning, Lord Westram. And I asked you a question.'

He bristled at the annoyance in her voice and the use of his title.

'It is for you to wear at the ball, Mrs Godfrey.'

She lifted her chin. 'I said I would not attend the ball.'

He shrugged and lifted his newspaper. 'As you wish.'

'I have decided we should not take breakfast at Sydney Gardens either. We came here for business purposes, not to gad about.'

She had decided. Interesting. 'I am afraid we have no choice. The Admiral is expecting us.'

'No such thing. He is visiting the doctor.'

'He sent round a note first thing this morning. His wife convinced him to change the time of the appointment and meet us for breakfast at noon.'

She glanced at the clock. It was eleven already.

Despite all of his good resolutions, Red had been congratulating himself on a job well done when the usually early-rising lady had not appeared at half past ten. While he had sworn to himself to keep his distance from now on, he had not expected *her* to want to run and hide.

He forced himself to keep his expression politely blank.

'I am not going,' She narrowed her gaze on his face. 'You can if you wish, but I will not.'

There was a note of panic in her voice. 'That would be rude. And I will not be rude to a man who served this country so well. Please give me one good reason why you should not go.'

The look she gave him seemed to speak volumes, but he had no idea what it said.

'Well?' he asked again.

'Lady Godfrey makes me uncomfortable. Perhaps she knows I am not who we say I am. If she was ever to find out I am your—' She blushed a fiery red.

'My what?'

She gestured with her hand. 'You know. Your…your paramour.'

He would kill the first person who said that about her in his hearing. He glared at her. 'You are nothing of the sort. Now, go and change your gown. We need to leave shortly.'

'You have no authority over me. You cannot tell me what to do. You cannot make me go.'

He felt his temper rise. This was just the sort of argument he used to have with his sisters.

He tried to keep his voice low and reasonable. 'You are right. I cannot demand that you accompany me, but I ask that you do so, because it is the right thing to do. It was your request that I give you time to find

Clark and, despite my misgivings, I agreed. I acceded to your request to tutor you. Why can you not do this one thing for me?'

The calm reason in his voice irritated Harriet more than his raised voice had on the first day they met. Perhaps she should tell him of the connection between her and the Admiral. Surely that would be a good enough reason for her to cry off.

Dash it. Until they'd met the Admiral and his wife, she had been looking forward to having breakfast in Sydney Gardens. Meeting them had spoiled everything. Just as they had spoiled everything for her papa. And the way Redford was looking at her, it seemed he thought she was being difficult. Then he smiled. 'I thought we were going to enjoy ourselves for the brief time we are here.'

And that smile weakened every resolution she had made.

Why should she let her grandparents spoil the only visit she was ever likely to make to Bath? They could not force her to admit the relationship, if indeed they even suspected it. There must be hundreds of families named Godfrey in England.

She glanced down at the gown she had crumpled in her hands. So pretty. And her favourite colour, too. And once they left Bath, she would never meet any of these people again. 'Very well. If you insist. I should not like to think you had wasted your money for no reason. We will go to breakfast and we will attend the ball.'

He raised a brow. 'How gracious of you.'

She had been grudging rather than gracious. She blushed. 'Thank you for the gowns. They are lovely.'

His eyes danced. 'You are very welcome.'

Well, he would be happy. He had got his own way. She marched back to her chamber.

Truth to tell, she was secretly glad he had insisted on something that would have been her right by birth, if only her grandfather had approved her father's choice of a wife.

In no time at all, Pomfret had her dressed in the other gown they had purchased together. Harriet gazed into the pier glass. What she saw was not a shopkeeper from Ludgate Hill, but a woman of fashion. The gown was a rich burgundy with dark green pinstripes. It fell from the high waist to a sweet Vandyke lace hem. The matching spencer had the same lace on the collar and the cuffs. It was modestly cut at the neck and thoroughly elegant.

The dressmaker had also sent along a bonnet in dark green with silk flowers dyed the colours of autumn.

The woman in the mirror looked elegant and quite unlike herself. She turned away.

Pomfret had draped the ball gown over the bed.

Harriet was going to be attending her very first ball. The only ball she would ever attend. Papa had always spoken of balls and routs and drums, always regretted that he had deprived her of those treats, even while affirming he did not regret his marriage one bit. Her mama was the only woman for him.

And she had not doubted it for a moment.

'It became a little creased, ma'am,' Pomfret said with

a cheerful smile. 'While you are out, I'll take it down-stairs and give it a press.'

'Thank you.'

She was going to miss the woman when she returned home, but she simply did not have a need for a lady's maid. And she certainly could not afford to pay Pomfret just because she liked her.

A knock sounded at the door and she glanced at the clock. Time to go. She put on her bonnet and went to join Redford in the parlour.

He stood at the window, looking down at the street, but turned at her entry.

He perused her from head to toe and smiled.

Heat warmed her cheeks. 'Will I do?'

'You look lovely. Stunning.'

Her heart squeezed at the compliment. 'It is all your doing.'

He looked quite lovely himself in a navy coat with silver buttons and his buff unmentionables. His linen as always was pristine and his cravat beautifully tied, but his waistcoat was a pièce de résistance in silver-grey, embroidered with sprigs of lily of the valley.

He took her arm and they walked down the hill. Upon arrival at Sydney Hotel, the maître d' guided them to their booth in the loggia on the right-hand side, a mirror image of those facing them across the square.

The booths were occupied by the cream of Bath society all in their elegant finery.

Harriet felt like a fraud. If they knew who she was, what she did for a living, they would be appalled. Likely they would turn their backs on her and give Redford the cut direct. She must do her very best not to disgrace him.

She took the seat held out by a footman and tried not to look about her in awe, but rather to give the appearance of someone who did this sort of thing every day.

The Admiral and Lady Godfrey arrived a few moments later. Redford seated Lady Godfrey beside him and the Admiral sat beside Harriet. In the centre of the square between the wings of the loggia, a band warmed up their instruments.

They ordered their food, making sure to include some Sally Lunn's Bath buns, which Lady Godfrey recommended highly.

'How fortunate we are with the weather,' Lady Godfrey said once the waiter had left.

'Indeed,' Redford said.

'Is this your first visit to Bath, Mrs Godfrey?' the Admiral asked. 'How odd that sounds. I think this is the first time I have ever met anyone with the same last name who was not a relative.'

Lady Godfrey pursed her lips and shook her head at her husband. 'It was her late husband's name, my dear.' She turned to Harriet. 'Where is his family from? Perhaps we are distantly related.'

Harriet had half expected this question and was ready with her answer, after having reviewed all she knew of her father's family and hit upon a county he had never mentioned. 'He came from Shropshire.'

Lady Godfrey looked disappointed. 'I know of no one in that county.'

'A Salopian, then,' the Admiral said. 'Wild county Shropshire. Too many hills and too far from the sea.'

'I have never been there,' Harriet said.

Lady Godfrey looked surprised.

'My father's family left when he was very young to reside nearer London and there has never been a reason to return.'

The waiter arrived with the food and to Harriet's relief the conversation drifted to other matters. She found herself enjoying the company very much, especially when the Admiral told stories of his life at sea, though it sounded quite shockingly hard.

Her father had never spoken much about his family, except to express his resentment, and it was fascinating to have a little window into their world.

'You know, my dear Mrs Godfrey,' Lady Godfrey said, 'I hope you do not mind my saying this, but you look a great deal like my sister-in-law. The resemblance is almost uncanny. Do you not think so, Admiral?'

Her spouse narrowed his gaze on Harriet's face. 'I do not see so well, these days, but, yes, I would say you have black hair and black eyebrows like my sister Maud, but it is a common enough trait. I see nothing to marvel in it.'

'But her expressions, dearest,' his wife insisted. 'Surely you see it?'

The Admiral shook his head with a frown that made him look terribly fierce. 'Wife, I think you are looking for connections where there are none.'

Harriet released the breath she'd been holding.

Lady Godfrey looked unhappy. 'I am sorry, Mrs

Godfrey. The Admiral is right. I have a son with whom I lost contact many years ago. I keep hoping…'

Harriet drew in a breath. Could it be that her father's family had changed their minds?

'We have only two sons now,' the Admiral said sharply, 'and neither of them is missing.'

The hope that had filled Harriet's heart faded. Though why she had hoped, she wasn't sure. She had never known the Godfreys. They meant nothing in her life. Sadness welled up from her heart.

His wife bit her lip and then gave a small laugh. 'Excuse me. Indeed, I am being quite foolish. Did you try one of Sally's buns? Do tell me what you think.'

'Delicious.' Harriet's voice sounded husky. She took another bite of bun to give herself time to recover her composure.

Chapter Twelve

Red wished the Admiral and his lady had not accepted his invitation to breakfast. He would have preferred to have been alone with Harriet. But then, in their absence, she likely would have refused to come at all.

And he would have been deprived of the pleasure watching her enjoy the event. He was proud of the way she stood up to Lady Godfrey's questioning, answering her with calm polite confidence. No high-born lady could have done any better. And some of them might have done a great deal worse.

Indeed, Eugenie could be rather stiff when meeting strangers as well as rather judgmental. She would likely have been quite irritated by the Admiral rambling on about his battles and near encounters with death and his salty tales of foreign lands. She would have deemed the conversation quite inappropriate in a lady's company.

Red had enjoyed the old chap's stories and he could see Harriet had also.

'What are your plans for after breakfast?' he asked

the Admiral when they had eaten the last of the buns and waved off an offering of another serving.

The old fellow groaned. 'The Pump Room.'

'Come now, Husband,' Lady Godfrey said. 'You agreed yesterday that the waters are working wonders for your gout.'

'You find them efficacious?' Harriet asked. 'I wonder if they would benefit my mother. She has terrible rheumatism in her hands.'

'They really help,' Lady Godfrey said. 'You must convince your mother to try them.'

'Eight glasses a day,' the Admiral said with a grimace. 'But I must say I have noticed an improvement, so I shall not complain.'

'You complain a great deal about the pain. And for the past two days, you have not uttered one word about your foot.'

'What do you young people have planned for the rest of the day?' the Admiral asked, clearly wishing to change the topic.

'If the day remains fine,' Red said, 'I thought we might take a walk up Beechen Cliff. The guidebook extols the view as extraordinary. Or perhaps a visit to the Abbey.'

'I won't offer to join you on either of those expeditions. Far too energetic for an old fellow like me.'

Precisely why he had thought of them. He smiled at Harriet. 'Which would you prefer, Mrs Godfrey?'

'I think I would choose the walk with the view,' she said. 'It will make a nice change.'

He assisted Lady Godfrey to rise and then Harriet.

The Admiral heaved himself to his feet with a grunt and bowed to Harriet and shook hands with Red. 'We will see you at the Assembly Rooms this evening, if you are not too tired.'

'I doubt a brisk walk will tire us,' Harriet said.

They strolled back out to Great Pulteney Street and there took their leave of each other.

'That wasn't too bad, was it?' Red said to Harriet once they were alone. For some reason, he'd found her quieter than usual.

'No, not bad. I had not expected to find the Admiral and his wife quite so genial.'

Faint praise indeed. 'Tales of the sea are not everyone's cup of tea, I suppose,' he said. 'I have to admit he went a little too far.'

'I really enjoyed the buns. Indeed, all the food was delicious.'

He frowned at her change of subject. Was it that she was uncomfortable in the presence of a peer? She had never seemed so with him. He let it pass and pulled out the guide book. 'Do you really feel like walking? That is Beechen Cliff.' He pointed to a steep hill overlooking the city.

'Yes. I would like that very much. I would also like to see the Royal Crescent, if there is time. And the Abbey.' She sounded a little wistful.

'We can visit those tomorrow, if you wish. Before we call upon Mr Clark.'

She nodded. 'If there is time.'

He was going to make sure there was time. He got his bearings from the guide book and tucked it in his inside

pocket. They strolled arm in arm across the Pulteney
Bridge and down to the river, where mills stood on each
end of the weir that crossed the river.

As recommended by their guide, they struck out
across fields and footpaths. The prospects were quite
lovely as the ground rose ever higher and steeper until it
became quite an arduous climb. At the top, they stopped
and gazed down at the city a mile away and tucked into
the curve of the River Avon.

A breeze blew playfully across the crest of the hill,
threatening to carry off his hat. It tugged and teased at
Harriet's skirts.

'How small the city looks from up here,' Harriet said.
'And the Abbey dominates everything.'

'As I am sure its architects intended. Look over
there.' He pointed. 'The Royal Crescent. And there is
the Pump Room.'

'And that must be Avon Street.' She pointed to a
cluster of crowded buildings beyond Sydney Gardens.
'Do you think we have seen the last of our friend in the
green waistcoat?'

'I certainly hope so.'

They walked away from the city to view the scenery
in the other direction and were impressed by the rolling
countryside of Somerset. 'How beautiful it all is from
up here,' Harriet said as she stared out at the view. She
turned her face up to him. 'Thank you for bringing me.'

He wanted to kiss that pretty smiling mouth. 'You
are very welcome.'

A cloud crossed in front of the sun and she shivered.
'Are you cold?' he asked.

'Not really. The breeze feels a little cool when the sun goes in.'

He glanced up at the sky. The clouds were gathering. They would not want to be up here if it rained. 'Perhaps we could fit in an hour at the Abbey.'

'Do you think so?'

'If we go down now, I think we could. Unless you wish to stay longer.'

'No I am quite satisfied. I do wish I was a painter so I could record what I have seen.'

'Perhaps we will find a print in Milsom Street you can keep as a souvenir.'

'What a good idea. I would like that.'

In Harriet's eyes, the Abbey was just as beautiful on the inside as it was outside. Fortunately, Henry VIII's reformation had not utterly destroyed it the way so many others had been put to ruin.

At James Leake's print shop on Terrace Walk, Harriet found an excellent print of the view from Beechen Cliff which, after a spirited argument with Red, she purchased from her own money.

Back on Milsom Street, they wandered along, peering into shop windows. Some of them contained the sort of bric-a-brac she sold in her shop.

'Goodness me,' she said. 'I have a little dog exactly like that.' She pointed to the spaniel. 'Mine is half the price.'

Redford eyed it for a moment. 'I expect the rents are higher here, given the desirability of the location.'

She sighed. He was right. 'And I expect the class of customer is better also.'

Indeed, the other pedestrians were clearly members of the beau monde, if not members of the nobility.

'I shouldn't be surprised. Would you like an ice? The guide book lauds the one on this street as being equal to Gunter's.'

'I have heard they are delicious. Are they not rather expensive?'

He looked startled. 'Are you saying you have never had an ice?'

She stiffened at the disbelief in his voice. It proved once again how different their worlds really were. 'I have not.'

'Well, this is something we really must rectify.'

Really? It was only food. 'I do not think it necessary—'

'Nonsense. I insist.'

Another man who wanted to run roughshod over her. She opened her mouth to object.

A scrawny figure jumped out in front of them.

Redford clapped a hand to his waist. 'You again. Go, before I call for the constable.'

The fellow in the green waistcoat put his hands on his hips. Harriet moved closer to Redford.

The fellow glared at them. 'Why didn't you swear out a warrant agin me?'

Redford grimaced. 'You didn't get away with my watch.'

'Was the second time I tried fer it. And I snitched your wipe.'

'I have lots more handkerchiefs, so why bother? I have a great many more interesting things to do than chase after a petty thief.'

'And you left me coat. You could have swiped it. Teach me a lesson. I had valuables in the pockets.'

Redford raised his eyebrows. 'I can assure you that your coat and any items it contained is of no value to me.' He gave the young man a hard stare. 'Do not, however, take my indolence as a sign of weakness. If you attempt to steal my watch a third time, or any of my property for that matter, I will not be so lenient.'

'Oh, no, my lord, never again will I touch anything of yours, not even if you drops it. I know a gent when I sees one and you been more than fair to me. There ain't a cove in Bath as will so much as steal a farthing from you or your lady and that's the bald truth. Not if Tommy Sand tells 'em not to.'

Harriet could not quite believe what she was hearing.

'Why?' Redford asked.

Sand winked. 'Ain't many gents that wouldn't raise the hue and cry after what I done. I owes you and I always pays me debts.'

'Why don't you get a proper job?' Redford asked. 'You will end up on the nubbing cheat or in the hulks sooner or later. Thieves always do.'

Sand shrugged and grinned. 'I can earn three times as much thieving in this city as I can shovelling dung in some lord's stable. I got me pride.'

'Pride is an expensive commodity, if you pay with your life.'

'Some of us don't have a choice. We ain't all born with silver spoons in our mouths.'

'If you could get something that paid well, what sort of work would you prefer?'

'Me da apprenticed me to a sweep when I was nought but a stripling. I decided it weren't for me and ran off.'

'I would have run off, too,' Redford said grimly.

In Harriet's opinion, the plight of chimney-sweep boys was scandalous. She was pleased Redford saw it the same way.

'I found other ways to make a living, but I always thought I might like to be a jockey,' Sands said. 'Got the build fer it, see.' He twirled, bowed and grinned. ''Cept I can't ride a horse. 'Tis no matter. I wanted you ter know you can go anywhere in this city and your watch is safe.' He held out a square of white linen. 'Had it laundered proper-like, I did.'

Redford hesitated.

Before he could refuse it, Harriet smiled. 'That is very good of you, Mr Sand. Thank you.'

Redford took the handkerchief. 'If you change your mind about a real job, come and see me.' He handed over his card. 'I will see what I can do. I cannot promise work as a jockey, but we might find something that pays better than a stablehand, at least.'

'Got a nice little crib here, me lord, not sure I want to give it up, but I'll think it over.' He touched a hand to his hat and strolled away, whistling.

'Do you think it possible he could reform his way of life?' Harriet asked. 'He might steal anyone who hires him blind and then run off.'

'It is a risk, to be sure. But some risks pay off.'

That was the sort of thing her father would have said. The same sort of attitude that had landed her family in the King's Bench prison. Men charged ahead doing what they wanted without a thought for its effect on others.

Redford shrugged. 'Besides, he seems like an intelligent young man. Not vicious, but merely light-fingered and cheeky. He knows the dangers in what he does, but I have no idea if he will take up my offer.'

They continued their stroll.

'Can you offer him work as a jockey?'

Redford shook his head. 'My grandfather kept racehorses, but my father sold the stud when he inherited the title. Far too expensive. The estate needed the finances. But I suppose I do have friends who would likely accept him on my recommendation.' He paused, looking thoughtful. 'I would have to tell them about his past, though.'

So they would know the risk. It was fair and right that he do so.

'Ah, here we are,' Redford said.

They entered a tea shop with small tables and customers drinking tea and eating cakes, and some with little glass dishes containing a creamy brightly coloured substance.

They were shown to a table and reviewed the list of ices the waiter provided. There were all sorts of exotic flavours: royal cream ice, chocolate cream ice and muscadine, as well as lemon and orange.

'I have no idea which to choose,' she said.

'Chocolate for me,' Redford said.

'I will try the orange,' Harriet said.

The waiter was back with their order in no time at all.

Harriet could not quite believe how deliciously sweet and cold it was. And it tasted just like an orange. 'Oh, my, this is good.'

'Try mine,' Redford said. 'See if you like it as much.'

She took a spoonful from his dish and closed her eyes as the flavour hit her tongue, creamy and tasting like hot chocolate, only sweeter and icy cold. 'Ambrosia for the gods.'

He beamed at her, clearly enjoying her reaction.

He was too sweet, really. As sweet as the desserts they were eating. She was beginning to want this to go on for ever. And it could not. She was going to miss him when they went back to their own different worlds. 'Thank you for suggesting this. What a treat.'

She wanted to kiss him. But, of course, she could not. Not in public. But she hoped her smile told him how happy he had made her.

Very pleased with their day's outing, they returned to their lodgings.

'Shall I order the tea tray,' she asked Redford, 'or would you prefer some other sort of libation?'

'Tea would be most welcome,' he said settling into the armchair.

Harriet rang the bell and, once the order was given, she went to her own chamber and removed her bonnet and spencer.

The ball gown lay over the armchair, not a crease to be seen.

She stroked the fine fabric. It wasn't right her letting him spend his money on ball gowns. And he had done so without asking her first, putting her under an obligation of sorts.

No. It would be different if she had asked him to take her to the ball, but instead he had ridden roughshod over her measured opinion. She just wished she knew why.

She ought to plead a headache. Tell Redford she was too unwell to go to the ball. Then she would not have to meet Lady Godfrey again and tolerate her intense scrutiny.

Hearing the sound of chinking teacups, she returned to the parlour. Redford was alone and sitting on the sofa behind the teapot, pouring out a cup. He grinned at her, a conspiratorial grin that caused her heart to leap in her chest.

'May I pour you a cup of tea?'

She shook her head at him. 'Could you not wait a moment for me to return?'

'You were gone so long I thought perhaps you were tired after our expedition and had decided to take a nap.'

She had not been gone that long, surely? She shook a finger at him. 'A nap? I am not a child, you know.'

He winked. 'Too bad. I was thinking of joining you.'

He was teasing, surely? Her insides tightened. Her body tingled. She forced herself to take a deep breath and smile. 'Funny man. It is still daylight.'

'All the better.'

Her stomach gave an odd little bounce. Excitement. 'Someone might hear us. You wouldn't dare.'

He rose to his feet, his expression intense. 'Is that a challenge?'

Red wasn't one not to pick up a gauntlet when one was thrown down. He prowled towards her, thinking to kiss her silly. She backed up, putting her hands up to ward him off. 'I thought you were jesting.'

He had been. But he'd also been wanting to kiss her since he first saw her this morning. Kiss her and more.

But, of course, it was up to her. If she said no, that would be an end to it, but she didn't know the delights she'd be missing.

'I thought you wanted me to tutor you.'

She looked puzzled and intrigued. 'You already did.'

He grinned. 'Did you think that was all there was to learn?'

Her eyes widened. 'How much more could there be?'

He sprang the trap. 'Well, you have learned to enjoy receiving pleasure, but how about learning to give pleasure.'

She pouted. 'You did not get any pleasure?' She gestured vaguely. 'From our…from what happened?'

'From our lovemaking? Most certainly I did. I enjoyed it most thoroughly.'

'Then?'

'Then, what if you want to be the one in control? If you wanted to please your partner, as well as yourself?'

Doubt filled her face. 'As you did? A woman can do that?'

'If it is what she wants.'

'And it would please you to make love in daylight?'

'It would.'

'And there is more to learn?'

He forced himself not to grin. She was looking so serious, studious almost. 'There is a great deal more, if you are interested.'

She inhaled a deep breath and gazed at him for a great many seconds. The longing on her face, the curiosity, almost undid him. In some ways she was bold, his Harriet. In others she was cautious. Asking him to tutor her had taken a lot of courage. But this was a much bigger step.

'Very well.' She sounded like a prisoner going to the scaffold. Terrified. Unwilling. 'You have been so kind to me, so generous. How could I refuse…?'

That was not what he had intended at all. 'My dear sweet Harriet, please, do not feel obligated. Feel free to say no. I promise, it is of no importance.' Indeed, he really should not have suggested it.

He would never have suggested anything like this to Eugenie. And Harriet was no less of a lady. He was a cur for even thinking it. 'Forget I spoke. I was teasing you. Nothing more. Please. Come. Join me for tea.'

She hesitated. 'If you are sure.'

He raised an eyebrow. 'Sure about what? Taking tea?'

She smiled, albeit a little weakly, and allowed him to seat her in the armchair opposite the sofa. He handed her the cup of tea he had poured, just as he knew she liked it, with milk but without sugar. 'Try one of these biscuits. Ginger snaps. They are really delicious.' He held out the plate.

She took one and bit into it. 'It is good. Nearly as good as the ones my mother makes.'

'I enjoyed our day today,' he said. He'd enjoyed it so much he'd forgotten himself and made an outrageous proposition to a respectable woman. He wanted to kick himself.

'It was lovely. The view was better than I expected and the ices were delicious.'

'I should not have invited the Admiral and his wife to breakfast, I am afraid. But I somehow felt obliged after they were so friendly.'

'I quite understand. I would have done the same if I were you. Breakfast was very nice. I found the Admiral's stories fascinating.'

'Too bad about their other son.'

'Yes. It is sad.'

She sounded wistful. Too wistful given that the Godfreys were strangers.

She gave him a swift, rather pained smile. 'Family does not always meet one's expectations, do they?'

'I know that only too well. But I would never cast out any member of my family, for any reason.'

'Not even if they committed some terrible crime?'

'What sort of crime. Murder? I don't think anyone— well, if it was not justified, I suppose I might think twice.'

'Justified? How could anyone justify murder?'

If he had known what Neville Saxby, his sister Marguerite's husband, had been up to, he might have committed murder himself. But that was water under the bridge. Saxby died in Spain, killed by French soldiers, and he could no longer abuse his wife.

'You are right. But I would never abandon my family. For any reason.'

She smiled tightly. 'I am glad to hear it.' She put down her teacup. 'You are still of a mind to go to the ball this evening, I presume?'

Was she going to back out of this also? 'Of course.'

'Then after our exertions today, I would like to bathe and wash my hair.'

Bathe. He almost groaned out loud at the idea of her in her bath. He could talk her into letting him join her. He knew he could. But she really wasn't ready to expand her sensual horizons that far. Not yet. 'Very well. I think I will take myself off to the Assembly Rooms to catch up on the latest news from London. I will be back in time to escort you to the ball.'

He bowed and left before he could change his mind about helping her with her bath.

Chapter Thirteen

Harriet knew exactly what Redford really meant when he said he wanted to catch up on the news. She had not been born yesterday. The beau monde loved their wagering. No wonder he needed his money refunded so urgently. Debts of honour! What was honourable about leaving poor tradesmen to go without their proper payment so gambling debts could be paid?

Fortunately, Redford's gambling could have no impact on her life. He could not dip into her money to pay his debts as Father had dipped into the money from the shop to buy artefacts that no one else wanted and got them all sent to debtors' prison.

She could not help worrying about Redford, though. Or feeling a little regretful. If she had agreed to his offer of a lesson this afternoon, he wouldn't have gone off to seek other amusement. Likely he would not offer again. But lovemaking in the middle of the afternoon? It was utterly scandalous.

Once more her pulse raced at the thought. Pushing

aside the images that forced themselves into her mind's eye, she rang the bell to ask Pomfret to arrange a bath.

The walk up the hill had been exceedingly energetic and traipsing around the city streets had left her feeling grimy. If she was going to wear the pretty turquoise gown and go to the ball, she wanted to look her best.

If. Would she have enough courage to attend? Or would she back out at the last moment with the excuse of a headache, or some such? She wasn't sure, but the nervous fluttering in her stomach every time she thought about going was making her feel queasy.

When Pomfret arrived, she did not look at all well. Her nose was red and her eyes watery.

'Is something wrong?' Harriet asked.

'A touch of the ague, madam,' Pomfret said and sneezed into the handkerchief clutched in her hand.

'Oh, dear. I think you better go straight to bed with a tisane.'

'But you need to get ready for this evening and—'

'And I can manage perfectly well. Go on. Off to bed.'

The woman sniffled in her handkerchief and blew her nose. 'Thank you, ma'am. I do feel that dreadful. I am sure I will be better in the morning.' She dragged herself out of the room.

While she was brushing her hair, Harriet had heard Redford return a few minutes before the clock struck the hour of five. No doubt he had been so engrossed in his gambling, he had forgotten to watch the time. Now, fifteen minutes later, dinner had arrived, but he had not yet appeared. Standing looking out of the window,

Harriet gripped her hands together. Perhaps she should tell him she had changed her mind about the ball. Except she was already dressed and ready. She glanced at the clock. If she was quick, she could change back into her own gown—

His chamber door opened.

Her jaw dropped. He looked splendid. He was freshly shaved and his hair had been trimmed and he was a vision of sartorial elegance.

He was looking at her, taking her in from her head to her heels.

She smoothed her skirts with a hand that trembled.

'My word, you look lovely,' he said, his voice containing real admiration. 'The colour suits you perfectly.'

His compliment took her breath away. The suggestion that they forget the whole idea died on her lips. 'Thank you.' How oddly shy she sounded.

He smiled. 'Are you famished? I am sorry I am late. I had a long wait at the barbershop.'

So that was why he was late. Or partly why. She turned back to look out of the window. 'How did your game of cards go at the Assembly Rooms?'

He frowned 'You sound disapproving.'

'It is none of my business how you waste your money.' She drew in a quick breath. She should not have said that.

'Come,' he said grimly. 'Let us eat or we will be late.'

She spun around. 'We will be late because you were late.'

'And if you do not sit down for dinner, we will be even later.'

Blast him. He was going to put the blame on her shoulders. How typically male.

She sat down and he carved the ham. She passed him the vegetables. He poured them both a glass of wine. Candlelight picked out glints of copper in his hair.

He lifted his glass in a toast. 'To a most enjoyable day and the prospect of an even more pleasurable evening.'

The double entendre was not lost on her. She lifted her glass and sipped the wine, hopefully hiding the rush of heat to her cheeks.

'Let us not argue, Harriet,' he said, his gaze intense over his wine glass. 'This is likely to be our last evening in Bath. I would have it be a good memory for us both.'

Her stomach sank at the reminder that soon this little daydream would come to an end, but she inhaled a deep breath and nodded. 'I am sorry. I am a little nervous about this evening. It will be my first ball.'

His eyes widened. 'Devil take it. I had not thought of that. You do know how to dance, I hope?'

'I do indeed. I may not move in your circles, my lord, but even us common folks enjoy dancing from time to time.' She'd had lessons. Mother, with vague hopes of the family one day accepting them, had insisted, before their money troubles had put a stop to that.

'I learned there will be minuets, before tea,' he said, 'and country dances after. No waltzing. You see I did not waste my time this afternoon.'

And he had been thinking of her. Her heart seemed to swell. 'Thank you. I am most grateful. It is good to know what to expect.'

'Please save a minuet and a country dance for me.'

She raised her eyebrows. 'I doubt I will need to save dances. I shall be quite happy to sit among the dowagers and wallflowers.'

'My dear Harriet,' he drawled, 'you do yourself an injustice. I fully expect to fight off every male in the ballroom in order to secure the two dances that are my right as your escort.'

She laughed and shook her head at his nonsense. 'You flatter me and I thank you for your kindness. I apologise for my crotchets.' And for misjudging his motives for going to the Assembly Rooms. 'As you said, Redford, this is our last night in Bath. We should not spoil it by quarrelling.'

'A sedan chair?' Harriet stared askance at the old-fashioned equipage, with its carrying poles front and back and two jarveys waiting to lift it. Painted green with gilt trim, its red velvet curtains and squabs had seen better days. 'Why would I need to be carried through the streets?'

A gentleman with two sisters knew exactly how to reply. 'Because that is the way it is done in Bath. The hills are far too steep for horses. And, yes, I know you are perfectly capable of walking, but you don't want your hems to get filthy before the evening starts.'

One of the jarveys touched his hat. 'You'll be quite safe with us, milady. Haven't dropped anyone yet.'

With a sigh of defeat, she climbed aboard. The men hoisted the chair and set off at a trot.

Red had discovered that everything about Bath was old-fashioned and rule-bound. No wonder most of the people one saw here were in their dotage. On Bennet Street, they joined a fleet of sedan chairs converging on the Assembly Rooms.

The jarveys halted at the portico and Red, having paid them off, helped Harriet to alight. He escorted her through the octagon room where men were deep into their games of whist and vingt-et-un and into the crowded ballroom.

By dint of a tap on the shoulder here and a gentle push there, Red got them through the press of women in ballgowns and feathers and their escorts. Rows of seats lined the walls and he found a pair of chairs side by side as far from the orchestra ensconced on the balcony as possible. 'Will this suit?' he asked Harriet.

'It will indeed,' she replied. 'Thank you.' Whereas a *ton*nish lady might make every effort to appear bored at such a parochial event, she gazed about her in awe.

Her interest and her delight pleased him more than he would have expected.

It was not many moments before the Perry ladies found them and sat either side of Harriet. 'How lovely to see you again, Mrs Godfrey,' the elder Miss Perry gushed.

Harriet smiled. 'You also. I thought to see you on the dance floor.'

Miss Perry made a face. 'Perhaps later. There are very few bachelors in Bath this early in the season.' She gave a quick glance and a smile in Red's direction, a blatant hint.

'And besides,' Miss Rose said, 'we prefer conversation to dancing.'

Red tried not to roll his eyes at this valiant effort to appear unconcerned. 'You ladies will do me the honour of a country dance after supper, I hope?'

'Oh, indeed. It will be our pleasure,' Miss Perry said.

One of the men he had played cards with that afternoon, a Mr Lamb, approached them with his wife in tow. The Perry ladies greeted the couple, then gave up their seats and moved on. The Lambs had a wide circle of acquaintances and soon Harriet and he were brought into the fold. Just as Red had predicted, Harriet was asked to stand up for every dance. Naturally, Red did his duty by the other ladies in the group, once he had established that Harriet would dance the supper dance with him.

Surprisingly, he was looking forward to their dance. After years on the town and his duties escorting his sisters, he had lost interest in attending balls, preferring the time spent at his estate. This evening, he was enjoying himself as if it was his first ball.

After he returned his most recent dance partner to her escort, he ran into the Admiral and his wife on the edge of the dance floor.

He bowed.

Admiral Godfrey greeted him warmly.

'I see Mrs Godfrey is in good spirits,' Lady Godfrey remarked. 'I do not believe she has sat down for one single dance.'

'Used to do the same myself at her age,' the Admiral said.

'You did indeed,' his wife said. 'Perhaps you will do so again when your foot improves.'

The Admiral looked doubtful. 'Will you and your cousin join us for supper?'

'Unless, of course, you have arranged to have supper with another party,' Lady Godfrey said with a hopeful smile.

'I will ask Harriet if she has made any plans,' Red said, not wishing to commit her to yet another meal with the Admiral and his wife, if it was not to her taste. 'I managed to secure the dance before supper.'

It seemed Harriet had wronged Redford even more than she had known. Clearly, he had gone to the Assembly Rooms with the intention of meeting people with whom they might socialise this evening.

Very pleasant, genteel people.

Mrs Lamb was a treasure. Sweet and friendly. And their friends were equally delightful. The young man she was dancing with was Mr Lamb's oldest son. He gave her a shy smile. 'Father said you were only in Bath for a few days, Mrs Godfrey.'

'Yes, indeed. We will return to London tomorrow.'

'It is a pity. If you had been staying longer, we could have got up a party for a ride out in the country.' He truly looked disappointed.

'Sad to say, I do not ride.'

'We could go by carriage, then.'

If he knew from whence she came, his family would likely be horrified to know he had invited her to ride out in his carriage. Indeed, he would likely not be speaking to her. 'You are very kind, Mr Lamb, but other engagements require our return to London.'

'Will you come to Bath again before the season is over? I hope you will. There are so few young people here, it is dashed dull most of the time. If it should occur, please, write to Mother and we can arrange an outing.'

She would never come here again and she was not going to lie to him. 'I am sorry, I do not think I shall return to Bath.'

His face fell. 'Perhaps when I have my come out next year, I will see you in London. Should I write to you directly, or to Lord Westram?'

Good Lord, she could imagine his mother's face if she saw the contents of her shop. 'Lord Westram.' If he did write, Redford would put him off and that would be an end to it.

The music ended and he escorted her back to her seat. Of Redford there was no sign and the next dance was his.

Ah, there he was, making his way across the ball-room, his red hair and height making him easy to spot.

He arrived as the orchestra struck the opening notes of a minuet and he led her out on to the floor. Unfortunately, the dance floor was so crowded there was no opportunity for private conversation, so they restricted themselves to pleasantries.

He was an excellent dancer. Lithe and graceful, yet manly.

'Thank you for convincing me to come this evening,' she said, smiling at him. 'I am enjoying it immensely.'

Gazing at her as if to be sure she meant what she

said, and finding that she did, he smiled. 'I am glad. It is a shame this must be our last evening in Bath.'

She raised her eyebrows. 'I think we should make the most of it, now and later.' The naughty words left her lips before she could think about them.

His eyes widened. 'Why, Mrs Godfrey, I do believe that is another of your interesting invitations.'

Laughing, she glanced around to see if anyone was listening. They did not appear to be. 'I believe you are right.'

'What can a gentleman do, but accept, with very great pleasure.'

Unreasonable joy bubbled up inside her. She had never felt quite this happy. Yet beneath the lifting of her spirits was the little bit of sadness that she would never see him again when they parted in London. But she must not think of that now and spoil everything.

'The Admiral and his wife have invited us to join them for supper. I told them I was not sure if you had made other plans. If you are tired of their company, I can easily find another party we can join.'

Part of her wanted to find a way out. But another part of her wanted to accept the Admiral's invitation. After all, she would likely never spend time with her grandparents again either, even if they did not know who she was.

She discovered that, although she was angry at her grandfather for being so stubborn, she wanted the chance to get to know her grandmother a little better. 'I would love to join the Godfreys.'

Red inclined his head. 'Then it shall be as you wish.'

How nice that he was prepared to take her wishes into account. 'Are you bored by the old gentleman's tales of his life at sea?'

He grinned. 'Not at all. He makes me very glad I did not join the navy.'

She tilted her head to look at him. 'Did you think you might?'

'At an early age, I was caught between wanting to be a pirate and wanting to be a heroic navy captain.'

'Really?'

'Indeed. But then I decided driving the mail coach would be just as exciting, particularly if it got held up and I was able to overcome the highwayman with a flick of my whip and a handily placed shot from my pistol. After that I thought the cavalry might be the thing for me. The one thing I did not want to be was a dull old farmer. Unfortunately, that is what I am.'

'Surely being an earl involves far more than farming. There is Parliament and laws to make and a country to run.'

'Yes, there is that, too.'

The dance ended and he escorted her into the supper room where they found the Admiral and Lady Godfrey seated at a table.

Chapter Fourteen

The Godfreys greeted them like old friends.

'You were not short of partners this evening, Mrs Godfrey,' Lady Godfrey said.

'Please, my lady,' Harriet said. 'Do call me Harriet. I feel like we have known each other for a very long time, even though it is only a few days.'

'And you shall call me Jane,' the older woman said.

Oddly Harriet hesitated, then smiled shyly. 'To do so seems a little forward.'

'Nonsense, my dear Harriet,' Jane said. 'We are friends. I am so sorry you are leaving Bath tomorrow. I shall miss your company.'

'How kind of you to say so. It has been a pleasure meeting you and the Admiral.'

A waiter arrived with their suppers which consisted of dainty sandwiches, fancy cakes and pots of tea.

Lady Godfrey took charge of the tea pot and the plates were passed around the table.

'Do you enjoy taking in a play when in London,

Lord Westram?' Lady Godfrey asked. 'I do not believe I have seen you at any performances in the recent past.'

A good thing, too. The only time he had been to the play was with Eugenie the last time they had been in London at the same time. 'I rarely attend.'

'What about you, Mrs Godfrey?'

'My husband did not enjoy the theatre,' she said.

It wasn't a lie, really. After all, how could a non-existent husband enjoy anything.

'That is a shame. I would love to invite you to join us in our box when we get back to town.'

'You are too kind, Jane,' Harriet said, looking startled. 'I sincerely doubt it will be possible. My family obligations make a great many demands on my time. I rarely go anywhere at all.'

Red felt a twinge of pain for Harriet's discomfort. Of course, she could not visit Lady Godfrey. It would not be appropriate at all. He did like the way she handled the awkward situation. Hopefully, Lady Godfrey would forget all about her invitation and Harriet after a week or two.

Which was more than Red could ever do.

The older woman pursed her lips. 'You know, Mrs Godfrey, I had a long think about you last night and I have recalled that my husband does have relatives, far flung and very distant, in Shropshire. We might be related, after all.'

Harriet froze for an instant. She took a deep breath and shook her head. 'Sadly, I doubt it. If there was any chance that my family had an admiral for a distant connection, I am sure you would have heard from my husband's Great-Aunt Lucia by now. I will, however, write to her and see what she says. She is very keen on relatives who might add to her consequence. If it should come to pass that she has connections to the aristocracy, she will be announcing it all over the village, in short order.'

Red hid his smile at the look of alarm on Lady Godfrey's face. She was clearly wondering if she was about to be set upon by Harriet's social climbing great-aunt-in-law.

'Perhaps I will look into it a little more, before we start making assumptions,' Lady Godfrey said tightly.

'It might be as well,' Harriet agreed calmly. 'The potted shrimp is excellent. Did you try it?'

'It is, indeed,' the Admiral said, helping himself to another.

Red could not help but admire Harriet's aplomb. And her tact. She had managed to put Lady Godfrey off, without making the woman feel rejected. To the manner born. The phrase popped into his head unbidden. She had certainly been a great deal more tactful than Eugenie would ever have been.

The more he compared Eugenie with Harriet, the less well his betrothed came off. So he had better stop doing it.

Supper over, they strolled back into the ballroom. Or rather pushed their way through the crowd.

'Is it my imagination,' Harriet said, leaning close so he could hear her over the chatter and the music, 'or are there more people now than before?'

'I think you are right.'

Mr King somehow manoeuvred his way over to them. 'Is everything to your satisfaction, Lord Westram? Are you in need of introductions?' He rubbed his hands together. 'It seems the season is getting underway. Soon we shall be turning people away at the door.'

And this was a good thing?

'I congratulate you on a successful evening, sir,' Red said. The man bustled away.

Harriet looked up at him. 'Do we have to stay? I have enjoyed myself. But the heat and the noise in here is quite overwhelming.' She glanced at the dance floor where a lively country dance was in progress. 'Bother. I promised Mr Lamb a dance after supper, so I suppose we must.'

'Did you promise anyone else?'

'Only you.'

'Then let us find Lamb. Have your dance and then we can leave.'

'You do not mind?'

'Why would I mind, when I can have you all to myself?' His body heated at the prospect.

After many friendly farewells, they made their escape to discover that, in the meantime, it had started to rain.

The falling droplets glistened in the Assembly Room's portico lamps and the smell of dust and coal smoke filled the air.

This time, Harriet did not object when Red hailed a sedan chair.

The porter handed him an umbrella. 'Send it back in the morning, please, my lord.'

'There is room for you in here,' Harriet said, squeezing over.

'I'm far too heavy. The umbrella will do me just as well.'

'Carried the Prince of Wales once, we did,' said the jarvey holding open the door. 'Huge he was. We managed, didn't we, Pat?'

'Arr,' the other man affirmed. 'No sense in getting your shoes wet, sir.'

'Thank you. I am sure you are fine strong fellows, but I am perfectly content to walk.'

The man closed the door and a moment later, she was off the ground and jolting along until the men settled into a steady rhythm. Through the side window, she could see Redford easily keeping pace.

At their lodgings, Redford held the umbrella over her while she climbed out. They made a dash for the front door and were out of breath from laughing when he finally got the door open and they staggered in.

One of her ostrich feathers must have missed the reach of the umbrella because it hung limp and dripping in front of her face, making her laugh all the more. 'After such a lovely day,' she said between gasps for air, 'who would have guessed it would rain so hard?'

'Certainly not me,' Redford said. He shrugged out of his overcoat and gave it a shake, sending a shower flying in all directions.

The porter came out from the back of the house to take her wrap and his coat. 'I'll hang them in the laundry, my lord. They'll be dry by morning. When I saw it raining, I took the liberty of having the fires lit in your rooms.'

'Excellent,' Red said, slipping him a coin. 'Very thoughtful.'

The porter touched his forelock and disappeared behind the green baize door at the end of the corridor while they made their way upstairs to their apartment.

The parlour was already toasty warm.

Pomfret, her nose red and her eyes watery, was waiting in Harriet's chamber.

'You need to go to bed, Pomfret.'

'They were going to make the tweeny stay up to help you to bed, ma'am. Poor little thing has to be up at four in the morning to lay the fires.'

Harriet knew all about the miseries of early mornings. She was up at the crack of dawn to prepare for her days in the shop. 'All I need is my tapes untied and I can manage the rest and you can get off to bed.'

Pomfret looked relieved, did as she was asked and was gone within ten minutes.

Harriet slipped into her nightgown and robe and returned to the parlour.

Redford handed her a glass of brandy and water.

She raised it in a toast. 'To our last evening in Bath.'

He smiled and lifted his in return and took a sip. 'While I hope our venture tomorrow is successful, I must say, Harriet, I am going to miss you.'

Her heart gave a little pang. 'I will miss you, too,' she whispered.

'If things were different—'

'But they are not. You will return to your betrothed and I will run my shop. But I shall always treasure the memory of our time together.'

He put down his glass and tipped up her chin and closed his eyes briefly. 'I cannot recall a time when I have felt so peaceful as I have these past few days. It is as if the worries of the estate, my sisters, even the dashed debt I owe, while still there, are less burdensome.'

He kissed her.

She closed her eyes and let the feel of his lips on hers, his hands roaming her body, carry her to a place deep inside herself.

How could she not have realised how delightful a man's touch could be? She was going to miss this dreadfully, but not nearly as much as she was going to miss Redford.

They drew back at the same moment and gazed into each other's eyes. No words were needed.

He took her hand and raised it to his lips, and she knew he was asking if she was brave enough.

She recalled her cowardice of earlier. Regretted it. She was not about to let this chance slip away. She smiled her assent.

Hand in hand they walked into her bedroom.

In a silence broken only by the sound of their rapid breaths, they helped each other undress. Excitement rippled through Harriet. Anticipation. happiness. A storm of feelings.

Naked, they stared at each other. He was beautiful. Nothing like a statue. As he moved, muscles rippled beneath his skin. The light from the candles glinted red in the crisp curls on his chest and encircling his engorged phallus.

She reached out, then pulled her hand back with an awkward laugh.

'Touch me,' he said, his voice low and hoarse. 'It will please me.'

He had promised to teach her how to please him, had he not? Tentatively, she reached out again and he took her hand in his and pressed her palm firmly against him. His member was silky to the touch, yet beneath the delicate skin the core was hard and surprisingly hot. He moved her hand in a slow firm rhythm and groaned when she squeezed a little harder. When she glanced up from her task to his face, his expression was strained, almost as if he was in pain, but there was pleasure there also.

The way she had felt when he had stroked her with his hand.

'You like that,' she whispered.

His hips moved in counterpoint to her strokes. 'Very much,' he gasped.

A shiver ran down her spine. The hairs on her arms rose. Her nipples tightened.

'You are cold,' he said. He lifted the sheets. 'Into bed with you.'

Reluctantly she released him and hopped up on to the bed. He climbed in beside her and she snuggled close and kissed him, revelling in the warmth of his big hard body along the length of hers. Breaking the kiss and rising above him, she gazed into Red's face. 'What else do you like?'

His ballocks tightened at the thought of the many sensual delights he enjoyed.

He adored that she took the initiative to expand her knowledge as well to put into practice what she had learned in only a few short hours.

Her curiosity about all things sensual delighted him more than he could have imagined. Her innocence remained in evidence in her hesitancy and wonder, but her bold nature allowed her to explore her own sensuality to the full.

He cupped her breast. 'I like to kiss you here.'

A thoughtful look passed across her face. 'You did that last time,' she said, nodding.

To his surprise, instead of laying back to give him access, she gracefully mounted him, presenting him with her breasts at just the right level for his mouth. The curls of her mons brushed against the head of his cock. Exquisite torture, when he wanted inside the wet heat he felt pressing against his belly.

He came up on his elbows and nuzzled and licked at each firm full breast. She rocked her hips in an instinctive search for pleasure. He suckled.

She gasped and froze.

He stopped.

'That…hurts.' She frowned. 'But I liked it. How can that be?'

'Some types of pain can give the highest form of pleasure there is. You experienced it already, did you not?'

She nodded slowly. 'Do it again.'

He raised an eyebrow.

'Please.' Then she laughed. 'Do not tease me.'

He pulled her head down and kissed her lips briefly. 'It is all part of the game, my darling.'

'Hmmm.'

She moved her hips in a slow circle, her gaze fixed on his face. He pulled her hips downwards so she was now firmly where he needed her.

She moved again.

He groaned and burrowed his hand beneath her, taking hold of his shaft, but she lifted upwards. 'I want you to do that again.'

'Playing tit for tat, are you?'

She laughed and her breasts jiggled delightfully. 'Apparently so.'

He groaned at the double innuendo and obeyed her wishes. After all, what else was a gentleman to do?

She gasped and sighed and moaned her appreciation of his efforts until he was nigh on at the end of his control.

What a pity this would be their last time as lovers. The thought gave him pause.

'Is something wrong?' she whispered.

How could she have noticed such a small hesitation? He shook his head. 'Everything is wonderful, but there are other things I like, if you care to know about them.'

The haziness in her face lifted a fraction. 'Fellatio?'

He almost swallowed his tongue.

'Yes. Certainly that is one thing we can do,' he somehow managed to speak without begging.

'I always wanted to try that.'

Dear saints in heaven, her boldness rocked him backwards. His head, or some other part of him, was going to explode. at the innocent way she announced her knowledge of the erotic.

'Yes,' he managed to say as he stroked the pretty breast temptingly suspended before his face.

'I think we can do it to each other at the same time.'

His whole body seized. If he didn't get things under control and fast, this was going to be over before it started.

Harriet peered into Redford's face. He was looking a little strange. Stunned, perhaps. 'Have I got it wrong?'

He made an odd sound in the back of his throat. 'No. Not at all.'

Was he laughing at her? He seemed to be struggling to breathe 'I bought a statue and when I asked the dealer what it represented, she said that was what the couple was doing.'

He took a deep breath and looked a little less distraught.

'We don't have to do it, if you don't want to,' she said.

'I would like it above all things. You surprised me, that was all.'

He lifted her off him and gave her a kiss. 'Let us give it a try. First you need to turn around.'

He helped her adjust her position and once she was at eye level with his phallus, it occurred to her there was an awful lot of it. In the statue, it had all but disappeared in the woman's mouth. 'It must have been half-way down her throat,' she exclaimed.

His hips arched upwards. 'Kiss it,' he said hoarsely. 'Grip it firmly at the base.'

With one hand curled around the thick hot shaft, she licked the tip. It tasted salty. The scent was dark and earthy and erotic. The soft sacks rolled like marbles in her palm.

He moaned and his hands cupped her buttocks and drew her towards him. A long, wet stroke of his tongue along her slit and dipping inside her at the last made her whole body tingle with white-hot sparks.

'Oh,' she moaned and opened her mouth and gently sucked.

He cried out. 'Whatever you do,' he gasped, 'do not use your teeth.'

Then he did something down there, licked and sucked and...

She fell apart.

He grabbed his member, drew it from her mouth and, with a few hard strokes of his hand, he shuddered to his own completion.

She lay unable to moved. Shattered.

He gathered her up and brought her up to lay her head on his chest. 'Oh, my goodness,' she managed to say. 'That was...'

'The most erotic thing I have ever experienced,' he muttered.

For some reason his words made her feel very proud, which was even nicer than the lovemaking. How strange.

But her mind couldn't seem to figure out why. Besides, she definitely needed a nap and Redford was already breathing deep and slow. He must have fallen asleep.

Red dragged himself from the depths of sleep. Something was wrong. Yet with Harriet curled up close at his side, it all seemed very right. Memories rushed back. Dear God, he'd almost disgraced himself. Thank the Lord she'd responded so quickly to his efforts or he might have made a mull of it.

Perhaps they could take things more slowly next time.

A bang on the outer door put paid to his thoughts along with his burgeoning erection and brought him fully awake. Regretfully, he removed his arm from beneath Harriet and slid out of bed, hoping not to wake her.

No such luck. She sat up. 'What is it?'

'We have a caller.'

He shrugged into his robe.

The porter was standing on the other side of the door, looking as if he smelled something gone bad. 'There is a person at the back door asking for you, my lord. He gave the name Tommy Sand. He refuses to leave until you speak to him.'

'What is going on?' Harriet said from behind him, pulling on her robe and looking deliciously dishevelled.

Resisting the temptation to kiss her, Red put a finger to his lips. 'Show him up.'

'I'm sorry, my lord, he is not the sort of person my mistress would want in her house. I cannot—'

'You can and you will. I will stand surety for him. Show him up.'

The man walked off, grumbling.

Red left the door open and turned back to Harriet. 'I sought Sand out this afternoon and asked him to see what he could learn about Clark. I am not sure why he is here, but it seems to me it must be important.'

'You did not tell me you went to see him.'

'I am sorry. I had planned to mention it, but you were so busy berating me about the evils of gambling at dinner I forgot.'

She made a face. 'No matter.' She picked up a shawl she had left on one of the chairs and threw it around her shoulders. 'I shall be interested in what he has to say.'

Sand sauntered in with the disgruntled-looking porter right on his heels. Red handed him a shilling. 'Wait outside.' His face lightened and he closed the door behind him.

Sand's gaze went from one to the other. 'So that's the way of it, is it?'

Red narrowed his eyes. 'I hope your information is worth getting us up at this time of the morning.'

'That's for you to decide. The gent you asked about... Well, he's back and he'll be gone by first light.'

'Clark? Are you sure? His butler said he wouldn't return to Bath until tomorrow evening.'

Sand shrugged. 'Wot he said and wot is, be different. He arrived around midnight. And his man went off and hired a yellow bounder for six in the morning.'

'You know this how?'

'One of my lads was watching the house. He came and got me after he followed the footman to the inn and heard him order the chaise.'

It seemed that Sand had taken Red's request far more seriously than he had expected.

'Do you know where he is going?'

'The post boy didn't know.'

Why on earth would Clark dash off, knowing that Red wanted to speak with him if he didn't have something to hide? No doubt the old fellow at the warehouse had probably sent him a message tipping him off. Devil take it. Instead of enjoying himself with Harriet he should have gone to Wells and tracked him down.

Damnation.

He flipped Sand a coin. Sand flipped it back. 'I don't want nothing from you, governor.'

It seemed his thief had a code of honour. 'I need you to do one more thing.'

Sand bowed. 'Whatever you need, guv. Say the word.'

'Keep a watch on Clark. If it looks as if he has changed the hour of his departure, come and tell me.'

Sand nodded. 'What you goin' to do, guv?'

'Mrs Godfrey and I are going to pay him an early morning call.'

'I'll be there to make sure he doesn't lope off before you can have a word, then.'

Red had no doubt he could handle Maxwell Clark by himself, but he could see how Sand's presence might be useful in the event the man refused to co-operate.

'Very good. I will be there at about a quarter to the hour.'

Red ushered Sand out and into the care of the porter lurking in the hallway outside.

He closed the door and leaned against it.

Harriet looked grim. 'I am coming with you.'

'Then you had better get some sleep while you can.'

She looked surprised, then pleased.

No doubt she had expected him to refuse to let her to go along. But this was as important to her as it was to him. They had set out together to discover the truth and they would see it to its conclusion together. 'I will ask the porter to rouse us at five. Will that be enough time for you to dress?'

'More than enough time.'

He went off to make his request.

When Red knocked on Harriet's door three hours later, she was up and dressed and looking tired.

'You did not sleep,' he said.

'I closed my eyes, but it seemed each time I opened them, the hands of the clock had moved but a few minutes.'

He crossed the room and took her in his arms, kissing her briefly and hard, hating the idea that their idyll was almost over, yet knowing it must be. 'Very soon, this will all be resolved. But no matter how it turns out, please know that I do not hold you responsible for any of it.'

She gazed up at him with a sad smile. 'I did not think you would, but I am glad to hear you say it.'

And there was nothing else he could say at that moment. There was an unpleasant feeling in his chest as if he had lost something important and knew he would never find it again.

He pushed the thought aside. Right now, he needed to focus on his business with Maxwell Clark. There would be time later to consider what this strange feeling meant.

They hurried out into the dark wet street, huddled beneath the umbrella he had borrowed from the Assembly Rooms, and arrived at Clark's lodgings at the appointed hour.

Sand appeared out of the shadows. 'The chaise ain't here yet, but there's been a lot of hustle and bustle inside. Candles ablaze in every room.'

There was no doubt in Red's mind that Clark intended to leave Bath in order to avoid him. Anger rose hot in his veins.

Harriet put her hand on his arm and he took a deep breath. No need for anger. Not yet.

'Which are his apartments?'

'First floor on the right-hand side of the landing,' Sand said.

They walked across the street and knocked on the front door.

An astonished-looking footman opened the door.

'We have an appointment with Mr Clark,' Red said and, before the footman could comprehend what was going on, he pushed into the hallway. 'We know the way,' he said.

'Sir,' the footman said. 'You cannot—'

'Milord to you, fellow,' Sand said with a cheeky grin.

'Mind yer manners. No need to follow us, if you know what's good for you.'

The footman blinked, then backed away at a glare from Sand.

Red and Harriet mounted the stairs with Sand trailing behind them. They squeezed past a pile of trunks and boxes stacked on the landing in front of the open door and walked in.

A middle-aged woman was seated on a sofa with two schoolgirls on each side of her. They were dressed in travelling clothes.

A small balding man with a huge grey moustache was issuing orders to a lackey while he gathered papers at a desk. Maxwell Clark at last, Red assumed.

Clark swung around when the woman, jaw dropping, pointed at Red and Harriet.

Clark's face reddened. 'Who the devil are you?'

Harriet felt sorry for the two young girls on the sofa shrinking into their mother. All three had expressions of dread. Pity filled her. She knew exactly what it felt like to discover one's father had feet of clay.

'We are here,' Redford said tightly, much as he had done when he first arrived at her shop, though he did seem to have his anger firmly under control, 'to claim restitution for a fraudulent idol you sold to my father, Lord Westram.'

Clark paled. Swallowed. Sank into a chair and mopped his brow. 'I have no idea what you are talking about.'

'Yes, you do,' Redford said. 'This is Miss Godfrey.

She has a receipt issued by you to her father. And in case you do not recall the item in question…' He pulled the velvet bag from his coat pocket and tipped its contents on the low table in front of Mrs Clark and his daughters. It glistened in the candlelight, but the ugly grey metal exposed in the break at the neck revealed its falseness. 'Well, sir. What do you have to say for yourself?'

'I—' He gasped and clutched at his chest. 'I don't feel very well.'

'I did not feel very well when the fraud was discovered. My father paid a great deal of money for this fake.'

'Maxwell,' his wife said. 'Can this possibly be true?'

Clark put his head in his hands. 'I am so sorry, my dear Wife, I was desperate. It was the year the *Sally Jane* went down and the cargo was lost.' He looked up at Redford. 'I always intended to buy it back. But time passed and I feared the repercussions should I admit what I did.'

'Time passed and you thought you had got away with it.'

Clark hung his head. 'Yes, there was that, too. It was an excellent forgery. It quite fooled me, but the man who sold it to me said it was a copy. But I did think it was made of gold. None of the experts who looked at it realised it was not the real thing.'

'Including my father,' Harriet said. She felt a great surge of relief. She had been right about her father's honesty at least.

Clark groaned. 'I knew in my heart it would come back to haunt me.'

Mrs Clark squeezed her children tighter to her sides.

'How could you?' she said, her voice rising. 'You will hang for this.'

Redford was staring at the sad-looking little family. He looked as if he, too, felt sorry for them. He glanced over at Harriet, as if to see her reaction. He fisted his hands on his hips and glared at Clark. 'How many others like this did you sell?'

Clark looked surprised. 'None. I assure you. There was only one.'

'Then where did all your wealth come from? Your grand house in Bristol. The carriage in your stables.'

'From my business. And investments.' He winced. 'I invested the money from the idol. And never again did I take foolish risks.'

'You have ruined us,' his wife said. 'You will be hanged and we will be put out on the street.'

'I do not think it need come to that,' Harriet said, hoping she was right.

Redford nodded tersely. 'I am not a vindictive man. I simply want the money my father paid for the idol refunded.'

What if he could not pay? Harriet furrowed her brow. 'I will, of course, return the finder's fee paid to my father. After all, he was supposed to be an expert in Egyptian antiquities and should have spotted a fake.'

Clark stared at them wide-eyed, his jaw slack.

'Well?' Redford said. 'Will you return the money?'

'Of course he will,' Clark's wife said.

'Yes. Yes,' Clark finally blurted out. 'Thank you, my lord. Thank you. I did not expect such mercy. I will go immediately to my bank and see that you are paid. Unless you wish to come with me and receive the money in gold.'

'That is what I would do,' Sand said. 'He might lope off the moment your back is turned.'

Clark bristled. 'I certainly would not. My word of honour on it, my lord.'

'I will trust Mr Clark to make good on his promise,' Redford said. 'He is fully aware of the consequences if he does not.'

Mrs Clark gave a little moan. 'He will, my lord,' she said. 'Have no fear on that score.'

'I assume your bank is in Bristol?' Redford said. 'I shall expect to receive the money two days hence and no later.' He would just about make Featherstone's date for restitution. 'I also require a signed confession.'

Clark immediately went to his desk and sat down to write. It took him several minutes, meanwhile the ticking clock and scratching of pen on paper sounded extraordinarily loud in the silent room.

Clark blotted the paper and handed it to Redford. He scanned it and handed it to Harriet. 'What do you think?'

Her heart swelled at his asking her opinion. She read it carefully. 'I believe it to be satisfactory. It is quite clear both your father and mine was duped by this man.'

Their quest was over.

So why wasn't she happy as a grig?

Because she was going to miss Redford terribly.

Chapter Fifteen

The return journey to London was passing so much more quickly than the one to Bristol a few short days before. Redford had insisted on travelling by post-chaise.

Worried about her mother, Harriet had been glad to give in gracefully despite the expense.

They left that morning, after Redford paid the shot at their lodgings as well as tipping Pomfret for her services. Harriet promised to write her a glowing reference and send it along to the agency the moment she got back to London.

She and Redford did not talk much during the drive. He was likely as busy with his plans for the future as she. Not to mention regrets. Her thoughts kept returning to their upcoming parting. She would be calm when saying goodbye. She would smile and thank him for agreeing to the journey in the first place and express her satisfaction that the matter had been brought to a successful conclusion. And wish him well.

She did wish him well.

He would marry his betrothed, raise boys who looked like him and a girl or two who...in her mind's eye they had black hair, but she had no idea what his fiancée looked like.

'Do you have picture of your fiancée?' she asked. 'A miniature?'

Clearly startled by the sound of her voice, as well as surprised by her question, he frowned. 'I do not. Our engagement has not been formalised as yet.'

What an odd way to put it. How very odd the aristocracy were. They threw their sons out when they chose not to obey unreasonable edicts and they tied themselves to each other for social or financial gain.

'What is she like?'

'She is sensible and dutiful.'

That told her nothing. 'Is she pretty? Do you like her?' Does she make your heart pound in your chest the way mine does when I look at you? Not a question she dared ask.

His frown deepened 'I do not dislike her.' He sounded defensive. Perhaps almost unhappy.

She turned her face away and leaned forward to look out of the window in the door. Something deep within her had the feeling he deserved more than this cold arrangement of a marriage. He was a good man. An honourable man. She wanted him to be happy and she did not get the sense he would be. Her heart ached. She clenched her hands in her lap. It was better not to dwell on the future.

'Why do you ask?' he said.

'No particular reason. I wondered, that was all. I wish you happiness.'

'I am sure I will be'

His voice held determination, as if he intended to work at being happy against all odds. Sorrow filled her. He had no choice. He had to marry. And the choice of a bride had been made for him.

She on the other hand was free to choose whomsoever she wished, or no one at all.

Thank goodness, since she couldn't imagine choosing anyone other than Redford. Being required to do the lovely things they had shared with some other man would be a nightmare. At least, so it seemed at this moment.

Perhaps in time? No. She doubted her feelings would ever change.

If she could not have Redford, and he was completely out of the question given his rank and her occupation, then she really could not imagine being with anyone else.

As they crossed London Bridge, the city greeted them with the noise and smells of home. She gripped her hands together, bracing herself to say farewell.

The chaise stopped at the posting inn nearest to her shop and they climbed down.

Redford picked up her valise.

'I think we should say goodbye here,' she said. 'I will send over the finder's fee I owe you.'

He looked doubtful.

'I promise I will send it.'

He shook his head. 'That is not what troubles me.

You know, you really should not be walking the streets alone.'

She laughed to hide the pain in her heart at his caring. 'And will you escort me tomorrow and the day after as I go about my business as usual? I think not, my lord. I am used to looking after myself.'

He nodded reluctantly. 'Very well. I bid you farewell, Harriet. I am glad we went on this adventure together. I would not have missed it for the world.'

Her eyes ached with the tears she refused to shed. 'I, too. And I am glad it worked out so well. Farewell, my lord.'

She turned to leave.

He touched her arm. 'Please, do not concern yourself about the finder's fee. It was an honest mistake. I do not need it. I shall return it if you send it.' The warning note in his voice was clear.

Once more he was proving just what a lovely gentleman he truly was. 'Thank you,' she said softly.

She walked away before she really did start to cry.

Three days later, back at his estate in Gloucestershire, Red picked the purse of guineas from his desk and hefted it in his hand. Usually he would have used bank notes for such a large sum. It would have been much safer and more sensible.

But the debt to Featherstone would be paid in gold. There would be no impugning his honour by asking him if he had the funds to cover the note or being told it was not considered paid until the notes cleared the bank.

Today was the date by which he had to repay the man. And today he would keep his word.

So why hesitate? This had been his only objective for the past many days. He tucked the purse and Clark's confession in his pocket and, gritting his teeth at the necessity to prove his honour, drove in the pouring rain to Featherstone's estate.

The butler admitted him and took his outer raiment.

'Is Miss Eugenie in residence?' Red asked.

'She is indeed, my lord,' the butler said.

Which meant he could kill two birds with one stone, if he had a mind. Clear the debt and re-establish his betrothal with Eugenie. If.

For some reason, he kept recalling the way she had looked at him as if he had deliberately tried to defraud her father.

And when Harriet had asked him if he liked his intended, to his shock, he had almost said no. He certainly knew that his sisters did not like her. He did respect her. Of course he did. But he did not like her in the way he had come to like Harriet. And likely he never would.

The butler knocked on Featherstone's study door and Red entered at the invitation.

Featherstone came around from behind his desk. 'Westram. Here you are. Two weeks to the day. I told Eugenie you would not fail. Cutting it a rather fine though, aren't you? Eugenie has been worried.'

The hairs on the back of Red's neck rose. 'Eugenie should have been in no doubt, sir.'

The old fellow rubbed his hands together. 'No easy

thing to lay your hands on that much in the way of ready funds.'

'I didn't.'

Featherstone stilled, his face turning red. 'I suppose you need more time. I suppose I have to put up with my poor little Eugenie moping around here for another week or two while you try to come up with the money. It really is too bad.'

The idea of Eugenie moping over him or anyone else was rather ridiculous. Eugenie had iced water in her veins according to Petra, his younger and most outspoken sister. And after having had a chance to put some time and distance between them, Red had come to agree with her opinion.

'I did not say I had not come up with what I owe,' he said stiffly. 'I discovered the name of the man who defrauded my father and had him refund the money.'

Featherstone stared at him. He dropped into the nearest chair and mopped his face with his handkerchief. 'I say, that is most enterprising. You actually discovered the perpetrator of the fraud and made him pay up?'

'I did.'

Featherstone's face returned to its normal reddish complexion. 'That is excellent news. You have done well. Much better than I would have expected.'

'I am no longer a boy out of the schoolroom who needs help at every turn, the way I did after my father's death.'

Featherstone must have heard the rising annoyance in Red's words because he looked at him sharply. 'No, no. I am simply glad to hear your father did not deliberately… I mean, not that I thought he had, but he was rather badly dipped, you know. He wouldn't be the first to sell the family jewels and replace them with paste.'

Enough was enough. Red drew the purse from his pocket and deposited it on the table. 'There is your money, sir. Do you wish to count it, or will you trust that I have paid you in full?'

'I have been thinking about that. If the statue had been real, it should have increased in value over the years I have owned it and—'

'I looked into that matter,' Red said, keeping his voice quiet and even, despite the anger making his heart pound. 'I am told the market for Egyptian antiquities is not what it was and that, in fact, over the past five years they have lost value. May I suggest you take the purchase price without further ado, or shall I deduct the amount that the market for those items has gone down?' He raised a brow in question.

Featherstone leaned back in his chair, narrowed his eyes and clearly saw that Red was serious.

'Well, well, what are a few guineas between friends, after all. Eugenie will be delighted. I'll have word sent to her to meet you in the drawing room.'

No doubt to set the date for their wedding. To the devil with that. Why would he offer marriage to her simply because she was calm, respectable, very well bred and rich, when he loved Harriet?

He closed his eyes as the realisation struck him like a blow to the heart, leaving him breathless and speechless. Harriet was the one he wanted to spend his life with. They liked each other. They worked well together. And he loved her.

'No,' he said. 'I do not need to see Eugenie. She and I have nothing to say.'

'But the betrothal,' the old man spluttered. 'You are promised…'

'You, with Eugenie's consent, ended our engagement, sir. And I can see no reason for its resurrection.'

'You impudent puppy. What about all the help I have given you over the years?'

'Your advice has been invaluable. If you wish me to pay for your time…'

The high colour washed back into Featherstone's cheeks.

Red took a deep breath. 'I beg your pardon. I have appreciated your help these many years. I always assumed it was freely given and I thank you. However, I have regretfully come to the conclusion that Eugenie and I would not suit.' He bowed. 'I wish you good day, sir.'

He left.

It was only when he was outside that he realised he had left without his umbrella and it was raining harder than before. He turned back to see Eugenie on the doorstep holding it out to him.

Cursing under his breath, he returned to collect it.

Eugenie glanced over her shoulder. 'Father said you have declined to offer for me again.'

He nodded tersely.

She smiled tightly and looked down her aquiline

nose. 'Take my advice, you are making a mistake. The Featherstone name would bring you much consequence.'

All her disparaging remarks about his brother and his sisters in just that tone of voice came to mind. Remarks he had tried to pass off as her trying to be helpful, when in truth they were nothing but a way of her proving her supposed superiority.

The anger fell away along with the guilt of letting her down. His sister Marguerite had been correct. She was blinded by her own self-importance.

'The consequence of the Westram name is quite enough for me,' he said.

'After all the scandal in your family?'

'You know, Eugenie, you wouldn't bear the Featherstone name if you married me. You would be a Greystoke and just as tainted by our scandals as the rest of us.'

Her jaw dropped. Clearly, she had never looked at it that way.

She thrust the umbrella at him. 'Do not dare propose to me again, Lord Westram, for I declare I shall not have you.'

She went inside and slammed the door.

Humming, Red strolled out to the stables to collect his carriage and his spirits were so light, he forgot to open the dashed umbrella.

Already more than a week since her arrival back from Bath and Harriet still had trouble getting back into her old routine. Instead of arising at six to light the fires and get ready for another day in the shop, once again she hadn't awakened until nearly half past seven. Shivering, she lit a candle and opened her clothes press to find her favourite shawl, knitted by Mother before arthritis had crippled her fingers.

On top lay the morning gown he'd bought on their first day in Bath. She had given the other gowns bought in Bath to Miss Pomfret to sell for whatever she could get when they had been in too much of a hurry to leave for London to return them. She knew it was what ladies often did for their maids and Pomfret deserved the token of appreciation.

Harriet had kept this one because she had told Redford she would wear it to church. She wouldn't. She could not bear to wear it again. It reminded her too much of their brief time together. A time that had come to mean a great deal.

She ran her palm over the expensive fabric. She really ought to sell it. Not yet.

No doubt he was well on his way to being married by now. The banns would be called. A grand wedding with invitations to members of the aristocracy were likely at this moment being written out. There would be a notice placed in *The Times*, announcing the marriage. She would not look. It was not her concern.

The shop was all that she needed.

Yet she did not rise with the same joy she used to feel. Her days seemed to stretch endlessly before her. It was nonsense. The journey with Redford had disturbed the order of her life. It was simply taking time to settle back into her normal routine, that was all. The fact was that she missed his smile and his little flashes of humour and even the way he sometimes took charge and let her rely on him for a change. Even if she would never tell him so.

A pang twisted in her chest. She would never have the chance. She dashed away a drop of moisture from her cheek. Dust must have got into her eye.

She rummaged around, found her shawl and threw it around her shoulders. She was ready to face the day and she would not think about Redford for another moment.

In the kitchen, she lit the stove, then cleaned out the ashes in the hearth in the parlour. She laid the fire, but did not add coal or light it. They used the kitchen during the day and only used the fire in the parlour for after dinner.

Rubbing her chilled hands together, she went down to the shop. There she lit the fire behind the counter and unpacked a box of trinkets that had been delivered during her absence.

When everything was ready, she put the open sign in the door and picked up her needlework. A handkerchief for Mother's birthday.

As the day wore on, only a trickle of customers interrupted her work and a few meagre coins entered her till. Being away for so many days had definitely caused a drop in custom. But things would have been a whole lot worse if she had not refused to accept the blame for that fraudulent statue and gone hunting for the fraudster.

Hopefully, word would get out that the shop was open again and things would start looking up. The bells on the door tinkled and, putting her work aside, she went to greet her customer.

She almost fell over backwards. 'Lady Godfrey!'

'Harriet.'

'Why are you here? Is the Admiral with you?'

'The Admiral remains in Bath. I needed an urgent fitting with my dressmaker so had no choice but to come to London. I return to him the day after tomorrow.'

Thank goodness she didn't have to face her grandfather. 'How did you find me?'

'Your mother wrote to me when my son died.' The old lady glanced around the shop and sniffed. 'Disgraceful. What have you to say for yourself, my girl?'

Harriet stiffened. 'What should I say? I am a shopkeeper and there is nothing to be ashamed of in that.'

Lady Godfrey thrust her chin forward. 'I am not talking about the shop. I am talking about you gallivanting around Bath with Lord Westram.'

'I do not see that is any of your business.'

'You are a member of my family. Is he going to make you an offer?'

'An offer?'

'Of marriage, of course. You did tell him of our connection, I assume?'

'You know I did not. Indeed,' she said hotly, 'I did all in my power to deny our relationship.'

'Still, I thought—'

'Lord Westram is betrothed. And he certainly would never think of making an offer for a woman who keeps a curio shop.'

'Nonsense. You are a Godfrey.' She frowned. 'Betrothed, is he? That is a problem. Still. He must in all honour make you an offer having debauched a lady.'

Harriet laughed. Even to her own ears it sounded a little hysterical. 'He did not debauch me. I debauched him.'

Lady Godfrey glared. 'Do not play those games with me. Where is your mother? I am sure she will see sense.'

Harriet's jaw tightened. She restrained herself from throwing one of the little statues on the nearby shelf at the old lady. 'After years of refusing to acknowledge my mother's existence, you now asked to see her? Does the Admiral know you are here?'

The old lady's face crumpled. 'I thought to tell him, once your marriage to Westram was settled.'

She looked so dejected, sympathy softened Harriet's heart. 'I am sorry, Grandmother, but really, my circumstances are as they always were and, with Father gone, we seek no claim upon his family.'

The stairs creaked. A moment later, Mother appeared from behind the curtain.

'Mother, what are you doing down here?' Harriet rushed to her side.

'I heard voices, dearie.' She squinted at Lady Godfrey. 'Jane, that is you, is it not? I recognised your voice.'

Harriet stared at her and then at her grandmother. 'You know each other?'

'Lady Godfrey visited once or twice before you were born. Trying to get your father to make peace with his father.'

'Both of them were too stubborn for their own good,'

Lady Godfrey said. 'But we should not have tried to separate him from you, Nancy. It was wrong of us. For years, I have begged the Admiral to change his mind, but he is a proud man. He would not even attend our son's funeral. Enough is enough and so I told him after I met Harriet in Bath. She is my only granddaughter and she looks so much like my sister-in-law Maud, there is no mistaking that she is a Godfrey. I followed her to London and had my husband's man of business track you down.'

Mother gasped. 'Against the Admiral's wishes.'

Grandmother nodded tersely.

'You are very brave,' Mother said. 'He always scared me to death when I was young.'

Harriet stared at her grandmother in disbelief. 'My father did not hide his whereabouts,' she said. 'You could have easily located him at any time.'

'Of course, I knew the antique shop in Mayfair. I was content that he was comfortable there. But then it closed. And no one could apprise me of his whereabouts. I assumed he did not want to be found.'

Father had been very ashamed of their time in prison. They had gone there in the dead of night. Perhaps it had not been so easy to find him after that.

'You have a beautiful daughter. And I have a beautiful granddaughter. I would dearly love her to take her proper place in society.'

'So would I,' Mother said.

Harriet folded her arms across her chest. 'My place is here. With you, Mother.'

'Dearie—'

'No. I am sorry, but if my grandparents want me, then they must accept you also.'

'Well said, Harriet,' Lady Godfrey said, a fond expression on her face. 'Did you know you sound just like your father?' She sighed. 'I cannot fault you for your loyalty, but I do think Westram ought to know who you are.'

That would be the very worst thing that could happen. 'Lord Westram and I had a business matter to conclude. It is now finished. There is no reason for us to see each other again. Nor do we wish to.'

'Lord Westram?' Mother said. 'That nice young gentleman who was here?'

'Yes, Mother. He had purchased something from Papa and we had to find the original owner and get his money back.'

'You didn't tell me he was a lord.'

'It wasn't relevant.'

Mother tilted her head so she could see better. 'Why are you blushing?'

'Because you are staring at me.'

'Will you take a cup of tea with me, Jane?' Mother asked.

'I would love to,' Lady Godfrey replied. 'I will tell my coachman to come back in an hour.'

The last thing Harriet wanted was for her grandmother to tell her mother all about her trip to Bath. Or at least what she knew of it, but she could hardly forbid them from taking tea. 'I will tell him,' Harriet said. 'Lady Godfrey, you will need to assist my mother on the stairs, her vision is poor.'

She certainly wasn't going to follow them upstairs and listen to their gossip. And she certainly was not going to be convinced to enter society where she might run into Redford. No, she must think of him and speak of him as Westram, or her grandmother's eyebrows would certainly be raised more than they already were.

Meeting Westram would be awful. She could not risk it. She loved him too much to be the cause of any embarrassment for him and his new bride. Heat rushed through her body. She loved him? Her heart gave a little skip. Of course she loved him. She had since the moment in their lodgings in Bath when he told her he thought she was beautiful. She just hadn't wanted to admit it.

No wonder she felt so at a loss without him.

She went outside, hoping the chilly air would cool her heated cheeks.

What on earth would her father have thought about this latest development?

Chapter Sixteen

Since returning to Gloucestershire, Red had found himself restless. He had to force himself to settle to each and every task. And he had missed Harriet like the very devil. Several questions had arisen these past few days, when he wondered what she would have thought of the matter.

What was it that Marguerite had said to him on her wedding day, when he had asked her if she was sure she wanted to marry Jack Vincent?

'When you find someone you respect and they instinctively know what makes you happy, you know you have made the right choice.'

He and Harriet had not met under the most auspicious circumstances. Indeed, for a time they had been very much at odds, but he respected her deeply and they had enjoyed their time together, hadn't they?

One thing was certain, he wasn't ready to let her go.

Sadly, it seemed she was quite happy to end their affair.

How was he to change her mind?

* * *

Strangely, Mother hadn't said a word about her conversation with Lady Godfrey the previous afternoon, but right now, over the breakfast table, she was looking at Harriet sideways with a knowing little smile.

'What is it?' Harriet asked, wiping her mouth with a napkin, in case she had toast crumbs on her lips.

'What is what?' Mother said.

'You keep looking at me as if you are expecting me to say something.'

Mother beamed. 'I am waiting for you to tell me about this young man of yours. Jane said she smelled April and May each time she met you together.'

Harriet sighed. 'My grandmother is wishfully thinking. Very well. I had a brief romantic interlude with Lord Westram, but that is all it was. I had a pleasant time and now it is over.'

Mother looked disappointed. 'Only pleasant? You were away for nigh on a week.'

'The purpose of our journey was to save you and I from being cast into prison. We were fortunate that Lord Westram was willing to listen to reason. Yes, I liked him a good deal, but I shall not be seeing him again.'

Mother pursed her lips. 'So you sent him to the right about. Told him that nonsense about preferring independence to marriage. I told Jane that was exactly what you would have done.'

'I told him the truth. Besides, surely Lady Godfrey informed you he is betrothed.'

Mother frowned. 'What sort of man goes gadding

around the countryside with an unmarried lady when he is betrothed to another?'

'Really, Mother. The gadding, if you can call it that given the nature of our problem, was at my behest, to save *us*. Lord Westram behaved honourably in all of our dealings. There is no more to be said. If Lady Godfrey has some notion of pressing him into marriage, I will not have it. Members of the aristocracy do not marry shopkeepers, not poor ones anyway. They marry for wealth or some other advantage. I will not have Redford coerced into marrying me out of duty.'

Mother's brows shot up. 'Redford, is it?'

Harriet rose from the table. 'I am not saying another word on the matter.'

She stomped downstairs to the shop.

Dash it all. Just because she missed the man, his kindness and the partnership they had forged in their common quest, and just because she missed him in her bed, did not mean she had to marry the man. This sense of loss would pass in time. It must.

The tinkle of bells made her heart leap. She berated herself. She did not want Redford to visit. After all, by this time, no doubt his wedding date had been set.

The man who entered was nothing like Redford. Harriet left him to browse.

Oh, good Lord. Even now, Lady Godfrey could be approaching him and informing him that Harriet was a member of her family. Insisting he 'do right by her'. Would he think she was trying to trap him into marriage? Would his honour require that he break off his engagement and marry her? Was that even possible?

Her heart picked up speed. She felt dizzy.

No! It would not do on any front. While she might have fallen in love with Redford, he had never shown the least indication that he felt the same way. And for Redford to marry so far beneath him would likely mean his ruin. She would not have him cast out of his rightful place, the way her father had been, because of an indiscretion. It was not his fault she had not been honest with him about her family.

The customer left without making a purchase.

But if Redford was caught unawares by Lady Godfrey, he might do something he would regret in the heat of the moment.

Harriet gritted her teeth. She would not have Redford put in such an awkward position. One thing she knew for certain, Lady Godfrey would not be making calls this early in the morning. Forewarned was forearmed, was it not?

Now, where had she put his calling card? Ah, here. In the counter drawer. She memorised the address, closed up the shop and set off for Grosvenor Street.

There was a chill bite to the wind and a dampness in the air that threatened rain. She pulled her shawl tighter about her. It being only nine in the morning, the streets were not yet crowded with fashionable shoppers, although common folk scurried about their business. Her ears rang with the sound of criers touting their wares and horses' hooves and cartwheels grinding on cobbles.

As she approached Mayfair, the buildings took on a more affluent appearance, with fewer shops and more residences lining the streets. Grosvenor Square had a garden at its centre surrounded by iron railings and a gate for which, no doubt, only residents of the square had the key. The trees and shrubs were mostly bare of leaves, and yet looked inviting.

The town house she sought was in the middle of the row on the east side of the square. Its front door was painted black and its brass doorknob shone as did the lamps on either side of the portico. A short bridge crossed the area—a narrow cobbled courtyard in front of the basement some ten feet lower than the pavement.

Down there was the servants' entrance.

The front door looked imposing. She could imagine the sort of man who would open that door. A toplofty butler or a liveried footman. He would take one look at her and shut the door in her face. If only she had worn the pretty walking gown and coat Redford had given her, she might have had the courage to knock, but dressed in her drab grey dress and apron, she knew that whoever opened the door would not let her in.

Perhaps if she went by way of the servants' door and said she had a message for His Lordship, she might gain entry. Or she could actually leave a message for him. She trotted down the steps and banged on a narrow black door.

A red-faced young woman in apron and mob cap opened the door. She looked Harriet up and down. 'Yes?'

'I have a message for Lord Westram.'

The girl held out her hand.

'I am told to deliver it personally.'

'Who is it, Bess?' a woman called out from within.

'A shop girl with a message,' Bess answered. 'Says she has to deliver it personal.'

A middle-aged woman with a florid round face and eagle eyes arrived. Bess moved out of her way.

'What is your message?' this woman asked.

Harriet drew herself up. 'Please tell His Lordship that Mrs Godfrey from Godfrey's Curiosity Shop has called to see him. I have information about something he is interested in.'

'His Lordship is out.'

'Then I shall await his return.'

'If you wants.' She started to close the door.

Another person appeared behind her, curiosity all over his face. Tom Sand? He looked exceedingly smart, in a dark coat and pantaloons, but his waistcoat was bright blue and embroidered with birds of paradise.

'I thought I knew yer voice,' he said. 'Best let her in,' he said to the woman, who Harriet assumed was the housekeeper. 'His Lordship won't want her standing outside in the cold.'

The woman shot him a glare. 'You have been here five minutes and you think you can dish out orders to your betters.'

Tom gave her a cheeky grin. 'I'm His Lordship's valet and you be a housekeeper. Who's better than who?'

The woman huffed out a breath. 'You ain't no valet yet. Training, you be.' She turned away. 'On your head be it, then.'

'Come in, Mrs Godfrey,' Sand said. 'His Lordship is at breakfast.'

She stepped over the threshold into a bright cheery

kitchen with gleaming copper pots hanging from a rack in the centre, a large modern stove and a blazing hearth. 'Then he is in.'

He nodded. 'Seems like it's what they does here. Tell everyone he be out, unless they are someone important.'

Naturally. He was a lord. The hoi-polloi needed to be kept in their place. They likely wouldn't keep Lady Godfrey standing on the step. 'Very well. Please let him know I am here and need to speak with him.'

Another man arrived behind Sand and pushed his way forward. Portly and elderly. He looked down his nose at her and at Sand. 'What is going on?'

'Mrs Godfrey needs to speak to His Lordship,' Sand said. 'I was going to show her up.'

'You will do no such thing, Mr Sand.' He glared at Harriet. 'Now listen here, madam, if you have a message for His Lordship you may give it to me. I will see that he gets it.'

During this haughty speech, Tom Sand winked at her and backed away, leaving her to deal with the butler, the coward.

The kitchen was now full to overflowing with curious maids, a grim-looking cook, a supercilious butler and an indignant housekeeper.

She met the butler's gaze. 'The message is private and personal.'

'I will be the judge of that.'

'I do not think you will,' a deep voice said.

Redford, his eyes twinkling, but his expression serious, had arrived. Sand must have fetched him.

The servants scattered.

'My lord,' the butler said. 'This person is demanding to see you.'

'Mrs Godfrey is a friend of mine.' He put his arm through hers. 'She will take tea with me in the drawing room.'

He escorted her through the kitchen and up to the first floor. He offered her a seat.

'Harriet, are you well?'

'Very well, thank you.'

Red thought she looked pale. 'I assume you walked here. You should have dressed more warmly. I was quite chilled when I rode out this morning.'

She smiled wryly. 'I didn't notice how cold it was until I was halfway here. I needed to speak with you.'

And he needed to speak with her. He had been tossing up whether he should throw caution to the winds and surprise her with a visit to her shop or send round a note asking if he could call on her.

And now here she was on his doorstep. He could not be more pleased.

'A cup of tea will warm you and then you will tell me what brings you here. How is business?'

'Slow. No doubt it will improve once word of our reopening gets about.'

He nodded. 'I do hope so. How is your mother?'

'She is well.'

Her stilted answers were troubling. 'Is something wrong?'

The butler arrived with the tea tray and they sat in silence until his departure.

Harriet sipped her tea. 'That is good. I feel warmer already.'

'Good. Now, how can I be of service?'

She put her cup down. 'I need you to give me your promise to do something for me.'

It was the first time she had asked him for anything. A warm glow travelled outwards from his chest. 'Anything.'

She pursed her lips as if trying to form her request in a way that would be acceptable to him.

'Out with it, Harriet. You are not one to stand on ceremony.'

She released a small sigh. 'When Lady Godfrey comes to call on you, please promise me you will not be swayed by anything she says. Promise me.'

Startled, he stared at her. 'Why on earth would Lady Godfrey come to see me? Besides, I thought the Godfreys remained in Bath for the next few weeks.'

'This is serious, Redford. I need your promise. Give me your word.'

The steely light in her gaze stemmed the flow of warmth inside him. Did she not trust him to keep his word without some sort of oath swearing? His jaw tightened. His back stiffened. 'What is going on, Harriet?'

Resting in her lap, her hands tightened convulsively. Her expression became anxious. 'Please. You must promise.'

He hated seeing her so upset. 'Very well. I promise. Now tell me what she has done that distresses you so.'

'She is my grandmother.'

His jaw dropped. His mind raced to catch up. 'You

told the woman you were no relation when she asked, if I recall.' A hole seemed to open in the pit of his stomach. Was she playing some sort of game with him? 'Why did you lie?'

Her gaze slid away. 'There is no relationship. Grandfather disinherited my father years ago. I'd never met the woman before we were introduced in Bath. I certainly did not want to embarrass you or cause a scandal by revealing my identity. I had no reason to think they wished to be reconciled.' She bit her lip. 'Except, it seems my grandmother has changed her mind. I hate to be cynical, but thinking that I might marry an earl may be the cause of her change of heart.'

He stilled. 'You think she *expects* us to marry.' The empty sensation inside him grew less. He almost smiled, but she looked so pale and drawn he quelled the urge.

'I am certain she does.'

His heart stopped, then picked up speed. Before he could speak, she continued.

'You know I do not want that.'

His chest tightened. 'I know you said you do not.'

She gave him an odd look. 'I explained to her that you are betrothed and that it was none of her business, but she refused to listen. I thought I ought to warn you.'

'I am not going to marry Miss Featherstone, after all.'

Her eyes were round, her expression—he could not read it.

She looked down at her hands in her lap. 'I see.' She straightened her shoulders and looked him in the eye.

'It is of no matter. I refuse to be forced into marrying to save my non-existent reputation.'

Forced. The idea that she would have to be forced hurt like the blazes. 'Naturally, I do not want that either.' He took her hand in his, rubbed the back of it with his thumb. 'I do miss you, you know. Terribly. We rub along very well together. Perhaps—'

'No.' She turned her face away. 'Please. We agreed it was to be a short-lived affair, to be concluded when we returned to London.' She gave a half-hearted tug at her hand, but he did not release it. He had the sense she was wavering. He nearly blurted out the truth of his feelings, but once said they could never be taken back. If she did not care for him the way he cared for her...

'Do you deny you feel something for me?' he asked instead.

'I cannot deny I miss you, Redford, but it is better that we do not see each other. I only came because—' Her voice broke.

'Because you did not wish me to be trapped into a marriage. What if I said it would not be an unwanted trap?'

Her head snapped around. Eyes wide, she stared at him. The longing he saw in her deep dark blue eyes gave him hope. They misted over. She shook her head.

'It would not work,' she whispered.

His stomach plummeted. 'Why?'

She swallowed, looked away and spoke in a low strained voice. 'An earl does not marry a shopkeeper.'

She thought him so shallow? But then he had been,

had he not? He had not permitted his sisters to do so. Had he told her that?

'Any number of noblemen have married daughters of merchants.'

'Wealthy merchants. I don't have a feather to fly.'

'I will provide for my family.'

'How can you say that so blithely? As I understood it, the point of your marriage was the wealth and position your wife would bring to the match in exchange for a title.'

It was likely the worst idea he had ever had. 'Things have changed.' He had changed. 'It will take a bit longer to bring my holdings up to their full potential, that is all.'

Doubt filled her expression.

'I know what I am doing. Marrying Eugenie was a shortcut to financial security thought up by my father. Things are in much better shape now than they were in his day.'

'And the reason you are marrying me is because you now believe I fit your definition of a lady and thus it is your duty to wed me.' She watched him expectantly.

'Harriet, you don't need to worry about such things. I will take care of everything. And I don't give a fig for what people say.'

'You would care what your sisters thought.'

He hesitated. His sisters had not liked Eugenie. And now they were married to noblemen would they think less of Harriet because she kept a shop? He winced. The items in her shop were not exactly the most genteel. 'If it bothers you, then no one need know but us.'

She shook her head. 'It is very hard to keep secrets. I am sorry. I do not think such an arrangement would work for me.' She stood up. 'And I certainly would not have you ashamed of your wife.'

An unexpectedly harsh pain in his chest robbed him of speech. A pain he had not experienced for a long, long time. The pain of rejection.

He rose to his feet. He was making a complete mess of this. There was something he was missing. Some reason for her refusal he did not quite understand.

He ached to hold her. To kiss her, tell her it would all be all right and change her mind, but in her determination, she looked so fragile he feared she might break if he took one step closer.

Besides, she had given him his answer. He was not going to beg. He took a deep breath. It hurt. There had to be something... 'If you ever need assistance, I hope you know you can always count on me as a friend.'

Her expression softened. 'Thank you.'

She strode across the room to the door, clearly distancing herself before turning to face him, pale-faced and in obvious distress.

'Thank you for the tea. I really must get back to my shop.' Head high, she walked out.

Chapter Seventeen

Outside the drawing room door, Harriet brushed away the tears that she'd barely been able to control when seeing Redford's rather lost expression when she'd told him she had no intention of accepting his offer.

She sniffled and found a handkerchief thrust at her. Mr Sand. He gave her a sympathetic glance. 'I will show you out.'

Mortified, she glared at him. 'I hope you were not listening in on our private conversation.'

He put a hand to his heart. 'Would I do such a thing?'

'Yes.'

He grinned. 'This way, miss.' He directed her towards an impressive set of stairs.

'This is not the way I came in.'

'His Lordship wouldn't want you to leave by the servants' entrance.'

Since she had no idea where the servants' stairs were, she pressed her lips together and descended to an imposing hall, decorated with chinoiserie wallpaper. It all looked so opulent. But then her father had hidden his financial difficulties beneath a cheerful manner and purchases he could ill afford, but that he was sure would make their fortune. For all she knew, Redford was on the brink of financial ruin. She shuddered at the thought.

She crossed the black and white marble floor where a footman stood ramrod-stiff beside the front door. He opened it as she approached.

Sand reached around him, pulled an umbrella from the stand and opened it for her as she stepped outside.

He shook his head. 'Can't understand it, I can't. You nobs are half-flash, half-foolish.' He ducked back inside.

Just as well. The tears were starting up again. Thank heavens for the umbrella. If Redford did happen to glance down into the street, her face would be hidden. It would never do for him to think she was not firm in her resolve.

She was. For his sake. She would not have him forced into marriage. Nothing in his reason for making the offer had in anyway suggested he felt more for her than he had felt for his erstwhile fiancee. He deserved to love and be loved.

When she arrived back at the shop, Mother was standing at door, peering into the street. 'You did not say you were going out.'

'I went to Billingsgate.' She held out the paper-wrapped surprise. It had been a rather long detour, but she had thought of it when she was almost home. 'It has been ages since we had a feast of whitebait.'

'Ooh, lovely, dearie.' Mother beamed. 'What a nice surprise. Such a good girl you are.' She retreated upstairs.

Harriet let go a breath. Now life really could go back to normal. She picked up her feather duster and flicked it at a statue of an entwined naked couple.

It was for the best. Truly.

Over the next two days, Harriet cleaned every shelf and rearranged the tiny window. With nothing left to do, she sat on the stool, her chin in her hand. How different she had felt in Bath. Like a completely different person without a care in the world. Happy. Now the very real prospect of financial disaster stared her in the face. She needed more customers.

But how?

The string of bells on the shop door chimed.

She shot to her feet. And closed her eyes briefly in disbelief. 'Lady Godfrey, if this is about Lord Westram, I must inform you—'

The old lady gave her a piercing stare. 'It is not. I am returning to Bath tomorrow. I wanted to invite you to come with me.'

Harriet blinked. 'Why would I do that?'

The old lady's lower lip trembled. 'You are our granddaughter. It is time you took your rightful place. I wrote to the Admiral and he agrees. Having met you and seen what a lovely young woman you are, he regrets the pride that separated him from his youngest son.'

Harriet lifted her chin. 'If you think I am going to

abandon my mother because you decide to drop your glove, you really do not know me very well.'

Lady Godfrey blinked rapidly as if trying to clear her vision. Her voice quavered when she spoke. 'You are so like your father and my sister-in-law Maud it is uncanny. And it is no more than I expected. Naturally the invitation is for both of you. We would like to introduce you into society and of course to the rest of the family. It is long past time to let bygones be bygones.'

The temptation was overwhelming. The life being dangled before her glittered like diamonds. Why shouldn't Mother finally be given the position she deserved? On the other hand, they would expect Harriet to marry according to their wishes and give up her independence.

Besides... 'You cannot introduce me into Bath society as your granddaughter. Everyone there believes me to be a widow, related to Lord Westram.'

Lady Godfrey shrugged. 'Oh, you can still be a widow. We can simply say that for financial reasons your deceased husband is distantly related to both families. I assure you, if we recognise the connection, no one is going to blink.'

Harriet paced to her counter. Clearly her grandmother had been thinking about this very hard. She strode back to face the old woman and looked her right in the eye. 'Have you discussed this with Lord Westram?'

Lady Godfrey's mouth turned down. 'He wasn't home when I called. His man said he'd left for his estate.'

Harriet breathed a sigh of relief. At least he wasn't being dragged into her grandmother's machinations. As yet. She had to make sure it could not happen. 'Please do not think I am being ungrateful, but I am perfectly happy as I am. I cannot see Mother being comfortable in Bath or in society. I am glad we met, at last, but I do not think we should meet again.'

The old lady's shoulders slumped, but she looked resigned. 'Godfrey pride—it will be the ruin of you, too. I'll say this, though, and mean it. If you ever change your mind, or need help, please do not hesitate to come to me. Promise me this one thing.'

It was little enough. 'I promise.'

The old lady leaned forward and, with tears in her eyes, kissed Harriet's cheek, then turned and marched out of the shop.

Harriet leaned against the nearest shelf. She felt horrible, as if she'd been cruel and hard-hearted. She made her way back to her stool behind the counter, wondering if she should tell her mother what had occurred.

Again, the bells at the door jingled. She looked up and groaned. Another unwelcome visitor.

'Mr Sand. What do you want?'

His cheeky grin made its appearance and he tugged at the edge of a bright yellow waistcoat decorated with scarlet cherries. 'His Lordship asked if you would mind accompanying him for a drive.'

'I would mind. Please tell him, no, thank you.'

'He has important matters to discuss. And he's waiting outside. He ain't going to leave till you agrees.'

Important matters? Had something gone wrong with

the agreement with Mr Clark? 'What sort of important matters? I cannot leave the shop.'

'I'll look after it for you.'

'What do you know about keeping a shop?'

'I've bought things.' He sounded indignant. 'You tell the customer the price and, if he wants it, he gives you the money. Nothing hard about that.' He leaned into her window and glanced out into the street. 'Quite a gathering of lads out there. Those high steppers be getting nasty. Wouldn't be surprised if they kicked out at one of those nippers.'

She sighed. Naturally the local boys would come to look at something so strange as a lord and his carriage. She certainly didn't want to start a riot. She got her coat and bonnet from the hook beside her back door and went outside.

Her eyes widened when she saw what His Lordship was driving. A very fancy phaeton with two beautiful black geldings in the traces. He tipped his hat when he saw her emerge.

Her heart leapt at the sight of him. Foolish organ.

'Cor, missus,' one of the lads called out. 'Bet you daren't get up there.'

It looked as though she didn't have a choice because those horses were definitely getting restless.

Westram reached down and, taking her hand, hauled her aboard.

'Really, my lord, what were you thinking, bringing this to my front door?'

He gave her a rather shy boyish smile. 'It worked, didn't it?' He set the horses in motion and manoeuvred them out on to Ludgate Hill and through the traffic. He was headed for London Bridge.

'Where are you taking me?'

'Somewhere we can talk.'

Across the bridge the traffic thinned out and they were soon in the country. He turned up a lane and pulled up outside a country inn.

An ostler grabbed the horses' heads and held them while Redford helped her down. They went into the inn's parlour.

She stripped off her gloves. 'What is so urgent that you must kidnap me in broad daylight?'

He gave her an odd look. 'If I was kidnapping you, we would be heading for Scotland right now.'

She laughed and sat down.

His expression turned serious. 'I am not jesting.'

Her pulse fluttered wildly. She forced a smile. 'What is the urgent matter you needed to discuss? Did Clark not keep to his side of the bargain?'

A maid entered with a pot of tea and some scones and scurried out again. Clearly, he had arranged all of this beforehand.

'This has nothing to do with Clark. When you visited me the other day, I was delighted until you made your purpose clear. I have been going over and over what you said and I realise there is much more to this.'

She gazed at him blankly.

He poured the tea. 'What have I done to earn your distrust?'

He sounded perfectly calm, but she sensed a deep hurt. Guilt assailed her. Clearly, he thought she had impugned his honour in some way. 'It is not that I do not trust you in particular. It is simply my experience of men in general.'

His gaze sharpened. 'Which men?'

The intensity of his piercing green eyes made her look away. She picked up her teacup. 'Father made a terrible investment against my mother's advice when I was fifteen. We were evicted from our shop and ended up in debtors' prison. We were there for weeks before he managed to pay off his creditors. If he would have listened to my mother...'

'Not all men ignore their wives.'

'What about my grandmother? She did not want to be parted from my father. She had no choice.'

He grimaced. 'The Admiral is a man used to command. I do not excuse him, but it is possible to understand...' He shook his head. 'These are things that can be worked out between two people, if they trust each other.' He hesitated. 'If they love each other.'

She almost dropped her cup. It rattled in the saucer and he took it from her.

'I love you, Harriet. Up to now I have avoided all thoughts of romantic love. My grandfather married for love and his besottedness over my grandmother brought the estate to its knees. When she died not long after my father was born, he disappeared inside a bottle. He lived to a ripe old age, ignoring all around him in his misery and there was nothing my father could do about it.

'Father drilled it into me that a good marriage, like the one he made, was based on mutual respect and financial advantage. Anything else was pure self-indulgence. He arranged marriages for all his children, except Petra, the baby of the family, who seemed to be able to twist him around her little finger.

'With all the responsibilities placed on my shoulders, I never gave love a thought until I met you.'

Heat rushed to her cheeks. Her whole body warmed. This blunt declaration she had not expected. 'Redford.'

He stopped her words with a look. 'What? I love you, Harriet. I want to marry you. Not because your grandmother requires it. Or because I feel guilty about our affair. Or because I want to ride roughshod over your opinions. I don't. I respect your opinions. Marriage to you would complete me. As well as make me happy. With you at my side, I feel as if I can tackle any problem. If the reason you do not wish to marry me is because you do not love me, then I need to hear you say so.'

'But you are an earl. You cannot marry a shop-keeper.'

He took her hand in his, gazing into her eyes. 'Is that what you truly believe?'

'My father was ostracised for marrying beneath him and he was a third son.'

'Did he care? Did it make any difference?'

'No. He loved my mother. We were a very happy family.'

'As we could be happy.'

She bit her lip.

'What is it, Harriet? What are you keeping from me?'

'When I was little, I thought my father was infallible. I adored him. He always acted as if he knew everything and on occasion would ignore my mother's advice, even though she had been involved in the antique business long before she met him.'

'Your mother must have hated him for that, I suppose.'

She recalled how remorseful Father had been for not listening. And how, in the end, he had made it right. Harriet's fear and disgust of debtors' prison had made her harbour her anger.

'She forgave him. I did not. I was terrified that some item would take his fancy and it would happen again.' She took a deep breath. 'He died not long afterwards and then I blamed him for leaving us to struggle alone. I decided I would never depend on a man again.'

'You have not answered my question.' His tone was gentle, but firm. He squared his shoulders as if to brace against the worst.

She had always prided herself on her directness. On her ability to confront the truth and deal with it. But since meeting Redford she had constantly lied to herself about her feelings.

Would she lie to him?

'I care for you, I really do.'

He shook his head. 'Caring is not enough. I care for my horses. I care for my friends. I care for my staff. Deeply. But that is not what I am talking about. I want you as my partner in life. My soulmate.'

The vulnerability of his words and in his expression shook her to the depths of her being. He meant it.

She took a deep breath. To deny the truth was wrong. 'I do love you, Redford.' There, it was out in the open.

Her heart seemed full to bursting, yet a small kernel of fear remained like a small dark cloud on a clear horizon.

He took her hands in his. Kissed the back of each. 'Thank you, my darling. However, I sense a "but".'

He knew her too well.

Tears blocked her throat. Stung the back of her eyes. Made her voice husky. 'What if we disagree on something important? In the end, by law, the decisions are yours alone.'

He frowned. 'Along with love comes trust. I trust that you will do right by me and you must trust me the same way.' He huffed out a small breath. 'I might make mistakes along the way, as might you. But I would never intentionally cause you harm. And I would certainly hope that we would make decisions, small and large, together.'

'You bought those gowns against my wishes.'

'Against what you said your wishes were. But you know, I did see the longing in your eyes.'

His boyish smile tugged at her heartstrings.

So it all came down to trust. Trusting her heart. Trusting his. Against all odds, all logic, it seemed she could not help herself. She gripped his hands tightly. 'I trust you. I really do. And I love you so much it hurts.'

A long sigh escaped him. 'Finally, you see sense.'

She laughed at his long-suffering expression, but froze when he dipped into his waistcoat pocket and withdrew a ruby and pearl ring.

He was grinning when he slid off the chair on to one knee. 'Miss Harriet Godfrey, will you do me the honour of becoming my wife?'

How could she refuse him? Whatever the future brought, she knew they would face it together. 'I will.'

From somewhere outside the door came a little squeal of delight. The little maid must have been watching them this whole time.

Harriet giggled and watched with joy as he slipped the ring on her finger. 'What on earth will people think of you marrying a shopkeeper?'

'I care not one jot what anyone thinks,' he said and kissed her so thoroughly she no longer cared a jot either.

Epilogue

Harriet gazed at the guests seated at the table running the length of the ballroom. She had wanted a small wedding. Redford had agreed. Only family and close friends would be invited to celebrate with them at his Gloucestershire estate.

He had gone ahead to prepare for her arrival. She and Mother had travelled north by easy stages.

This wedding breakfast proved that they had a great deal more family than she would ever have expected.

Beside Redford, sat his older sister Marguerite and her husband Jack, Earl Compton, sitting with their three girls, behaving like perfect little ladies. Catching her gaze, Marguerite waved. Harriet waved back.

On the other side of the table was his other sister Petra with her husband Ethan, Lord Longhurst, and in Petra's arms their new arrival, a baby boy named Phillip. Beside them were Lord Avery and his wife, Carrie, who had once been Redford's sister-in-law. Their two children, ages three and two, were at present playing hide and seek around the table chased by a frazzled-looking nanny.

Her side of the family was also present. Her mother right beside her, the Admiral and his wife and her father's two brothers and a sister and their spouses along with one or two of their grown-up children. She had met them all, but was still not quite sure who was who. They were a cheerful bunch who seemed happy to welcome her into their family.

If only her father had been alive to give her away and to see this reunion, the day would have been perfect. One look at her mother's happy expression gave her the feeling that perhaps he was here in spirit.

'You look thoughtful, my dear,' Redford said in a low murmur, lifting her hand and pressing his lips to her knuckles in a way that spoke of pleasures yet to come.

'I love having family,' she said.

He glanced around. 'Just as well. There is rather a lot.'

'I think we have a great deal to thank Mr Clark for, don't you?'

He grinned. 'Why, I suppose you could look at it that way. And I should perhaps send Eugenie a note to thank her for dropping that idol or we might never have discovered the fraud.'

'And we would never have met. Indeed, we have a great deal to be thankful for.'

He gazed into her eyes. 'There is nothing I am more thankful for than you.'

'I love you so much,' she said softly.

Lord Avery, an exceedingly handsome man and a

duke's second son, rose to his feet. 'Something tells me our bride and groom are about to depart this august company. So before they leave, I would like to propose a toast. To the bride and groom.'

The company rose to their feet. 'The bride and groom.'

Redford rose to his feet and raised his glass. 'Thank you all for sharing this happy day with us and thank you for all your good wishes. A toast to my beautiful bride.'

Harriet's face felt fiery as everyone drank to her. Her heart felt so full of love, she couldn't say a word.

He leaned closer to her. 'Time to go, my darling.' He drew her to her feet and, to warm laughter and good-natured hoots, they left as they had planned by the door behind them, hoping to make a quick escape.

Outside, a barouche was waiting to take them to his hunting box on the far side of the estate where they would spend their honeymoon.

As the barouche drove away, the guests flooded out of the ballroom on to the balcony overlooking the drive-way and a chorus of farewells sped them on their way.

* * * * *

*If you enjoyed this story, why not
check out these other great reads by
Ann Lethbridge*

Rescued by the Earl's Vows
An Innocent Maid for the Duke
The Matchmaker and the Duke

And be sure to read The Widows of Westram series

A Lord for the Wallflower Widow
An Earl for the Shy Widow
A Family for the Widowed Governess